The Devil Inside

Book II of the Dark World Series

Danielle Q. Lee

The Devil Inside

ISBN 978-0-9865680-5-3

Other Books by Danielle Q. Lee

Dimensions of Genesis

Inhuman

Nightmara

Dark World

For those who've read every word

...and can't wait for more

Acknowledgments

Thank you to my sister Jaclynn, and my friends Lea and Melanie for all their help. Thank you to my husband, Chris, for listening tirelessly to my brainstorming and constant insecurities about the storyline. And thank you to all those wonderful fans who keep me inspired every single day.

Dark World would not exist without you.

Blood on her skin, dripping with sin,
Do it again
Living Dead Girl

Rob Zombie

Prologue

"I am Lucifer, Lord of the Dark," he wrote, the golden ink glimmering by candlelight as the words danced upon the enchanted parchment. With every letter, every turn of the pen, the king doubted his actions. This would change everything; everything he'd worked for, all his hopes and dreams for Dark World would be forever altered by his actions this day.

But he had no choice. Malus had forced his hand. He'd known of her plots and scheming for decades, but he had no idea she'd go this far.

Any day now, any moment, an evil agenda was about to unfold. His spies could only uncover so much before they never returned. Lucifer had lost many men in this silent war against his wife. Yet she behaved as though nothing was amiss.

Lucifer sighed, his broad chest heavy, filled with regret. He despised doing this. Hated to let her have her way.

But he had no choice. Her plan to assassinate him was near. He had to retaliate with the only thing he had left: Magic.

He still had the upper hand, but not for long. He had to work quickly. The Crystal Pyramid needed to be silenced, the crevice closed.

It was the only way to defeat her.

He only hoped his son could forgive him—and find the secrets he'd need to win the war.

Part I

Two Worlds

1

"It's been...six weeks since our Scarlet vanished," Mrs. Prince said as she choked back tears. Mr. Prince stood steadfast at her side, though his grey eyes were empty, void of the trademark twinkle. "If there's anyone out there who knows anything, anything at all, please come forward." The Edmonton television crew looked somber as they held their positions behind the camera and microphones.

Oh Scarlet, Shelby thought, pain burning in her chest. *Where are you?*

For some reason unbeknownst to her, Shelby truly believed Scarlet was still alive—somewhere, somehow. It was like she had spidey senses and they tingled with some supernatural knowing that her best friend still existed, that she lived and breathed somewhere. It was illogical, she realized, but she just couldn't shake it. She just *knew* she'd see Scarlet again.

Shelby's gaze roamed over the large crowd that had gathered at her high school, Scarlet's high school. So many people, so much support. It brought a lump to Shelby's throat. Scarlet would have loved this. How tragic it had to be under these circumstances that people would finally appreciate how wonderful Scarlet truly was. She'd always been shunned by the teenage masses of high school, an outsider like Shelby.

They weren't cheerleaders, cuddling up to the jocks, drowning in booze and drugs on the weekend. They weren't eccentric like the Goths, with their black lipstick and pierced lips and eyebrows, moshing in the pits of depression.

No, they were just the girls next door. Average, even boring to some. Yet somehow, it seemed as though they'd been penalized for having their priorities straight.

Scarlet was the proverbial good girl. An intellectual.

A nerd.

But a beautiful one at that, Shelby concluded as she pretended to brush a strand of curly red hair from her face, but in actuality she was catching a runaway tear that had escaped her eye and navigated the curve of her cheek. She pulled in a shaky breath, glancing around to see if anyone had noticed. She had to stay strong, not just for Scarlet, but for the Prince family as well. They had enough to worry about, there was no need to add Shelby's ailing psyche to the pile.

Her teary gaze panned the length of the room, hundreds of heads bowed, praying for Scarlet's safe return. Despite the diversity of the crowd, the myriad of faces expressed a constant theme: teens concerned for a fellow student and angst for parents who now held their children a little closer.

In the midst of the sorrow, Shelby came to a bittersweet dawning: the reminder that at any given moment tragedy could strike with the speed and venom of a rattlesnake bite. It was amid these kinds of trauma when mortality unveiled its frailties, that the rush and tedium of modern day life could be halted by a single moment of senseless evil.

Her eyes blurred with fresh tears as she scanned almost every face in the room, watching loved ones and gazing upon all the affection. All this love, it would seem, had an invisible expiry date, though no one ever spoke of those moments. Only now, with reality disfiguring their illusion, did they realize the true meaning of love: that it should be cherished, every second of it.

Then her eyes rested on a lone figure at the back of the gym and the blood chilled in her veins. Through the throng of supporters, she saw *him*—Rory Dean—his head lowered in feigned reverence, the slightest hint of a smirk pulling at his lips. Hate and suspicion quickly overshadowed Shelby's sorrow, her tears hastily drying as anger consumed her.

Even though he'd been questioned repeatedly by the Edmonton police, she couldn't help but feel he was responsible somehow. He was, after all, the last person to see Scarlet.

He and Scarlet had been on a date when she'd gone missing. Scarlet's dream date, and her very first. She'd harbored a secret crush on Rory for years and then out of the blue, he asked her out. Mr. and Mrs. Prince were against Scarlet dating, mostly because of the scary disappearances around Edmonton, but Scarlet lied to them and ventured out on the date anyways.

Any other night it may have been alright, her parents might have relented, but it was October 1st, bathed by the light of a full moon—the recipe for the local myth to come alive. It was the one night everyone in the area knew as sinister, an urban legend that had proven itself worthy of fear time and time again. Teenagers would vanish without a trace—just like Scarlet did.

Shelby thought it horribly ironic that Scarlet would eventually end up a missing person on the very night her parents were most afraid of, like it was some prophecy made reality, courtesy of worry and paranoia.

And why had it only been Scarlet that night? If she'd been abducted by the serial legend, why had she been alone? It had almost always occurred in threes. Except for the first two incidences with Sybil and Vincent Kavanagh, of course, they'd been singular and only a year apart.

Shelby cast a disgusted gaze in Rory's direction, loathing every aspect of his face, wondering what he knew and what he had done to her best friend.

He alleged that while at the movie, Scarlet excused herself to use the washroom and simply never returned. She just vanished, her car and personal items never recovered. The cops tried to say that she'd simply run away, but everyone who knew Scarlet knew that was ridiculous. But all they had was Rory's version of what happened and unfortunately there were no witnesses to discredit his story, so the police had no choice but to take his word for it.

But Shelby knew better. Rory knew something. He did something. Shelby just had to prove it.

"Hey babe," said Greg, Scarlet's older brother, as he slid his arm around her waist, his body heat soothing her distress. "Let's get outta here." He was trying to sound tough, like none of this was bothering him, but the hitch in his voice betrayed him. Despite their bickering and sibling rivalry, Greg and Scarlet had been very close.

He led Shelby out of the gym, companions in pain and in hope. They'd started dating shortly after Scarlet's disappearance, a welcome distraction for the both of them. Scarlet's absence had left a gaping hole in their lives. In everyone's life.

As they rounded the corner to leave the school gymnasium, Shelby and Greg came face to face with one of Scarlet's many missing persons posters. Greg immediately diverted his gaze, but Shelby stared into Scarlet's ocean-blue eyes and thought, *Oh Scarlet, if only you knew just how much you're missed—wherever you are.*

2

A ghostly phoenix soared high overhead, its feathers but wisps of black smoke. Once a flaming beauty, the vaporous bird now wandered the skies as a specter, a soulless phantom cursed to a dark destiny. It navigated the snarling stalactites, twisting as it dodged a gargantuan pillar, one of the many that held the heavy ceiling over Dark World.

In the distance, the Crystal Pyramid shadowed the horizon, its silhouette a reminder of what Dark World once was, and could be once more.

Perched atop the Great Wall, the divide between Necrosia and the rest of Dark World, Fate's luminescent white stare penetrated the forever night, her gaze wandering the turbulent lands to which she'd been damned. Her life, or rather her death, didn't look like anything she'd imagined. She was an abomination, a beautiful monster that fed upon the essence of the living, spawned from evil and dark magic. But unlike many of the shades in the underworld, she retained a glimmer of her former self, a faint spark of the light she'd once been.

When she'd considered death as a mere human girl on the Surface, she'd imagined going to a Heaven rather than a Hell. She assumed naively that she'd ascend to a place of peace and white light with a palace full of angels, certainly not a land imprisoned in perpetual darkness crawling with demons and monsters born of black magic.

And she definitely didn't imagine herself as a creature of such power and destruction. She was a shade, a race born of hate, oppression, and greed. The opposite of who she had been on the Surface.

So much had changed, yet what remained of her soul was untainted, as glorious as the day she was born human. She only hoped she could keep it that way. The pain, the hunger, the temptation she endured day after day, minute after minute, threatened to consume her at every turn.

With a ravenous beast burrowed deep within, she worried she could lose herself at any moment. If she gave in, even for a second, she could become the very thing that frightened her most—a killer.

This Hell would have been intolerable, filled with unimaginable sorrow and loneliness, if not for one soul—Kane.

Her black demon prince, her soul mate, her lover. Had she not fallen into this darkened world, she would never have known such a love.

She wondered a moment if Heaven and Hell were simply a state of mind rather than a destination. If so, she had been damned to Heaven. For anywhere Kane was, was home.

A soft fluttering stirred Fate from her thoughts. To her left, a large silver griffon landed, cocking a curious eye at her. The half-eagle, half-lion creature then melted into a pool of molten steel, reforming into a humanoid shape—a necromancer.

"Hi Aura," Fate said casually, a smile warming her black lips.

"Hey," Aura replied with a grin, completely unabashed at her nudity. "Whatcha doing?"

After removing her cloak and handing it to Aura, Fate pulled in a breath and spread her arms before her, replying, "Just seizing the day."

Aura's silver-blue lips turned up as she donned the wrap. "Yeah, it's a good day."

Comfortable silence drifted between them for a moment, then Aura asked, "What do you remember about the Surface?"

Fate pushed her long white mane off her shoulders, answering, "Well, I recall more every day, but not everything."

"Can you tell me what you do remember?" Aura's necromancer eyes swirled like a starlit galaxy, staring at the shade with barely contained excitement.

Fate took a deep breath into her undead lungs as she searched her memories of the Surface, disquiet stirring within. She'd sensed something lately, something far away, something from her past. A sadness. A loneliness she couldn't shake. "I remember my name was Scarlet, and that I went to high school," she offered. "I had a wonderful family, a friend…" her voice trailed off as a dull ache nestled into her chest.

"What about the sky? The stars? I read about them in the necromancer library. Do you remember those?" Aura pleaded, obviously desperate to regain her own memories of the Surface, though it was uncertain she'd ever remember her life previous to this one. Aura didn't even recall her brief incarnation as a zombie.

Fate nodded. "Yes, vaguely," she started, trying to ignore the burn in her heart. "But mostly I remember my murder."

"Your...murder?" Aura replied, her face falling.

"Yes," Fate said, adding with a chill in her voice. "Rory Dean killed me." *And when I find him someday...I'll make him pay.*

"Hello ladies," a familiar voice said from behind them, freeing Fate from her prison of dark thoughts.

"Vale!" Aura swung her legs around, jumped down from the wall and wrapped her arms around the rogue shade.

"How are my favorite girls this morning?" he inquired as he planted a gentle kiss on Aura's lips, then tossed a grin up at Fate.

Grateful for the interruption, Fate stood and leaped down from the wall, landing with the grace of a panther. She smoothed out her black leather pants, then faced her comrade with a welcoming smile. Vale had earned a spot in her heart, what with his dashing smirk, devious wit, and inexhaustible devotion to his sister, Sybil. Fate was pleased that he'd recently found love with her favorite zombie-turned-necromancer.

Vale and Aura had been inseparable since the brush with death only weeks before when Malus and her evil posse had crashed Aura's inauguration party, killing almost everyone—including Aura. Thankfully, she and the other fatally wounded necromancers were resurrected by the power that had given them life to begin with, the Soul Nexus.

Kane's near-death experience, however, had been even more traumatizing—for him as well as Fate. She'd nearly lost the love of her life at the hand of his sadistic mother. Talk about the ultimate mother-in-law from Hell.

Fate's gaze fell on Vale who was tenderly tucking a stray piece of Aura's short, blue hair behind her ear. If not for Vale and his sister, Fate would have lost Kane forever. The three had discovered, quite by accident, that when they combined their powers, they could heal, even bring someone back from the brink of death. Kane had reawakened without so much as scratch.

Ever, unfortunately, had not been as lucky.

3

Kane ran his finger along his daughter's soft, ivory jaw line, cerulean eyes wrought with worry. She hadn't awakened after the incident with his mother. Except for the slow rise and fall of her chest, she showed no other signs of life.

Ever's long white hair spilled over the side of the bed, her once glowing blue eyes sealed behind their lids, hands folded over her stomach. So still. So like death.

Kane's heart cracked inside his chest. His baby. His little girl. What had his mother done to her?

"Ever?" he whispered, hoping she'd hear him, open her eyes, smile. Anything.

Kane lowered his head and sighed as sorrow settled over his heart, a wayward strand of his blue dreadlocks falling forward and resting on his cheek. He had failed in so many ways: he'd failed to protect his father so long ago, then Seren, and now his daughter.

And Legion, his crumbling underground home. If he didn't find his people a new place to live soon, there wouldn't be a place to call home. The buried Atlantean palace had served them well for over a century, but the weight of the Crimson Desert deeply burdened the shoulders of the city. As their leader, reluctant as he may be, it was Kane's duty to find them a new home.

Home, he thought wistfully. *Where is my home? With the other demons? Here, in Necrosia?*

Kane had to admit, the Necrosians were warm and welcoming, a far cry from his own suspicious and intolerant race. This place, even in the short time he'd been there, was quickly becoming a home away from home.

As much as he wanted to be a proud leader to his people, he couldn't ignore their waning faith in him to protect them from capture, from slavery. With Malus now dead, however, he hoped the task would be easier. But Dark World was so unstable, so unpredictable. Without their leader, the queen's shades would be free to roam the lands without any repercussions. Free to devour any and all souls that crossed their path. At least the queen had kept her ravenous minions contained within the walls of the Blood Palace—until she bid them otherwise, that is.

The only way to save his people and Dark World now was to obtain all the scrolls, rekindle the light of the Crystal Pyramid—and claim his birthright as the devil. He cringed at the last requirement, disquiet stirring within. His father had been a great leader, admirable, strong. Kane didn't feel the royal power coursing through his veins. The responsibility smothered him, confined him, not unlike the shackles adhered to his wings. A prison.

Suddenly, an ironic and tragic realization struck him with the force of lightning: *With Malus gone, the enchantment that keeps the shackles on my wings, on all demons' wings, can never be removed!*

She was the one to affix them to almost all of the resident demons of Dark World; therefore she was the one needed to whisper the enchanted words to remove them. He and his fellow demons would be forced to live with them for all eternity—if there was to be an eternity. If he didn't fulfill his obligations, Dark World's population would die anyways.

"Any improvement?" a voice asked, pulling Kane from his dark brooding. Vrill, the leader of the necromancers drifted into the room, his silvery-blue skin aglow from the hundreds of candles illuminating the room.

Kane shook his head. "Nothing. It's like she's under a spell."

Vrill nodded, wisdom shining behind his eyes. "Yes, I believe that is exactly what it is."

Frowning, Kane asked, "What do you mean?"

The necromancer hesitated, then crossed the room and settled into a chair created entirely of bones, as was nearly everything in Necrosia. Finally he spoke, "When the queen attacked Ever in the ballroom..." his voice trailed off.

"Yes?" Kane eyes lowered with the memory.

Vrill sighed, then said, "She may have...transferred her soul. I believe Ever is undergoing some kind of. . .metamorphosis."

Kane's heart stopped. The thought had crossed his mind, but until now, no one had dared speak the words aloud.

"But..." Kane began as he stood and paced the room, shaking his head. "Vale killed Malus before the ritual was complete, Ever's soul could still be her own...couldn't it?"

"I'm sorry your highness, we just can't be sure—until she wakes up," Vrill said quietly, his gaze resting on the sleeping princess. "And I'm not sure we should take the chance."

"What are you saying?" Kane growled, brow furrowed and fists clenched, barely restrained from charging the passive necromancer.

Vrill raised a patient hand to subdue the angry prince, stating, "We can't know for certain that she's still your daughter. The queen's soul could be in charge, Ever might be a prisoner in her own body. We cannot take the chance that the queen still lives. If she's in there, in her granddaughter's body, she could harness the power of a hundred devils. She will be unstoppable. We should..." Vrill lowered his eyes. "...put an end to her, now, before she can awaken."

"Put an end to her? How can you say such a thing? That...*monster*...is not in there," Kane raged. "She is Ever!" He moved protectively to his daughter's side, stared at her angelic face, and whispered, "She just has to be."

4

Fate closed the door behind her, wincing as the lock clicked into place. The bedroom, decorated with the many bones of unfortunate creatures, seemed to watch her, judge her.

She clutched her stomach as hunger pangs ate her insides, the lust for souls growing with every passing moment. Desire clawed at her, weakening her will. She'd gone to the Soul Nexus too many times to count in the last few days, attempting to quell the growing desire within—but the hunger was winning. The Nexus could not quench the thirst, her voracious craving for souls.

The other shades in the city seemed completely satiated by the pulsating orb located in Vrill's private quarters. Their need to kill temporarily eliminated—but not hers. Hers was a relentless obsession that threatened to consume her if she dropped her guard but for a moment.

Fate crossed the room quickly, towards the dresser with glowing white eyes targeting the top drawer. She opened it, slipped her hand in and pulled out the amethyst vial. The elixir Ever had held until the moment she fell into her inexplicable sleep. The elixir meant for Fate.

She cradled it in her palm, the ornamental bottle cool and glinting like a purple diamond against the flicker of candlelight. Thick liquid sloshed within, Fate's apparent cure, created by the blind shaman that dwelt within the hidden city of demons.

Fate eyed the vial, considering it carefully. It was meant to fix her, stop the hunger and end her suffering. If it worked, it would save lives. But there was no guarantee. Nothing like this had ever been attempted before, especially on a shade like Fate. She was different. Fate sensed the evil influence simmering beneath the surface. An uncontrollable and terrifying power that awaited its chance to be free, to destroy the living.

And what would happen to her? What would she become this time? Would her suppressed human side resurface, revealing a kinder, gentler version of herself? It confused her that she should have two identities buried within. Scarlet was most certainly in the submissive role whereas Fate was the dominant personality. Was everyone that way? Did everyone have dueling alter egos? She felt like some kind of undead schizophrenic.

She eyed the bottle again, curious. Without the hunger to control her, it would be interesting to see how she might change—if the potion worked, that is.

She sighed, placing the bottle back into the drawer and covering it with some clothes. What if the old demon got it wrong? What if he couldn't be trusted? Demons and shades were mortal enemies. Forever on opposite sides of Dark World. What would prevent him from betraying her?

Fate shook her head. The shaman was a sweet old guy, harmless. But, even so, she didn't know if she should risk it and tempt unleashing the dark side. For all she knew, the cure could be her own personal poison. But her greatest fear wasn't dying; she'd been dead before.

No, she didn't fear death—she feared becoming an unstoppable killer.

5

Kane watched his little one sleep within her poisoned slumber, her ivory skin as smooth as white satin, hair as long and fluid as a cascading waterfall. He remembered her as baby, as a toddler. Even then she'd been magical, her sweet nature gracing everyone she met and everything she touched. Ever was all things love, all things beauty. No demon disliked her, no demon ever said an unkind word of her.

Despite the visual similarity to her grandmother, she was nothing like her. Malus was inherently evil, manipulative and would do anything to gain power. Ever was so very good, so very gentle, tender with animals and empathetic to everyone she'd ever met.

It pained him to think that Ever's body could be being ravaged at that very moment by a parasitic version of his mother, writhing, festering, and growing like a virus.

What if Vrill was right? What if his mother was alive in there.

"Your Highness, you know it is the right thing to do," Vrill said solemnly. "We cannot risk Necrosia…or Dark World. We should finish this before it can go any further."

Kane's chest ached, his heart twisting as he listened to the necromancer. He knew it to be true. If there was even the slightest chance that the queen had survived, it was his duty, his obligation, to stop her at all costs—even if it meant killing his own daughter.

Vrill exhaled, his hairless brows creasing. “I understand your pain, your highness, but the queen…”

“I know!” Kane growled, spinning about to face the silver being, his fists clenched. He then inhaled deeply as he closed his eyes and added quietly, “I know. But what if we’re wrong? What if she is just Ever in there? What if my mother is truly gone?” He fought against the tears burning behind his eyes.

Vrill nodded. “The devil can fool us all,” he said cryptically. “She can take many forms, split her soul and spread the seeds of evil, all unbeknownst to those around her…even the one she inhabits.” His eyes swirled, resting on the princess. “Even if Ever awakens, she herself may not know the beast resides within. All of us, no matter how good, carry a bit of the Devil inside.”

With that, he folded his hands together and walked silently out of the room, allowing Kane to make the hardest decision of his life.

How? He thought. *How am I to decide the fate of my only daughter? How can I make the decision to sacrifice her on the presumption that she might hold my mother’s soul?*

Vrill’s words resonated inside his mind. What if he was right? What if his mother planted a seed of herself inside his only child? What then? How could they know?

A soft knock at the door stirred him from his sorrowful deliberation.

"Supper is served in the dining room," a female necromancer announced, bowing before she exited. Kane nodded, then turned his attention back to his daughter.

It's impossible, he thought as he scanned her delicate features. *This body couldn't harbor that beast, could it?*

Maybe Vrill was right, maybe it was irresponsible of Kane to think that his mother hadn't survived. What else could explain her condition? Perhaps she was a cocoon for his mother's wretched soul, an evil metamorphic vessel locked within the butterfly.

Even then, Ever was in there as well, conceivably trapped alongside a soul of pure malevolence, tethered to Hell itself.

Kane exhaled, taking his daughter's frail hand into his own, cradling it. What was he to do? His obligation, his duty, was to destroy his mother. But how was he to do so without killing his only daughter?

"Are you coming for supper?" a voice asked gently from behind him.

The large, black demon stood and turned about, smiling at Fate. "Yes, of course."

With one last longing glance at his lifeless daughter, he crossed the room in just a few strides and took Fate's hand in his.

"How are you?" she asked with worry in her eyes, holding the back of his hand to her cheek.

He took a deep breath in before replying, “I am concerned.”

Fate nodded in understanding. “Aura says their witchdoctor will return from his mission soon, and he may be able to help her.”

“I hope so,” Kane said, his soul aching. He sincerely hoped so.

They walked in silence for the remainder of the journey to the dining room, hand in hand, Ever’s condition weighing heavily between them.

Beyond an ornately designed door constructed primarily of skulls and finger bones, silverware clattered and wineglasses tinkled. Two silver-skinned necromancers opened the doors with gracious servitude, allowing the prince and the shade to pass.

“Ah, my friends, welcome,” Vrill called out upon their arrival. “Please, sit.” He gestured to several empty chairs nearest him. The table, rectangular and nearly ten feet in length, was draped with a deep burgundy cloth and adorned with gold place settings, lit candelabras fashioned from spinal chords featured every foot or so. The necromancers enjoyed a macabre, yet classy style.

Aura and Vale, seated near the center, waved when they saw the couple enter. Sybil, however, was strangely absent.

The room, the company, was all so friendly. So warm. Kane couldn’t help but marvel at the diversity of the room. Necromancers, demons—and especially shades—all eating a pleasant meal together was a rare vision indeed. Of course, the shades didn't indulge in any real food as they'd usually appeased their hunger via the Nexus before supper, but politely sipped on wines and enjoyed pleasant conversations while the others ate.

Ever would be especially pleased with this scenario, Kane thought wistfully. Not so long ago, many would look upon a scene like this as pure treason. *Many would still,* he considered bitterly, thinking of Syphon and the elder demons back home.

Kane took the seat nearest Vrill and Fate sat beside him, next to Aura. The two young ladies immediately started chatting about the day's activities and what they were going to do tomorrow. Seeing the two together made him miss Ever all the more. Her soft, sincere laughter, her incessant mothering nature, and her smile. He yearned to have her back. To have her awaken.

And most of all, to know that she was still Ever—and not a monster.

6

As place settings were filled with dishes of succulent foods, Fate's insides churned even more voraciously. How she wished she could simply devour normal food to nourish her body, to silence the inner demons. It was getting harder and harder to pretend she wasn't ravenous. The sound of her loved ones' blood pulsed through their veins, enticing her, their oblivious souls tugging at her weakening will.

Vale wasn't an issue, he didn't have a soul to steal, but the others, Aura, Kane, and even sweet, lifeless Ever, were quickly becoming too much of a temptation.

"Oh, do you want to go to the shopping district with me tomorrow? Master Sherla makes the most beautiful pixie-bone necklaces," Aura gushed, an expectant grin adorning her silver lips.

Fate nodded and smiled back, her heart full as she admired her new friend. She had a classy, yet fun fashion. A semi-sheer crimson dress flow the length of her long legs, hugged the contours of her body, then parted ways at her navel into two lengthy scarves that just barely covered the essentials as they caressed her shoulders and fell down her back. Aura's short ocean-blue hair had been coiffed into elegant waves, similar to iconic styles Fate recalled from the Surface, ones like Bette Davis and Marilyn Monroe would wear.

As Fate admired her friend's beauty, the ambiance suddenly changed. Like a storm had rolled in, smothering the sun with clouds of pure black. Her vision narrowed. The air thickened, charged with malevolence.

Fate's eyes locked on the necromancer like a cat watching a mouse. A foreign heartbeat began thrumming alongside her own. Aura's heartbeat. The young necromancer's soul seemed to whisper to Fate, sing to her, seduce her. Like the soft echo of a lullaby, it serenaded Fate's subconscious—the home of the beast.

Even though Aura's soul signature paled in comparison to the average living creature's, being that she shared one soul with all necromancers, it still called to the shade. Tempted the monster.

Fate gazed longingly at the necromancer's chest and the soft hollow between her breasts, the easiest route to her soul. Her mouth watered and she was instantly disgusted with herself. Had she such little will? Such pathetic power over this body?

"Fate? Hello?" Aura giggled, waving her hand in front of Fate's eyes. Fate snapped to reality, shame filling her as the lid to Pandora's Box slammed shut inside of her.

"I'm sorry...I don't feel well," Fate stammered, starting to stand. She had to get out of there, away from the souls, before she did something terrible.

Kane's brow furrowed and he started to rise from his seat. "Are you alright?"

Everyone stared at her. Vale, Aura, Vrill, Kane, and countless kind necromancers and friendly shades that sat around the table. All her friends and allies, yet she had to fight not to hurt each of them, to rip open their chests and steal what made them whole. A dark, unnameable beast was moving through her insides, snaking through her system. She felt hot and cold at the same time, dizzy as the world warped around her. Had she let it go too long? Had she lost herself?

Suddenly, Vrill clapped his hands together, commanding a server, "Bring Fate her meal, quickly."

My meal? Fate wondered, her fears rising. *What is he bringing me? I can't eat something here, now, in front of everyone!*

7

"Thanks for helping me with this," Mrs. Prince said to Shelby as they sorted through the stacks of missing persons flyers to deliver door to door, Scarlet's bright and smiling face decorating the front.

How odd to use such a cheerful picture when the purpose is so sad, Shelby thought wistfully as she held the paper in her hands, though she did love to see Scarlet's face again.

"Of course," Shelby replied, looking up and giving her best friend's mom a warm smile. Scarlet's mom smiled back, but the sadness in her eyes overshadowed any attempt at true happiness. Dark circles hovered under her blue-grey eyes and new wrinkles had formed almost overnight. The poor woman had aged ten years in a matter of weeks. But who wouldn't in this situation?

Mr. Prince wasn't doing too much better. Greg told Shelby he'd found empty bottles of vodka and whiskey hidden in a cupboard in the garage, with new empties added every day.

Greg, too, was pulling further and further into himself all the time, the mischievous twinkle in his eyes fading to a dull glimmer.

The family she'd come to love and admire was falling apart. Quickly.

Shelby couldn't even imagine how horrible it would be to lose a daughter, all of this was hard enough on her and it was just her best friend. But Shelby still had hope. Since she was a kid, she just *knew* things. A sixth sense. And she knew that Scarlet would come home.

She just hoped it was before the Prince family was completely destroyed.

The next day at school, Shelby meandered through the throng of students, the air in the hallway thick with impending weekend excitement. Everyone had plans with friends and parties to attend. Everyone, it felt, but Shelby. Her world had been turned upside down by Scarlet's disappearance, yet the rest of the world continued on like it had never happened. How is it that tragedy can strike and the universe doesn't have the dignity to at least pause, take a breath, and remember the hole left behind? Did it have no heart, no empathy?

"Hey Rory, go long!" a male voice hollered from behind her, a football sailing overhead and narrowly missing her. Rory, suddenly right behind her, nearly knocked her over as he lunged forward and caught the ball.

"Hey!" Shelby shouted, turning about and shoving Rory hard in the chest with both hands. "Watch it, asshole!"

"Ooo," Rory's friends taunted as they rallied beside their friend, who simply stood there and smirked.

She glowered at him, making certain he saw both hatred and accusation in her eyes. Before she turned away, Rory uttered under his breath, "Bitch."

Shelby spun about fast and stormed up to him, raising her five foot frame as tall as she could. Only inches from his face, she looked him right in the eye and growled, "At least I'm not a murderer."

"What did you call me?" Rory snarled back with a flicker of something sinister behind his eyes.

Even Shelby was taken aback by her accusation. She believed Scarlet was still alive—didn't she? All of the sudden it hit her: What if she'd just been in denial all these weeks? What if her best friend really was gone?

A strangled cry escaped her throat as she turned from Rory and his friends, broke through the gathering crowd, and ran down the hall towards the bathroom.

How could she not have seen it? How could she believe that Scarlet was alive after six weeks? What was she thinking? That Scarlet had simply camped out somewhere? Gone savage and lived off berries in the woods?

Scarlet was gone. Dead. And Shelby knew she had to face it.

Hot tears streamed down her face as she made her way to the girls' washroom, shoving past several seniors who stood gawking at her. She finally ducked into a stall and slammed it shut, weeping.

"Are you okay?" an anonymous voice inquired on the other side of the stall.

"Yeah, I'll be okay," Shelby mumbled through sobs and sniffling. *I'll be okay, alright, when I find Scarlet's body...and put Rory Dean behind bars!*

8

The servant brought out a covered plate and set it in front of Fate.

"What's this?" Fate asked apprehensively, praying it wasn't some cute little creature that had wandered too far onto necromancer territory. While the silver-skinned race was polite, they did seem to have a morbid fascination with death—and bones. Judging by the vast quantity of bones used to build the city of Necrosia, many thousands of Dark World's creatures must have been slaughtered. She hoped this wasn't going to add to the bone pile.

"Please," Vrill said, eyeing her intently. "You must eat."

The entire table seemed to be holding their breath as Fate reached for the lid. Aura's forkful of food was held hostage in midair as she, like everyone else, waited to see what Fate's lunch would be. Holding her own breath, Fate pulled up the lid.

The moment her meal was revealed, Aura exhaled loudly, Vale smirked, and Fate simply laughed. It was a plateful of Bloodstone, the rarest gem in Dark World, but also the only other substance Fate could consume that would keep her hunger at bay.

"Thank you," Fate said, sincerely grateful. She was positively thrilled there wasn't some kind of rodent or cute animal running around under the dome. There were at least six large crimson stones on the plate, more than enough to sustain her for a few days. But then guilt surfaced. Bloodstone was a precious rarity, a near extinct power source that the demons needed to keep themselves alive ever since the magical light of the Crystal Pyramid was extinguished by Kane's father.

She cradled one of the larger stones in her palm, closed her hand around it and used her formidable shade force to crush it. Fate then tilted her head back and opened her mouth, letting the stone's liquid bleed onto her tongue. Immediately relieved, the ache inside temporarily quenched, she felt her strength—and willpower—return.

The table fell into quiet conversations, everyone enjoying their meals and one another's company. Vale whispered sweet nothings into Aura's ear while Vrill and Kane discussed political tactics and policies. There were several other shades and necromancers at the table, but Fate was too shy to start a conversation with them.

Why did she always feel so out of place? Even here, where literal freaks of nature were commonplace, she still did not feel at home. On the Surface, she recalled being accepted by her family and one friend, Shelby, but she didn't feel she'd ever truly belonged anywhere. She was always on the outside looking in. Most people had some sort of niche, a place in which they fit. Why didn't she feel that way? Would anywhere ever feel like home?

"Fate?" Aura's voice broke her bubble of self-pity.

"I'm sorry, what?" Fate asked with a shy smile, shaking her head.

"I was just saying to Vale, you must be getting excited to start your training? What do you think your hidden power might be?" she asked, tilting her head to one side inquisitively.

The table seemed to quiet down, as though everyone was awaiting her answer.

I probably won't even have one, she thought glumly. But she knew better. A lot better. Single-born shades harbored great power, dark power. Vale and his sister, Sybil, had proven that beyond a shadow of a doubt. Both of them had been born of this world like Fate, alone and pulsing with power. Sybil was a prophet, a psychic phenomenon. Her ability to see into the future unsurpassed within the underground world.

Vale had the ability to wisp. To vanish in a cloud of smoke and reappear several meters away, a talent unrivalled in Dark World. Though he'd used his ability to steal several of the pages of the Devil's Bible from their guardians around Dark World, he'd also used it to save Fate and kill Malus.

With gazes around the table cast her way, Fate wondered what her ability might be. What dark force lingered within? Frankly, she was afraid to find out.

Fate cleared her voice, heat racing to her undead cheeks. She forced a smile, replying, "I couldn't even hazard a guess."

9

After supper, Kane and Fate left the castle for a walk. The balmy evening was filled with promise—and maybe even a bit of romance.

Fate turned her gaze upward, the ceiling of rock snarled down at her like a mouthful of razor-sharp teeth. Blood-red mist hovered amidst the fangs, giving the illusion that it had just devoured a fresh meal. She shuddered and forced her sight away.

How she missed the sky. Sometimes it felt like she'd never really known the baby blue air overhead with its hot sphere of gold, or the pitch of night enlightened by an ancient moon and a billion stars. Had it all been a dream, this other life as Scarlet Prince? Had she really existed on the Surface? It didn't feel real anymore. She was Fate now, some inhuman creature with silver hair, magical powers, and an unquenchable lust for souls.

The latter would have been nothing more than fantasy on the Surface, a tale woven by fanciful writers, but it was reality that didn't resonate with her any longer.

Still, a sliver of her former self lingered within. A spark of what was once Scarlet still flickered deep inside. It was her family and Shelby that kept the fire alive. The part of her that was still Scarlet held hope that she might see her loved ones again. Someday.

She sometimes envied Vale and Sybil. Despite the circumstances, that they had been torn from their lives on the Surface by Malus's minions, they still had one another. Even though Vale had searched for Sybil for a hundred years in the underworld, time had not made their hearts forgetful. They held each other as dear as they did on the Surface, if not more.

"I wonder where Sybil was tonight," Fate pondered as she and Kane walked hand in hand through the streets of Necrosia. She wasn't sure why, but she kept glancing around, expecting to see judgment in the eyes of the citizens. But everyone just smiled at them, accepted them. It was a place where all races were welcome: shades, necromancers, and anyone else who joined their community. It was a rare and beautiful place.

"The Oracle? I don't know," he replied nonchalant. "Why?" He looked down at her with a soft stare that made her heart quicken.

She shrugged and looked away. "I just wanted to ask her something."

"About what?" he asked as he led her to the left, towards a jewelry vendor. Earrings and necklaces made of bones, animal scales, and precious gems hung from the makeshift store walls. Some very beautiful, some macabre.

"Nothing really, just wondering if she had any sense of what my hidden talent might be," Fate said, then asked quickly, changing the subject, "Have you and Vrill decided what you'll do to find the scroll on the Surface?"

He shook his head as he leaned over a small box on the vendor's table, blocking Fate's view with his muscular arm. "No, we also must speak with the Oracle. She might be able to see its location."

Fate nodded, frowning as she rose onto to her tippy toes to see over his shoulder. "What are you looking at?"

He was silent for a moment, ignoring her. Then, after handing something to the vendor, he turned to her with a shy smile. "Close your eyes," he ordered softly.

Her brows pulled together in confusion, but she complied by shutting her eyes.

She felt his body draw closer, his warm breath feathering her face. Her head swam at his nearness, her senses blurred. His scent was more than intoxicating, it was alluring, seductive. It confounded her how just being close to him could completely throw her off her game. But instead of analyzing it, she just let it happen, falling back into the bliss.

He then took her hand into his, heating it with his hot demon skin, and she felt him slide something onto her finger.

She gasped, her eyes opening with a start. Kane lifted her hand, kissing the back of it before allowing her to see what he'd given her.

"But..." she sputtered.

Kane leaned into her, pushed her silver-white hair from her ear and after kissing her earlobe, whispered in *Attra,* Dark World's native tongue, "*Vosira mea anima.*"

I give you my soul.

10

Shelby's breath was slow and even, eyes closed, her mind wandering the ethereal realms. She held a special necklace, a bloodstone pendulum in the shape of a rounded arrowhead, over the map of Edmonton. The amulet was still, wavering only slightly with every exhale. Every so often she'd open her eyes just a crack in hopes that the stone would be moving, it needed to move in a circle to show that the spirits were near, helping her find her best friend's whereabouts.

It wasn't often that Shelby would resort to supernatural aid; too many things could go wrong. She'd once had an evil spirit terrorize her family for months after messing around with the Ouija board. It was a séance gone terribly wrong. Shelby was only trying to contact Granny Harris, to see if the old woman could tell them where she'd hidden the ten carat diamond earrings she'd left to Shelby's mother in her will.

Apparently something else, something dark, decided to pretend it was her dearly departed grandmother and wreaked havoc in their normally peaceful home.

She'd since learned to be careful with the Other Side. There seemed to be a lot of dark entities that were just waiting for an opportunity to sneak through the gates into the third dimension.

But this was an emergency. She had to contact the spirit world, to see if they could help her find Scarlet.

Of course, most people thought she was nuts for her paranormal antics. Her parents supported her, especially after the poltergeist-terrorizing-the-house incident wherein they had to call on a priest to exorcise the house. She hadn't even told Greg the depth in which she believed in the unknown. She was pretty sure he wouldn't understand. Most people didn't.

But she believed, no, *knew* about the other realms. She hadn't seen them, but somehow had knowledge of them. It was like she had one foot on either side of the veil; one was locked firmly in reality while the other traveled the spirit world. She couldn't help it, she was just born that way.

The bloodstone pendulum hung stagnant in the air, the spirits seemingly ignoring her. Shelby blew out a breath of aggravation via her bottom lip, her springy red bangs flapping up, then falling back against her forehead.

"Okay, Shelby, relax," she soothed herself, closing her eyes and emptying her thoughts. "Relax."

"Shelby! Supper!" her mother's voice rang out from downstairs, shattering what remained of the supernatural ambiance.

"Okay, I'll be right down!" Shelby called back, dropping the pendulum onto the map in frustration. How the heck was she going to figure out where to look for Scarlet? Where had Rory taken her that night? It seemed to be an impossible task. Edmonton was smack dab in the middle of Alberta, surrounded by mile after mile of farmland, littered with thick spruce trees and wheat fields. It would take a team of hundreds with bloodhounds just to cover the outskirts of the city.

And she was just one, with no bloodhound.

Shelby rose from her bed with a heavy sigh, slightly defeated. Rory was going to get away with it if she didn't find evidence, something that tied him to Scarlet after they went to the movies.

It's hopeless, she thought as she opened her bedroom door, glancing back at the necklace strewn across the open map. *I need a miracle.*

Just as she was about to close the door, she heard a soft sound. It was an odd noise, a rustling, like something being dragged across paper. Her heart skipped a beat and she flung her bedroom door open, carefully studying the empty room.

Then she saw movement.

With wide eyes and pounding heart, she crossed the room, slowly and carefully as not to disturb whatever supernatural forces might be at work.

She couldn't believe what she was seeing. There, on the bed, the jade-streaked pendulum was inching its way across the map, the tip of the stone leading the way like an arrow, pointing her in the right direction.

It moved ever so slowly, but surely, past the center of the city, beyond Yellowhead Trail, towards the outskirts of Edmonton—and then stopped.

Shelby waited a few seconds, her breath caught in her chest, to see if the necklace was done. It didn't move anymore, so she took a step closer and leaned over the map.

The stone pointed to two words.

Shelby read it with a tremble in her voice, "*Devil's Gate.*"

11

Fate had no words. The ring Kane had put on her finger was beautiful, perfectly spellbinding. The band appeared to be forged of white gold while a tear-drop shaped crystal shone sapphire in the light.

"Kane...I...thank you," she said, tears filling her eyes. She didn't want to speculate as to what this type of gift might mean. A ring could mean very different things in Dark World in comparison to the Surface. But she couldn't deny the swell of excitement in her chest as she eyed the glistening stone.

His dark cheeks flushed a reddish hue and his pointed tail flicked back and forth. "It's a Soul Crystal."

She gazed at it, holding her hand up, watching its many facets glint against Dark World's reddish hue. "Soul Crystal? I've never heard of it before."

"There's a myth behind it, a love story," Kane said as they turned from the vendor and continued walking down the street.

"Really? What is it?" Fate inquired, her eyes fastened on him.

He smiled, then began, "Eons ago, even before demons roamed the underworld, an angel fell from the heavens. A being so pure, so powerful, she could scarcely be looked upon by mortal eyes. All alone in this strange new world, she searched for another like herself, a mate. Another immortal to love and share eternity with. The angel searched for ages, a millennium, before she realized that she was completely unique, a rare light in this world of darkness."

Fate watched his lips as he spoke, falling deeper in love with both him and the story with each passing word.

He continued, "One day, when she realized she would never find her other half, she decided to use magic to conjure a mate. Only, she didn't know that her inherently good magic could not be used in the underworld. Good magic used in a dark magic realm creates a curse against the user."

"That's so sad," Fate said, eyebrows pulling together. "All she wanted was love."

Kane nodded, then finished the story. "So, she used her magic to create a mate, only he was made of dark magic, and she, light magic—then the curse manifested. She got to see him just once before he was transformed into a beast and hidden from her. These crystals..." Kane pointed to Fate's new ring. "…are said to be the angel's tears, pieces of her lonely soul, searching for him. When one finds him, the curse will be broken and they can finally be together. So that is why it is tradition in Dark World to give the one you love a Soul Crystal, to carry it with you and help the angel find her mate."

"How beautiful, yet tragic," Fate said softly.

"Yes," Kane agreed. "But it is just another of Dark World's myths. My father used to tell it to me as a bedtime fable, I…"

"Kane! Fate!" a voice cried out from behind them. "I'm so glad I found you! Vrill asks for you to come to the palace at once!"

Kane and Fate spun around, coming face to face with an out of breath necromancer. It was Petra, one of Vrill's assistants.

"Petra, what is it?" Kane asked, his eyes wide. "Is it Ever? Is she awake?"

12

Shelby pulled her purple VW bug to the side of the dirt road and parked. She scanned the tree line, squinting through her Prada knock-off sunglasses. There were no real signs to tell her she was in the right place; she was just going to have to go with her gut. The bloodstone necklace had hopefully pointed her in the right direction, now she had to do the rest.

"I'm coming Scarlet," Shelby said aloud as she climbed out of her car and started into the woods.

The afternoon sunlight streamed through the lattice of branches, skeletal without their leaves. Despite the cool bite of November's air, snow had not yet fallen. And for that Shelby was thankful. She probably wouldn't be able to find any evidence after the snow fell, which could be any day now. Courtesy of the warming climate, Alberta's winters were far less harsh than they'd ever been.

She hadn't wanted to come here at night. Too risky, not to mention too scary. At least in the middle of the day she could see where she was going if she needed to run out of the woods like a bat out of hell. Despite her need to find evidence, she was suddenly terrified she might find more than she'd bargained for, like some Rory Dean cult-like hideout, or worse, a dead body. Scarlet's body. As much as she wanted to find

Scarlet, finding her corpse would leave emotional scars on Shelby that could last a lifetime. Her greatest hope was to simply find some evidence, something that could lead her and the cops in the right direction.

Nature breathed around her; the crisp autumn air still owning the phantom scents of summer. The tall poplars groaned as they swayed with the light breeze, white bark peeling from their trunks to reveal a blackened core. A gust of wind rushed through the trees, dehydrated leaves shuddered overhead and the branches scratched at one another. A whirlwind swept a pile of leaves up behind her, scattering them as effortlessly as feathers.

Despite the cheerful songs of chickadees and chattering of squirrels around her, the woods felt eerie. The whole area was desolate, as though untouched by human hands. No technology. No signs of life. Yet she didn't feel completely alone, like she should out there in the middle of nowhere. She felt like someone—or something—was watching her. There was a power here, an energy that pulled at her core.

An evil she couldn't name.

She shook it off with a shrug of her shoulders. *I'm just being paranoid,* she told herself, pulling her short jean jacket tighter around her body. She wasn't sure what she was going to find, probably nothing. But what if she did? What if she found Scarlet's broken body out there in the forest? What would she do?

She knew she should have told Greg where she was going, or anyone for that matter. But she couldn't risk being talked out of it, or worse, have someone else tag along. This was crazy enough for one person, no need to drag someone else to Looneyville with her.

She reached into her pocket and wrapped her hand around her cell phone for comfort. At least she had one way out. She'd punched in her exact location into the phone's GPS App, ready to send with one touch of her finger. Then at least if something happened, they'd know where to find her.

A narrow trail meandered before her, weaving through the thick copse of trees and bushes. This just had to be it. It was exactly where the bloodstone amulet had pointed to.

The woods loomed around her, herding her towards something. *Why would Scarlet have come out here? Did she go willingly?*

Horrific thoughts poisoned Shelby's imagination. Images of Scarlet being attacked overwhelmed her. Was Scarlet dragged out here, into the middle of nowhere? Raped? Murdered?

She swallowed hard, forcing the disturbing thoughts aside. She had a job to do. She had to focus.

Narrowing her eyes, Shelby could see something ahead, amidst the matrix of copper and honey foliage. She pushed her legs to go faster despite the bite of thorny branches on her ankles. Within moments the forest seemed to part, ushering her through a gateway, and she was free of the woods. Before her was a meadow encircled with trees. Beautiful, yet creepy.

A fairy ring, she thought absentmindedly, recalling the ancient folklore of witches chanting and dancing by moonlight, leaving a perfect circle in their wake, the enchantment preventing the growth of anything but grass within its border. Her insides quivered at the notion of this place used for Satanic purpose. But it was, after all, called Devil's Gate.

Slowly, she walked towards the center, instinct urging her. Like Scarlet's voice was calling to her, leading her. Shelby gut twisted suddenly, knowing she probably wasn't going to like what she was going to find.

Dry leaves and dead grass crunched beneath her feet as she pushed forward. Soft gusts of cool wind blew random strands of red hair over her face, tickling her pinkish nose and cheeks. Clouds overhead churned dark gray and ash with the threat of snow.

She shivered, pulling her coat tighter around herself, wishing she could just turn back, go back home and pretend like nothing had happened. But she couldn't. Scarlet needed her.

When she neared the middle of the field, she could distinguish a marking on the ground—and her blood ran cold. This was the place. This was what she'd been brought out here to see.

Her hand over her mouth and eyes filled with tears, she fell to her knees before the symbol, and whispered, "It's a *pentagram*."

13

"Vrill!" Kane shouted as he stormed through the French doors of the necromancer's private chambers. A quick glance at the back of the room told him his daughter was safe, but she still lay motionless upon a pedestal-like bed. "Is it Ever?"

Vrill shook his head. "No, she remains the same," he replied, clasping his hands together as though in prayer, the long sleeves of his crimson robe shimmering alongside the soft candlelight. "But there is hope."

Kane's brow pulled together. "Hope?"

"This is Kraton," Vrill said as he waved a dramatic arm towards an odd-looking character: a necromancer with various swirling tattoos all over his silver skin, a pointed blue Mohawk, and bone piercings scattered about his face. "He's our witch-doctor. He has just returned from a spiritual retreat."

Kane eyed the new addition suspiciously. How was this person to help his daughter? What voodoo would he perform? The Oracle was the only psychic he trusted, and she was away on a secret assignment, at his request. Previous to her transformation back to Sybil, the Oracle had embraced her own unique, somewhat creepy style, but this character, he looked simply ridiculous.

"Pleased to meet you," Fate piped up when Kane didn't respond.

The witchdoctor nodded at her, his swirling necromancer eyes seemingly amused by the drama unfolding around him.

"Kraton is a master of the dark arts," Vrill stated with pride. "And mediumship."

Kane narrowed his eyes. "Mediumship?"

"Yes," Vrill replied. "He'll attempt to connect with Ever's soul, to speak with her or..." He paused, clearly reluctant to mention the possibility of the queen's presence within princess. "...draw out the...*other*."

"No, he won't." Kane glowered at Vrill and his quack doctor; he'd have nothing of the sort done to Ever. He'd heard of others meddling with souls and no good ever came of it. If his mother was inside there, the witchdoctor could just as easily bring her to the surface instead of Ever.

"But Kane," Fate interjected, setting a cool hand upon his demon skin. "What if he can help her? Maybe he can reach her."

Kane softened, facing her. "It's too risky. If Malus is in there, it could give her the power she needs to possess Ever's body. Ever would be lost to us, forever," Kane said, his voice wavering, emotion threatening to surface.

Fate took his hand and replied softly, "Yes, but he might also be able to show Ever the way home."

14

Shelby wasn't sure how long she'd sat there staring at the evil black symbol spray-painted on the grass. Could this truly be where her best friend took her last breath? Or was this just some stupid cult thing, where teenagers hang out, do drugs, and pretend to be Satan worshippers?

She needed proof. Proof that Scarlet had been here. Shelby stood, brushing away any dried grass that had clung to her black pants, and looked around. The sun had started to dip lower in the sky; she'd have to leave soon.

"Come on," she whispered as she scoured the ground, shivering as a cold wind blew through the meadow. "There has to be something." But as much as she wanted to find something, something that could prove Scarlet had been there and put Rory behind bars, she was terrified of what she might unearth. Anything, any item of Scarlet's that she found, would be evidence of her friend's death. Evidence that she was never coming back.

Death, Shelby pondered, a lump rising in her throat. *If she's dead, why do I feel like she's still alive? Why do I feel her presence all around me? Is she a ghost now?*

Shelby shook her head. No, ghosts felt different. They left the tiny hairs on her arms and back of her neck defying gravity, and left a shadow of emptiness in her soul. But the thought of Scarlet filled her up inside, expectant that her best friend would appear before her at any moment. Like she was so nearby, her energy signature so close.

Was she just in denial? Just clinging to some shred of hope that didn't exist?

She kicked at the ground with the toe of her shoe, hoping luck would guide her.

Then it did.

The smallest hint of something shiny and black peeked out from behind a charred piece of wood. The more she looked at the area, a circular pattern emerged.

There was a fire here.

Shelby bent down, brushing dead leaves and blackened kindling aside. Beneath them was a thick layer of ash, and then something she recognized.

It was the heel of a boot—her boot—the boot she'd lent Scarlet the night she disappeared.

15

"What are you going to do to her?" Kane growled at the witchdoctor.

Fate stood beside the agitated demon, her arm linked in his—mostly to hold him back if he decided to charge the odd-looking character. The witchdoctor, Kraton, was practically naked except for a well-placed tan loincloth. Swirls of black and white tattoos covered his silver-blue skin, tribal art that would have been considered pretty cool on the Surface. The dozens of bones stuck in his face and wild blue hair that rebelled against gravity, however, were less than appealing.

Kraton stepped forward, surprisingly calm and unafraid of the hulking black demon before him. "I must perform a ceremony, call to her spirit and make contact," he said, his voice soothing and guru-like.

Kane seemed to relax. "I want to be here when you do," he ordered.

"Of course," Vrill interjected bluntly, one brow raised in Vulcan-like fashion. "She is, after all, your daughter."

"When?" Kane demanded, his hands clenched tight at his side.

Kraton took a long breath, his gaze falling on the sleeping princess, then said, "By the light of next full Surface moon."

Kane scowled. "How are we supposed to know when that is? It can't be seen down here."

The witchdoctor just smiled.

"He's creepy," Kane scowled as he sat on the bed and reached for a Bloodstone from his pouch, his usually gleaming blue eyes dim and tired-looking.

Fate laughed, sitting beside him, rubbing his back. "I agree, he is a little...different."

"Different," Kane scoffed, tilting his head back, crushing the red stone and allowing the liquid to saturate his tongue. Power flooded his eyes immediately, the strong glow returning. He sighed, his muscular chest rising and falling. Fate eyed him hungrily and leaned in for a kiss. He returned the favor, wrapping an arm around her and pulling her closer. "Hey now," he smirked, kissing her ebony lips. "Aren't you a bit young for an old guy like me?"

"Pfft," she replied, stifling a giggle. "You're *only* three hundred years older."

"Actually, it's only two hundred and eighty-three," he stated. "You were seventeen on the Surface, right?"

"Almost eighteen," Fate replied, feigning irritation.

"Oh, forgive me," he grinned, his fangs flashing white. "My mistake."

"I might forgive you," she purred as she ran her hands over his broad chest, the smoothness of his blue-black skin like velvet beneath her palms. It was then that the glint from her new ring caught her eye. She brought it to her face, exclaiming, "Hey, look, it changed color!" What was originally soft blue had now shimmered to a bright yellow. It reminded her of the sun, sending a fleeting and unexpected pang of homesickness through her.

Kane nodded. "Yes, it will change with your moods. Apparently," he mumbled as he nuzzled her neck, "you are very, very happy."

"Well," Fate confessed as he nibbled on her earlobe, pushing her longing of home aside. "At least we know it's accurate."

16

Shelby pulled up to the police station a little too fast, earning a few stern glances from the cops standing outside. With evidence in hand—her scorched black boot—she exited the car and raced up the steps.

Out of breath, she approached the front desk and dropped the ash-laden boot onto the counter, a sprinkling of dust raining down. "I need to speak with Constable Jack," Shelby said to the female officer behind the desk.

The woman looked up from her work, narrowing her eyes. "And who may I tell him is here?"

"Shelby Harris."

Slowly, the cop reached for the phone and punched in three numbers. "Hey, there's a Shelby Harris here to see you," she said into the receiver and after a nod, put down the phone and said, "Okay, you can go on back." The officer unlocked a little half-door for Shelby and escorted her through. "Third door on the left," she said pointing to a hallway near the back.

"Thanks," Shelby said as she made her way to Constable Jack's office. She weaved around bustling policemen and narrowly sidestepped a thrashing criminal handcuffed to a desk. This place made her very uncomfortable, but she had to tell the authorities what she'd found. It was the only way to help Scarlet, and the only way to nail Rory.

Shelby knocked on the third door on the left, just as she'd been told.

"Come in," a deep voice called from the other side.

She opened the door and walked in. Constable Jack, a rotund, older gentleman with silver hair and kind blue eyes, was on the phone. He held up an index finger, telling her to wait a moment. The room smelled of cologne and old sandwiches, likely his way of showering and eating supper during those overtime hours catching bad guys and doing paperwork.

"Yeah, okay, yes ma'am," he mumbled, munching on the side of his brown and silver mustache. "Yes, ma'am, we will. I understand. Yes. No, your neighbor shouldn't be standing naked in his front room window and waving at people. We'll talk to him." He glanced over at Shelby as she sat across from him and rolled his eyes. Shelby smirked. "Okay, bye. Yes, ma'am. Bye," he said hanging up the phone a little too hard and sighing as he turned his attention to her. "Well, what can I do for you Miss Harris? You're with the...Scarlet Prince case, right?" he asked, shuffling some papers on his cluttered desk as though Scarlet's case file was nearby.

Shelby nodded and cleared her voice, then said, "Well, sir, I found something you might be interested in. I went into the woods," she started, then paused. How was she going to tell him how she'd found the remote location? She'd lose all credibility if she claimed to be assisted by supernatural means.

So she skipped ahead, hoping he wouldn't ask. "And found this near a pentagram, buried beneath a bunch of ash." She held up the charred remains of her boot.

He eyed the footwear, his skepticism obvious. "And why would that be related to the Prince case?"

"It's mine," Shelby declared. "I lent her my clothes—and these boots—when she went out on her date that night."

He sighed again, and Shelby knew immediately that he wasn't taking her seriously. She was just some teenage girl with an overactive imagination. "Miss Harris," he began with a patronizing tone. "I understand that you need to find closure, but finding a scrap of boot in a random location with nothing tying them to the case is, I'm sorry, but absurd. And unless your name is somewhere on there, we can't prove it was linked to you or to Scarlet."

Tears welled in her eyes and her shoulders fell as all hope seemingly abandoned her. She realized he was just being realistic, but she just knew it was her boot—and that Scarlet had been the last to wear it. But he was right. There was no way she could authenticate it as her own, not to mention it had nearly been incinerated, so any hairs or fibers linking it to Scarlet were likely destroyed.

"Thank you for your time," Shelby muttered around the lump in her throat and stood, turning to leave.

"Oh," he added with a touch of exasperation, "and next time, don't touch the evidence with your bare hands, it would render it worthless in court. If you *must* move something, cover it up so you don't get your prints on it; otherwise, leave it for us to deal with." He gave her a tired smile and turned his attention to his mountain of paperwork.

She nodded, tucking the desecrated boot under her arm and moved towards the door.

"Miss Harris," the constable said quietly, Shelby stopped without turning around. "It's not that I don't believe you, but we need more proof. If you can find evidence to link the boot to Scarlet, or anything about the location to a crime, then I promise, I'll back you."

Determination renewed, she straightened her shoulders, wiped her tears and said, "I will."

17

Kane loaded his plate up with fried eggs of various colors and sizes, eight long strips of dark meat that looked like bacon, and a pitcher of green juice.

"Hungry?" Fate asked jokingly as she eyed the heap over-flowing on his platter.

He smirked. "I have a healthy appetite, thank you very much. Even as a young demon, I ate quite heartily."

Fate smiled at the thought of her big, strapping demon boyfriend as a wee lad. "What were you like as a kid?" She imagined him as a shy, elusive youth.

He shrugged, swallowing before he answered, "Didn't get to be a child for very long, my father was killed by the time I was twelve. I was raised in the mines after that."

Fate suddenly felt awkward for prying into his past. "Oh, sorry," she said, wishing she hadn't brought it up.

But he only smiled. "It's okay, I like that you want to know about me. I want to know everything about you too. Like, when is your birthday?"

Fate blushed. "December 25."

Kane looked puzzled, asking, "Why did you give that look with your answer?"

"Well, you know, it being Christmas day and all."

His eyebrows pulled together. “What day?”

Her jaw nearly dropped until she realized what she’d said. Christmas and Hell probably didn’t go together very well. She laughed lightly. “Never mind, Surface thing. When is yours?”

He filed in a forkful of eggs, but finished chewing before he replied, “In the winter.”

“Don’t you know the day?”

He shook his head. “We don’t have the same system as humans for time. We go by seasons.”

“But Dark World doesn’t have seasons, does it?” She was suddenly very confused.

He nodded. “Yes, right now is our winter, just as it is on the Surface.”

“How do you know what season it is if you can’t see up there?”

Kane wiped his mouth with a napkin, scrunching it up before setting it on his now empty plate. “We have calendars, ancient calendars, that show us.” He suddenly looked pensive, as though he just had an epiphany.

“What is it?” she asked.

“Oh nothing, just something Kraton said earlier about the full moon.”

She tilted her head inquisitively, urging him to explain.

“Well, he said he would perform the ritual on Ever during the next Surface full moon. As far as I knew, the ancient calendars for following the moon’s phases were lost centuries ago.”

Fate thought for a moment. "Maybe he uses the cycle of shade births? Isn't the full moon part of Malus's ritual?"

He nodded, but looked uncertain. "That's true, but so many of the shades have been born outside the rules, we can never be certain."

"So how does he know when the full moon will be then?"

Kane shook his head. "I don't know, but I'm quite curious to find out."

"Ahh, there's my girl," Vrill clapped his hands together as he approached Kane and Fate in the breakfast room. "Are you ready?"

Kane and Fate exchanged confused looks. "Ready? For what?" Fate asked.

"Today you begin your training!" The necromancer beamed.

For once, Fate was glad she didn't eat real food; her stomach was suddenly writhing like it was filled with worms. "Oh, that should be...interesting," she said, trying to sound remotely excited. *Nothing better than a dose of good old-fashioned embarrassment first thing in the morning.*

"Don't worry my dear, it will be fun," Vrill stated as he waggled a silver finger at her, urging her to follow him as he turned and sauntered down the hall.

Fate stood, sending a pleading glance to Kane. "Go on, you'll have fun," he said too nonchalant, smiling and nodding.

Fun? Fate thought, mildly annoyed. *What could be fun about it? I get to learn how talentless I am.*

She thought of Vale and Sybil and how awesome both of their powers were, hopefully she was as lucky as them. Frankly, though, she couldn't imagine a new ability that could be cooler than theirs. Who wouldn't want to be a prophet and predict the future? And Vale, his power was just amazing: turning into a cloud of dark mist and wisping from one place to another. She'd kill for that ability.

"This way," Vrill said without looking back. His emerald robes trailed long behind him as he led her through the castle of bones. Torches held by disembodied skeletal hands lit their path down a hall she'd never been. Before long, the hallway turned into a stairwell, winding and forging deep into the ground. The further they descended, the darker it got. He was leading her into the bowels of the castle, the dank and dark soul of the old palace.

Fate let her fingertips brush along the jagged, rocky walls on either side of her, the path seeming to narrow with every step into the underground. "Why are we going down here?" Fate inquired, hoping her voice wasn't as filled with nerves as she was.

"It's...safer," Vrill replied, his voice echoing off the walls of stone.

"Safer?" Fate repeated, her eyes widening as her infrared eyesight strained through the darkening tunnel. Just as she was about to mention the lack of light, Vrill snapped his fingers and a string of glowing lights illuminated above them. Like tiny suspended lightning bugs, the lights streamed downward, spiraling and twisting with the winding stairwell.

Vrill nodded. "Yes, my dear, some powers are very dangerous and must be...contained."

Fate swallowed hard. What kind of dark magic had been down here before her? She couldn't even imagine the multitude of horrors these shadowy walls might have seen. Not to mention, what breath-taking abilities had been discovered. She truly hoped she wouldn't disappoint the old necromancer, or herself. Like money and prestige on the Surface, one's power was everything here.

In an attempt to quell her insecurities, Fate tried to keep the conversation going. "What kind of power do you think I might have?"

The necromancer stopped, pivoting on a single stair to look her in the eye. "Honestly," he whispered, fear veiled behind his starlit eyes, "I can't even imagine what kind of power lies within a shade of your...uniqueness."

18

Despite the early hour, the square was already teaming with shades and necromancers. Kane kept his eyes down, avoiding contact with anyone. He hoped no one recognized him, but soon realized that was ridiculous since he was the only one of his kind in Necrosia. He'd contemplated wearing a dark cloak, but a seven foot demon is hard to hide.

Kane weaved in and out the crowd, dodging necromancers carrying large baskets of macabre wares and shades performing acrobatics and magic for onlookers. It was a regular party here all of the time.

So different from the demons, Kane thought as he watched the citizens of Necrosia with growing envy. *My people are so serious, so bitter; they don't enjoy life like this.*

He couldn't even think of a time where there'd been a celebration in the underground city. Of course, there'd been plenty of parties, balls, and fun when his father ruled Dark World. But the world was different then. The demons were at the top of the food chain. The shades, then humans, were their slaves, a weak and inferior race.

Then the world changed. Flipped on its axis. Like karma had decided the humans deserved better and the demons needed to be punished.

It was then, discovered too late, that the queen had been plotting for years, centuries even. Scheming with the humans and dealing with the enemies of King Lucifer. Not that he had many, but she managed to find a few that would happily stab him in the back.

Kane sighed, guilt trickling through him. Despite the pain and suffering his mother had caused this world, she also did something wonderful: she set the humans free.

As much as Kane despised his mother for killing his father, damning Dark World, and throwing her only son into the mining pits, he realized that humans had been treated the same, if not worse, for centuries. It wasn't their fault they'd been victims of the great earth divide, swallowed into the belly of oblivion when the continents split in two.

Their uprising against the demons had been nothing less than a slaughter, but it spoke volumes as to their rage. They'd been treated unfairly for too long. And Kane finally understood their bitterness.

It was only after the demons themselves were forced into slavery, treated as mere mortals, that Kane had begun to comprehend the injustice his kind had placed upon the humans. Only through pain and humiliation could he learn true compassion. True empathy.

Kane turned into a narrow space between two marble buildings, taking cover from prying eyes. She was already there, waiting for him.

They nodded at one another in greeting, then he asked with hope in his heart, "Did you find her?"

The woman clad in the long black robes gazed up at him, her glowing shade eyes meeting his, and replied, "Yes sire, I found her. I found your wife."

19

"Again," Vrill commanded as Fate closed her eyes and willed another ball of light from her chest. The first dozen had misfired, leaving large, crater-like holes in the walls of the cavern. Vrill wanted her to hold onto to them, keep them obedient within her palms, but they kept escaping, ricocheting off the walls and obliterating anything that was minding its own business in the room.

She was getting tired, very tired. The Bloodstone she'd consumed earlier was waning in her system, and the hunger was returning with a vengeance.

Vrill seemed to sense her fatigue. "You must learn to be one with what powers you have, respect them. You cannot be at the mercy of your weaknesses. Don't let the hunger control you, embrace the hunger, only then can you defeat it."

"But how?" Fate growled through gritted teeth, annoyance surfacing as she held an unstable brilliant white and blue orb between her hands.

The necromancer smiled. "That is why we are here."

Fate exhaled, exasperated as the sphere spun off into the corner and chewed off yet another slab of rock. "What about these mystery powers I'm supposed to have? When do they come?"

Vrill closed his eyes, seemingly at one with some invisible energy in the room, then spoke in an airy, guru-like voice, "They will arrive when you surrender."

"Surrender?" Fate repeated, dropping her hands to her sides. She flopped into a nearby chair, her energy level hitting bottom. "What do you mean surrender? To what? To whom?"

Vrill smiled, raising his hands in front of his body. A wave of translucent turquoise appeared, danced with the movements of his hands, wrapping itself around his body like a ribbon of Northern Lights. As he manipulated the band of light, left and right, up and down, he spoke, "All around you is energy, an ocean of unseen power. We breathe it in, yet never own it. It lives, vibrates, and hums around us, just waiting for us to yield to it, to become one with it."

Fate watched him, mesmerized. "How did you do that?" she asked, her voice small and tinny against the cavern walls.

He just smiled. "That is the secret, one in which you must find on your own. Now," he added, closing his open palm, the power vanishing as though on command. He then clapped his hands loudly and gestured for Fate to stand, proclaiming, "Again!"

20

Shelby lay on her bed, staring at the ceiling as though it held the secret to her universal questions. What was she going to do? The cops didn't believe her. Even if she could prove it was her boot she'd found in the clearing, she couldn't link it to Rory. She couldn't sit by and do nothing; she couldn't let Rory live free and happy after what she suspected he'd done.

Insecurity suddenly crept in. What if she was wrong? What if Rory was telling the truth, that he didn't do anything to Scarlet? There might be another killer out there, a serial killer, skulking amid the shadows of Edmonton's alleys, preying on young, innocent victims like Scarlet.

What if she was wrong about Rory?

I'm not, she thought, shaking her head in defiance. *Rory's the one, I know it. I just have to prove it. But how?*

Exasperated, she rolled onto her side and picked at a frayed string on a decorative pillow. This was one of those times when she'd call Scarlet. These were the hardest times to endure, the ones where she needed her best friend. Scarlet was always the rock in the relationship, the logical, level-headed one that could figure out any puzzle, solve any problem. This kind of stuff, figuring out what to do next, was not Shelby's strong suit.

Shelby recalled an incident when they were nine years old, when Shelby's purebred Shih Tzu, Freckles, went missing from the back yard. Akin to Sherlock Holmes, Scarlet followed clues like a bloodhound, Shelby as her pathetic excuse as Watson tagging along behind. Within only a few short hours, and tons of searches on Kijiji, Scarlet found a couple looking for a male Shih Tzu to breed with their female.

Shelby's parents had received a phone call only a few weeks before, a couple had called to ask about their dog and if they could buy Freckles from them. Her parents declined and thought nothing more of it. After a reverse search of the phone number on the internet, Scarlet found their address and bingo, they'd found Freckles.

Scarlet was always the sturdy one. The reliable, stead-fast, calm one. Shelby felt lost at sea without her, floundering. Drowning.

Maybe she should go to Greg. He was, after all, her boyfriend and the one person who could possibly understand what she was going through. Despite Greg and Scarlet's sibling animosity, there was genuine love and loyalty there. He would help her, Shelby knew he would. But she didn't want him to know her suspicions about Rory. Being a testosterone-rich male, Greg would more than likely march over to Rory's house and rip him limb from limb.

With that thought, Shelby sat up in her bed and gasped.

She suddenly knew exactly what she needed to do.

21

"You found her? Are you certain?" Kane's throat tightened, he hadn't expected to find her so fast.

Sybil nodded. "Yes, she was where you said she might be, in the Valley of Shadows."

"Did anyone see you? Did...Seren see you?" Saying her name aloud made his heart ache. He knew he had to do this. He knew he had to see her.

"No sire, I was unseen," the shade said, her eyes narrowing. "What will you do now?"

Kane inhaled, then spoke, "I must find a way to leave Necrosia...without Fate. She cannot know what I'm doing."

"I understand, you know where I am if you need me further." The oracle shade bowed to him, taking her leave and disappearing into the alley like a ghost.

A cold knot tightened in Kane's chest. Seren, his wife, his first true love. It felt wrong to keep anything from Fate, but this, this was different.

He made his way back to the necromancer castle, indecision gnawing at his core. Could he look Seren in the eyes and still stay on course? Would she remember him? Would she be coherent enough to hear him? To reply to him? Kane didn't know all the answers, but he knew it was imperative that he speak with his wife, and soon.

Upon entering the castle, Vrill greeted him. "Your highness, I was just looking for you."

"Oh?" Kane raised a brow. "What can I do for you, Vrill?" The necromancer waggled a finger at Kane, signaling for the demon to follow him into the den. Kane, though his mind was in a hundred other places, reluctantly complied. While he liked the odd necromancer leader, he tended to drag conversations on for far too long. "Where is Fate?" Kane inquired, realizing his love was last with Vrill.

"She is resting," Vrill replied with a guilty smile. "I suspect I've tired the poor girl out for the day."

"Ah, and how is her training coming?" Kane asked, crossing the room and lowering himself into one of the high-back bone chairs, adjusting his large, black wings accordingly as not to aggravate the shackles attached to the stems.

Vrill sat across from the demon, folding his fingers together as though conjuring a prayer. "Very well, where she lacks in control, she gains in will."

Kane nodded, then asked in his baritone voice, "So, what did you want to speak to me about?"

"We need to discuss the scrolls," Vrill stated bluntly, which surprised Kane as the necromancer enjoyed mulling over topics in great length before getting to the point.

"Yes," Kane agreed. "We are in possession of four, but must obtain the other two." It was crucial to reactivate the

Crystal Pyramid, to re-establish the power of the light to Dark World. Without it, the demons would eventually dwindle away; dying of old age and sickness, resulting in their eventual extinction. Dark World needed to be brought back to life, and the only way was to obtain all six scrolls and re-open the fissure to the Surface.

"I've been studying them," Vrill began, "and their riddles. Your father was fond of creating a mystery." He chuckled.

Kane smiled wistfully, nodding. Yes, his father enjoyed mind games, usually harmless, but playful nonetheless.

"The first discusses the devil's heir, the second makes reference to the races...*To rise, to ascend, the races must blend...*" Vrill quoted with Kane listening fixedly. He continued, "*Must blur the lines of disparity, must come together, with the pages united.*" He stopped, his eyes focused on Kane's.

His father's words, his legacy, left Kane speechless. No matter how many times he heard it, it still sent a fleet of chills up his spine. He cleared his voice before asking, "What do you think it means?"

The necromancer paused, his smooth, blue forehead creasing. "I believe he means that along with the pages, all the races must be present to open the fissure."

Kane bristled, the memory of his disagreement with the wraiths surfacing. He'd all but declared war with them when he fought for Fate's freedom from their tornadic barrier. How was he to return to them and ask for their assistance? There was great mistrust there now, great animosity. He replied, "*All* the races?"

Vrill nodded. "Yes, all of them. But only one from each lineage. One banshee, one wraith, one necromancer, one demon, and one...reaper." He shuddered as he named the last.

Kane's large chest heaved as he exhaled a sigh. It wouldn't be easy, gathering them all; despite the fact he already had two out of the five. He frowned, realizing something. "What about the shades? Are they one of the races?"

"Yes and no," Vrill pursed his lips. "I believe that's what the queen meant when she said that Fate was the key to the Crystal Pyramid."

Now it was Kane's turn to suppress a shudder. One of the last words she'd said before she turned her feral shades on him was that she hadn't needed Fate's body, to possess it, she needed her because she was the key to opening the fissure. Up until now, Kane hadn't given it much credence; he'd thought it the rants of a demon gone mad.

"You think she needs to be present? Along with the scrolls and the races?" Kane asked.

"Yes," Vrill stated. "I believe that's what your father intended."

"Why?"

The necromancer pondered a moment. "He had to make it nearly impossible, didn't he? To open the fissure again. I think he knew he had to make it a joint effort, a cooperation between the races."

Kane's mind whirled. Did his father see good in the shades all along? Did he foresee the disparity, knowing that coalition was the only answer? What respect he had for his father multiplied in that moment. The king was truly great in all ways. It made Kane wonder how he could ever live up to those standards.

"Alright then," Kane smiled, suddenly energized. He could open the fissure, turn the Crystal Pyramid back on and give his people their mortality back. This would make him a great king, one worthy of respect, like his father. "We just need to gather the races, retrieve the remaining scrolls and save this world."

With that, Vrill appeared ill at ease, his swirling eyes of light churning with concern. "What is it?" the demon asked, leaning forward.

Vrill took a deep breath in, then released, and said, "I have a confession to make."

"Confession?" Kane repeated, anxiety climbing onto his shoulders. "What kind of confession?"

Vrill hesitated, his eyes trained on the floor. "I have been dishonest with you Prince Kane."

Kane cringed with the reference to his royal name, followed by refreshed angst. What had the necromancer withheld? "How? How have you been dishonest?" the demon inquired through gritted fangs, unsure if he really wanted to know at all.

"The scrolls we have," he said quietly. "Not all of them are...authentic."

Kane's heart stopped a moment, his breath caught in his throat. It was several moments before he could reply, "I don't understand. What do you mean by 'not authentic'?"

His gleaming silver skin dimmed momentarily. "Some of them have been…duplicated…if you will," he confessed with reluctance.

Kane absorbed this a moment, fearful to know more details. He was tired of being deceived. Tired of games and dishonesty. Exhaling, he asked, "How many are real?"

Vrill paused again, a glimmer of fear behind his eyes. "One."

The demon stood, rage exploding from him. "One! Which one?"

"Yours," Vrill answered, then added, "The rest are forgeries."

"What happened to the originals?" Kane's hooves pounded against the marble floor as he paced back and forth before an enormous fireplace.

"We had them duplicated, conjured if you will, by careful hands," Vrill confessed, standing and adjusting his long emerald robes. He pressed his palms together and approached the fireplace, igniting it with just a flick of his finger. The hot flames licked the air, threatening to escape the onyx enclosure but dissipating just as it appeared to have succeeded.

Frustration and hurt settled inside Kane. When would he learn? Hadn't his years with Syphon and the demon elders taught him anything? They'd lied to him. Omitted important truths, yet here he was, again faced with betrayal by someone he'd grown to trust. Finally, Kane's fury was overshadowed by duty. "Who has them?"

The necromancer lifted his eyes to the demon, fervent respect embedded in them as he uttered her name, "*Myth.*"

22

Turbulent dreams rolled through Fate's subconscious, images of terrific beasts flashed, pictures of horror. Ghoulish fiends reached for her, hatred broiling behind their fiery eyes, their talons tearing at her skin and hair. Blood-drenched demons with their wings ripped from their bodies, snickering wraiths—and Malus, her ivory face distorted, laughing wickedly. Death and sadness bombarded her, a wretched past or terrifying future, she couldn't tell. Was this the old Apocalypse...or a new one on its way?

And then there was the whispering. From a voice she could not name, a voice she'd heard before. "*Privus liberum,*" the voice said over and over, softly, ever so softly. "*Privus liberum.*"

Fate woke with a start, sweat trailing over her brow. She pushed her damp hair from her face, heart pounding in her chest. "Privus liberum," she uttered through shaky lips. "What does it mean?"

She lay back down, curled into a ball and pulled the blanket over her shoulders. Exhausted, she wanted to go back to sleep, but was almost afraid to do so. The dream had been so dark, so disturbing.

She groaned as she turned onto her back, her entire body ached from the long session with Vrill. He'd been relentless in his training, never allowing her to stop but for a moment to catch her breath. It was like he wanted to wear her down, to take her to the breaking point.

It was kind of annoying.

As she laid there, the hunger chewed at her insides, the desire expanding like a black hole in the center of a galaxy, never satiated, growing as it devoured more and more of the solar system. Fate reached for the night stand, retrieving the last of the Bloodstone she'd received at supper only a few nights ago. She eyed it undecidedly, should she use up the last of her sustenance? It was only a matter of time before she'd have to go back to using the Soul Nexus, which hadn't been able to sustain her needs for long. The stretch between 'meals' grew shorter and shorter each time she used the Nexus, like a drug that adapted to her system each time she abused it.

She sighed, folding her fingers around the rock and crushing it. She had no choice; she'd have to deal with the hunger as it came. The ruby liquid wet her tongue and a fire of energy surged throughout her body. The hunger recoiled like a cobra, but never truly went to sleep; it only waited for its next opportunity to strike.

Fate lay there a moment, savouring the brief normalcy. How long before she couldn't contain it? How long before she became the monster that she barely kept at bay?

How long before she killed?

She got up off the bed, shaking off the nightmare and her worries. The Bloodstone would last a day at most before the hunger would begin to emerge again; she wasn't going to waste those precious hours with worry.

The drawer caught her eye. The drawer that held her *cure*. What would it do to her? She was more afraid that it wouldn't do anything at all than do something horrible. What was more horrible than craving the souls of living creatures? What could make her feel more a monster than robbing innocent beings of their essence?

Fate opened the drawer, tempted again by the prospect of being free of this curse, but remained hesitant. She didn't know what stopped her from taking it: fear of betrayal by the demons or more change in an already chaotic afterlife.

23

Shelby sank low in her seat, the last thing she needed was for Rory to see her skulking outside his house. She'd borrowed her mom's car instead of using her own, which would have been far too recognizable since hers was a bright purple Volkswagen Beetle.

Part of her knew this was a stupid idea, but the other half of her was stoked for the adventure and nailing Rory's balls to the wall. Her plan was simple: wait for him to leave, break in, and search his room. It's well-known that serial killers have a penchant for keeping souvenirs from their victims. If he was guilty, she was bound to find something. Besides, what could go wrong? Other than she had no idea how she was going to get into the house—and did they have a dog that would be happy to chew her leg off?

For once, she wished she knew a bit more about Rory Dean.

Visually, she understood why Scarlet would have liked him, well, she more than liked him, she was head over heels for the guy, but it was only his face that Scarlet knew. Only the handsome, rugged good looks—the outer shell. But did Scarlet know anything about the guy beyond that?

Of course Greg, her own boyfriend, was gorgeous, but Shelby saw more than that. She saw a spark. A nameless power behind his eyes, a softness. Shelby wondered what else Scarlet saw in Rory. Had she seen a kindness in him? Some unsurpassed intelligence or outstanding characteristic that Shelby had simply overlooked?

She was pretty sure she hadn't.

Because of Shelby's innate ability to read people, she'd sensed something dark about Rory right from the beginning. Even back in grade nine when Scarlet first laid eyes on the guy, Shelby had seen something she couldn't quite name, something that sent chills up her spine. She tried to tell Scarlet that this guy was no good, but there was no talking her out of it. It was like he was part of some twisted destiny for her. A dark and magnetic fate, like all this was meant to be.

Shelby sighed, she was getting bored and her back hurt from slouching. She could practically hear Scarlet telling her she was crazy. Maybe she was. Maybe all this was just pointless and Rory was innocent.

Nope. No way, Shelby thought, narrowing her eyes. *Besides, innocent until proven guilty, and that's just what I intend to do—prove he's guilty.*

Finally, after three hours of playing Bejeweled on her iPhone, drinking two bottles of pop, and devouring three bags of chips, Shelby saw Rory step out his front door. She'd almost abandoned her post ten minutes previous as she had to pee so bad from the pop that she was worried her bladder might actually break. Not only was she anxious to break in and search his room, she was desperate to use his bathroom!

Crouched low in her seat, she watched as Rory got into his black '67 Chevelle, backed up out of the drive, and cruised down the road. She waited until he was completely out of sight before she even sat up. Donning a pair of black gloves she'd brought just for the occasion, her heart thrumming in her chest like a hummingbird on caffeine, she slowly opened the car door and climbed out of the car.

She'd never done anything like this before. Sure, she'd snuck out of the house a hundred times and ventured a couple of blocks to scale the lattice beneath Scarlet's window, but this was different. This was illegal.

And if she was right about Rory, it was the most dangerous thing she could possibly be doing.

The sun was tucking itself in for the night, putting the time at about six o'clock. She confirmed it as six twenty on her phone. Shelby never wore a watch, it made her feel claustrophobic.

As she walked swiftly up the sidewalk, she felt incredibly conspicuous, like she should be hiding behind trees and doing ninja rolls between bushes to keep from being seen by the neighbours. If her bladder wasn't screaming bloody murder, she might have considered it. It had occurred to her, of course, that she could just drop her drawers and squat against a tree or something, but that was just something she couldn't do. Ever. Seemed so—uncivilized. She could wait, but not much longer.

When she reached his front door, she stopped cold. This was incredibly stupid. What if she was the one who ended up in jail and not Rory? That would suck. A lot.

"I have to do this, for Scarlet," she whispered, giving herself a little pep talk.

Since a lot of people, especially men, didn't lock their doors, Shelby figured she'd try the door knob first.

No such luck.

"There's got to be some way in," she muttered under her breath, searching around for a hidden key. "Strike two," Shelby said after checking under a few rocks and a ratty old doormat. "Now the windows."

After a few minutes of crawling around and peering into the basement windows, realizing the place was like Fort Knox, she finally just grabbed a big rock and tossed it at an already cracked pane of glass.

"Sorry, but I gotta go," she said aloud, cradling her bladder and praying that none of the neighbours heard the crash or saw her vandalizing Rory's house.

She sat down on her butt, kicked away some of the excess glass and shoved her legs through the hole. It was a tight squeeze and hard to lower herself down without landing on glass, but after wriggling a bit and clinging to the window frame, she found her footing.

"Okay, first things first," she said as she ascended the basement stairs, desperately searching for a bathroom. "Ahh, yay!" she exclaimed aloud, racing into a small half-bath on the right.

After her happy release and a not-so-quiet flush, she got down to business.

"Okay, let's get us some evidence." She clapped her hands together and rolled up her sleeves.

For whatever reason, she figured she should check his bedroom first. Still cautious despite the raucous crash from the window shattering and the bathroom break, she tiptoed down the hall.

She peeked around every door frame like an FBI agent, left then right, making sure there was really no one home. Her hours of staking out his house, though, had convinced her he was the only one home. It was then that she realized something strange: Rory appeared to live alone. As in no parents.

How odd, she considered. *He's only seventeen, why would he have this place all to himself? How does he pay for this?*

She wandered through a darkened hallway, scoping out the two bedrooms. One was littered with what was obviously Rory's dirty laundry and the other was set up as an office. Nope, no parents here.

Shelby walked through the living room, and while the furniture simply appeared out of date, she was perplexed as to how many antiques were placed about the room. Some even looked over a hundred years old.

She picked up one in particular, a beer stein made of russet and white porcelain with countryside scene painted in blue on the side. From the looks of it, it was made in the early 1900s. She knew this because her great grandpa had one in his collection before he died. And he was eighty-four.

Shelby set down the antique, wondering why a teenage boy with no parents would have such a bizarre collection.

An inheritance, maybe? She shrugged and continued looking through his things. Something linking him to Scarlet must be there. It had to be.

She went back into his bedroom, that's where most people kept the most personal and secretive things. Careful not to disturb anything despite the chaos in his room, she panned over every item. Sweaters, jeans, rolled up socks; while the rest of the house seemed out of the ordinary for a teenage boy, his bedroom was certainly stereotypical. It didn't smell that fantastic either.

Shelby had almost given up when she saw something interesting, half-hidden by an Edmonton Oilers jersey. In the corner was a black duffel bag—covered in dried grass.

24

A fountain of silver waters reflected like an undulating mirror, pouring over the smoothened surface of ancient stones. Voluptuous trees filled the rounded courtyard, their boughs heavy with a multitude of unnameable fruits not seen on the Surface. Everything breathed here, lived and moved with some enchanted purpose. This place didn't just look magical, it was made of magic.

Necrosia's courtyard was one of Fate's favorite places in Dark World, other than the garden within the demon city, of course. How she hoped to see it again one day, with its magical color-changing trees, millions of flowers, and spirited pixies. Even the old, cranky Night Mare with his mane and hooves of fire clung to her memories.

Spark, Fate's phoenix friend spun and dove overhead, his flaming wings leaving a stream of heat waves with every pass. He was getting big. When he and Fate had arrived in Necrosia only a few weeks ago, he was just a hatchling. Now, he appeared almost a teenager.

Fate's thoughts turned to her lost friend, Ick. The adorable gargoyle she'd found in the first days of being in Dark World. She missed his soft, white fur, his orb-like green eyes, and his penchant for getting into trouble. Since she'd lost him in the

Crystalline Forest, she longed to go back and search once again for her friend. Even though Vale was technically responsible for scaring Ick away (chasing him through the Crystalline Forest to steal his soul) Fate didn't hold it against him. She understood the cravings far too well now.

"So how's your training going?" Vale asked as he entered the courtyard and sat beside her, ruffling her hair like an annoying older brother.

She grimaced as she smoothed back her mane. "Not great, I'm afraid."

"Why?" he asked.

She shrugged. "I don't think I'm strong enough to control the powers."

"What does strength have to do with it?" he said with a wink. "It's all about believing in yourself and what you can do."

"That's just it," she replied. "I don't believe I can do those things. How can I do it if I don't even know what the power is?" She flung her hands up and let them drop in frustration.

"Your power will be the greatest of them all," Vale reassured. "It's your destiny."

"Pfft," she scoffed. "How can someone so insignificant and small do something so great?"

"How big do you have to be to do something great?" Vale smirked, his wise eyes twinkling. She'd forgotten how old he really was. Over one hundred years. That's a long time to live, even on the Surface, that's closing in on Guinness Books of World Records status. For a split second, she wondered how long it would take for her to get sick of immortality. On the Surface, there's fear of death, but it's believed to be a time of peace, a well-earned rest from the chaos of living. If only they knew what really awaited them. Of course, she'd only seen this side of eternity; she wondered what the opposite was like. If this was Hell, what was Heaven?

"Smart ass." She grinned at him, shoving her shoulder into his.

"Where's Kane?" Vale inquired, glancing up at the castle walls as though Kane were visible somehow.

"I'm not sure, I haven't seen him since this morning," she replied. "Why?"

"No reason really," he answered looking away. "I was just wondering what he and my sister were talking about in the alleyway this morning."

Fate crinkled up her nose. "What? That is odd. I thought she was gone."

Vale shrugged. "I guess she's back. I just can't figure out what they'd be doing hiding away somewhere to talk."

"Hiding away?" Fate felt a streak of jealousy run through her. Vale had a point. It's not like Kane and Sybil were really close or anything. There shouldn't be any reason for them to meet secretly. "Did you see them personally?"

Vale shook his head and grinned mischievously, stating, "No, I have eyes and ears on the street." Then he stood, wiping invisible lint from his shoulders as though he really did brush the subject off. "I have to go find Aura, talk to you later."

Fate watched him walk away, dumbfounded by the news. Kane was always so upfront with her, so honest. Why would he keep something from her? What could he possibly have to discuss with Sybil that he couldn't discuss with her?

Stop it, Fate, she told herself. *You haven't even seen him since this morning; he'll probably tell you as soon as you see him.*

She nodded, agreeing with herself. She'd wait, giving him the benefit of the doubt—for now.

25

Kane paced the width of the den, his ebony hooves clacking furiously against the polished marble tiles. Vrill sat virtually motionless, his eyes averted guiltily to the floor.

Why this? Why now? Kane fumed. *Victory was within our grasp. The Crystal Pyramid nearly restored…but now, more delay.*

He wondered if his father had encountered such setbacks over the millenniums. Had he, too, navigated such insurmountable odds? Kane was certain he did, he could not have become such an admirable king otherwise.

Inhaling deeply, Kane pressed on. "Who is this...Myth?" he demanded of Vrill.

Vrill's eyes brightened a little. "She is our creator, the source of our souls," he said reverently.

Kane thought back to a previous conversation they'd had, when he'd first learned that the necromancers had stolen the scrolls. "The one who is dying? Who needs the Crystal Pyramid to be reactivated to live?"

Vrill nodded enthusiastically.

"And the scrolls are with her?" he pondered rhetorically, then added, "And just where does this *Myth* live?" Kane asked, feeling drained by the news. He'd planned on things going much smoother. He thought he only needed to acquire two more scrolls, but now it would seem that he needed all but one.

The necromancer looked uneasy.

Great, more bad news, Kane thought, exasperated as he prepared himself.

Vrill cleared his throat. "Exile Island."

Kane's jaw dropped. When he regained composure, he sputtered, "Exile...Island?"

The necromancer cringed, obviously knowing full well the implications of such a journey.

"But," Kane started. "That's impossible. Why does she have them anyways? If she is dying, why do you not have them in your possession for safe keeping, so we can use them to reactivate the Crystal Pyramid the moment we have them all?"

"It was," Vrill said sheepishly, "for safe keeping."

"How did you get them there?" Kane was suddenly suspicious. Exile Island was clear on the other side of Dark World, in the center of the Black Ocean. A dark enchantment surrounded the island: No one could enter, no one could leave.

Vrill's eyes clouded over as he spoke, like he was reliving a nightmare. "*It* just came one day, shortly before you arrived. Took them from us, took them to her. And left us with the perfect copies."

"*It*?" Kane reiterated, raising one brow.

The necromancer's silvery blue skin paled. "Death."

"Death?" Kane repeated, confused.

"A pale rider, cloaked. The Fourth Horseman," Vrill explained, hand shaking as he raised his cup of tea to his mouth.

The demon chuckled. "The Fourth Horseman. He's a legend. A fairytale for the suspicious."

"Be that as it may, it is who arrived on the doorstop only days before you. It is who took the scrolls and left the others in their place," Vrill said, his disturbed gaze fixed on the flames in the fireplace.

Kane narrowed his eyes at the necromancer, his patience growing short. "This *Myth*, this creator of yours, she sounds evasive. How do I know if I travel all that way, risk my life, that she will surrender the scrolls to me?"

Vrill inhaled deeply, reflecting a moment before he answered, "Because she is dying, she needs the light of the Crystal Pyramid to heal, to live. If she doesn't give them to you to relight the monolith, she will die—and so will every being in Dark World."

26

Fate wandered the castle, searching for Kane. Her mind spun, trying to think of what he might have been doing in the alleyway with Sybil. He had mentioned the other day that he needed to talk with her about the scrolls, maybe that was it? But something didn't sit right with her. Why would he feel the need to hide? Why wouldn't he just meet Sybil in the castle?

A seed of jealousy germinated in her stomach. Maybe Kane had developed a penchant for shades now. Maybe Fate wasn't interesting enough for him because she couldn't develop her powers like Vale and Sybil.

Her eyes narrowed and she folded her arms over her chest, heat churning in her core. She'd have to interrogate him. Get the answer out of him. There was no way in hell he was going to cheat on her and get away with it.

But is he cheating? Fate's logical side asked, her heart softening.

She took in a deep breath, then another, exhaling slowly. She had to learn to trust him. This was Kane, the demon who'd risked it all to be with her. Set aside his own mistrust for shades and professed his love for her regardless of the controversy and upheaval it would create within his xenophobic demon race. Why would he suddenly throw that all away?

He wouldn't.

Suddenly she felt better, the claws of doubt retracted into their suspicious lair. But still, why was trust so hard for her? Kane had been more than loving with her in the last few weeks, despite his worry for Ever and the destiny of his world. If anything, his attentiveness was remarkable considering the situation.

"I'm so selfish," Fate muttered as she climbed the steps to her room, nearly reaching the landing.

"Selfish?" a deep, baritone voice queried from the top of the stairs.

"Kane!" Fate exclaimed, placing a hand over her now racing heart. Immersed in her self-wallowing, she hadn't heard his approach. She gazed up at Kane, her sweet demon, and realized that all her worry and jealousy had been for naught. It was in the way he looked at her, with such devotion, such eternal love, that she knew he would never do anything to hurt her. An inkling of shame wove itself around her conscience. How could she think he would slink around behind her back? Go against all they stood for?

He smiled warmly at her, closing the gap between them and taking her into his arms. He kissed her once on the forehead, then said quietly, "Why are you calling yourself selfish? You're the most unselfish person I know."

She raised her face to his, puzzled. "I am?"

"Of course," he stated with an unwavering smile, tucking a strand of her silver hair behind her ear while gazing down at her. "I've never known anyone who puts aside their own needs for the sake of others as much as you. Speaking of which, you must be starving." His eyes narrowed with worry. "Do you have any Bloodstone left?"

Fate thought of the last of the stones Vrill had given her as a meal several days ago, and shook her head. She'd taken the last that morning. It disgusted her that she *needed* this so badly. She felt like a heroin junkie or something, desperate for her next fix. Pathetic.

"I have some in my bag, you can have it," Kane stated as he took a step towards his room.

Fate shook her head. "No, I can't let you do that. You need it too." She took his hand into hers and guided him from the door. "I'll be fine with the Nexus, I promise," she said, holding her hand up like a boy scout swearing an oath.

He gave her a sideways glance, glowing blue eyes sizing her up. "Are you certain?"

"Of course," she replied with a smile, wrapping her arms around his torso and laying her head on his massive chest, hiding the pain in her eyes as the white lie turned black inside.

27

Shelby fell to her knees before the black duffle bag, her heart throbbing against the inside of her chest so hard and fast it made her dizzy. This was it, she knew it. She could feel it.

After locating the start of the zipper, she slowly opened it. The bag opened wide like a gaping maw, darkness staring back at her. What if she found what she was looking for? What if she didn't? The prospects swirled around inside her head, the consequences if she was wrong, the significance if she was right. Personally, she wasn't sure she wanted either scenario to unfold. If she found nothing in the bag, or in Rory's house, she would have to face the fact that there was another killer out there. Or maybe none at all. Maybe Scarlet's fate had nothing to do with violence. Maybe Rory had been telling the truth all along, that she disappeared during the movie and simply ran away like many a teenager had done.

Shelby closed her eyes, shaking her head. Impossible. Scarlet would never do that to her family, or to Shelby for that matter. Besides, Scarlet was the least streetwise person Shelby had ever met. It would take a certain kind of wit and mindset to exist on the cold, cruel streets of the city.

But, on the other hand, if Shelby did find something to implicate Rory, she'd have to face certain realities. One being that

Scarlet was truly gone, and probably not in the most pleasant of fashions.

Either way, Shelby knew she needed the truth about what happened to her friend, Greg needed closure, and Scarlet's parents needed closure.

And it was all down this moment, and Shelby knew it.

She pried apart the sides of the bag, cautiously peeking inside. At first she could see nothing but black fabric, like a dark blanket made of thick cotton. She pushed the blanket aside, feeling around the sides. Sweat gathered on her brow and she tried in vain to silence her thundering heart. Why couldn't this be like a scene in a thrilling movie, easy and almost cheesy, the evidence left out in plain view while gaudy, suspenseful music played?

She swept around both sides of the bag, her breath shallow and forced. "It has to be here," she said aloud, then gave a paranoid glance around. She had to be more careful, just in case Rory came back, or there was someone in the house that she'd missed.

With that thought, images of Scarlet poured through her imagination. What if Scarlet was being held hostage somewhere? In this house—or another location? Shelby cringed with the notion that her friend might be enduring evils far worse than her young, teenage mind could conceive of. Maybe death in this case was part of a far better option. For Scarlet's sake, Shelby hoped she was already dead, put out of her misery rather than suffer at the hand of a rapist or torturer.

Suddenly, her hand hit something hard—and sharp. The edge of a cold blade sliced through her glove's pointer finger, missing her skin by mere millimeters.

Her mouth went dry as a psychic sensation rippled up her arm. This was what killed Scarlet. This was what murdered her friend.

Warms tears slid down her cheeks as images bombarded her mind, images of terror and blood and violence. For the first time, she'd come to realize that her best friend, her sweet Scarlet, was truly gone.

But why then did she still *feel* her? Like she was alive? Was she simply unable to face the truth?

It wasn't going to be easy convincing Constable Jack that this was probably the murder weapon, but she'd have to try. She knew it without a shadow of a doubt.

Shelby steeled herself, taking a deep breath in before she pulled the item of death out of the bag. She needed to take it to the cops as soon as possible. They could do some of their DNA testing on it; prove that Scarlet's blood was on it, and put that bastard in jail.

Not to smudge any precious evidence, Shelby withdrew it from its hiding place holding it by the top of the hilt. The blade slid out, serrated edges gleaming like rows of shark teeth. Shelby gasped and dropped the knife, the weapon clattering loudly against the hardwood floor as she backed away from it.

It was true—Rory Dean was a killer.

28

The various skulls within the bedroom seemed to watch him with quiet sentience. As though their desiccated, eyeless sockets had some kind of magical sight, they scrutinized him, judged his every thought and movement. Kane closed his eyes, willing the world back to the way it was so long ago. When everything was in balance. Back to when his father had it under control, under his seemingly flawless rule. What he wouldn't give to make it that way once again. Only it was impossible. Without a king like Lucifer, Dark World was damned to be the wasteland his mother created.

He had to wonder if she had preferred it that way, chaotic and existing without reason or purpose. She invaded cities like a tsunami, destroying everything in her path. Most of the villages surrendered to her without a fight, but a few of the brave fought back without success. Everyone soon discovered that if you weren't for her, you were against her. No one had a say, a voice, only silent submission.

Several of the larger cities were spared her tirade—but for a steep price. Every deal was different, for some she spared the children if the adults consented to work in her mines, others were forced to offer up their first-born if the head of the house was too old or lame to work.

The wraith city, Cryptica, had been left untouched. Kane wondered what deal they'd made with the devil to achieve that. Certainly their freedom would have come at a heavy expense. Other towns, like the banshees' Sensua and the necromancers' Necrosia were also left untouched, but Kane was certain that was due in part to the well-known deadly powers they held. The reapers also had a renowned reputation as formidable killers, but since their city's location was so remote and mysterious, Kane was sure his mother had let them be as well.

Kane's head ached, his entire body tired but restless after the discussion with Vrill. How could one being's existence be crucial to every living creature in Dark World? This Myth, how was she tied to *everyone* in the underworld? And how was it that she was a virtual phantom within the world? So little was known of her. How had she made it this long as a mystery to both himself and his mother? Malus had spies everywhere. She knew everything—or so she thought.

Frustration crawled through his system. He had so much to do, and so little time to do it. His first concern was the scrolls. Not only did he have to contend with one of the harshest terrains in Dark World, Exile Island, but he wasn't even sure how he was to obtain it from this secretive and powerful super being.

Then there was Ever. Stricken with an unexplained and potentially fatal illness, he wasn't even certain his daughter still owned her body. His sick, twisted mother might inhabit it. To top that off, a crazy-looking witchdoctor wanted to do some mumbo jumbo voodoo ceremony on her by the light of a full Surface moon.

Then, he had to embark on a mission through the Valley of Shadows to find his wife. That alone was a journey wrought with peril. Of course, it was a personal mission, but dangerous none the less, especially with what he had to ask of her.

For a moment, Kane wondered if the humans on the Surface faced such stresses. Did they have the day to day worries, the heaviness of duty bearing down on their shoulders? Or did they live a carefree life, bathing in the golden streams of sunlight and basking below an ocean of blue sky?

Once he had all of the scrolls, he intended to find out. He needed to see what the humans saw, what they lived with every day: the open sky, the brilliance of a nearby star—and their night. What would an evening sky be like sprayed with stars? Open and inviting, a universe of mystery just waiting to be explored? Had the humans explored the space above them?

All these questions and more grew inside Kane. The anticipation was as plentiful as the envy.

Dark World's heavens only snarled when gazed upon, the dangling fangs of a million stalactites poised as though ready to pierce its prey. It's all he'd ever known. All he'd ever seen. His father had promised to take him to the Surface, before the war started anyways.

Until it was sealed, the demons had always traveled to the Surface through the crevice, the narrow, winding gap that led from one world to another. They were always careful, though, if not hidden.

Some wayward demons liked to toy with the humans, playing harmless, paranormal tricks on them to get a rouse. But Lucifer kept a firm grip on the secrecy of his world. The humans, though mortal and powerless, were abundant compared to the population of Dark World, even in the early days. Despite their weaknesses, the humans posed a threat to the underworld, hence Lucifer's wariness to alert the Surface race to their existence.

"Hello?" Fate's voice pulled him from his deep ponderings. "Did you hear me?" She stood at the end of his bed, hands on her slender hips and head tilted to the side. So innocent, so sweet, he had to smile.

He shook his head, giving her a sheepish grin. "No, I'm sorry. What did you say?"

"I have to go soon, more training fun with Vrill," she said with a roll of her eyes.

"Okay," he replied. "I want to visit Ever before lunch and then..." he trailed off, his mood darkening. "Then I have to find that witchdoctor, to see when this ritual is to take place."

Fate nodded, blowing him a kiss. "Okay, see you later."

"Good luck," he offered and she tossed him an insecure grimace, closing the door behind her.

After she'd gone, he lay down on the bed, fatigued from the constant worry circulating in his system. What would happen to Ever when the witchdoctor performed his ceremony? Would he be able to find Seren and have his questions answered? Would he be able to find the scrolls, retrieve them from Myth, and relight the Pyramid?

Sighing, he rolled onto his side and wished for the darkened world to go away.

29

The golden flicker of candlelight lit her path as she descended the staircase of bones. Her pale hand slid along the smooth banister, the rib of what was obviously a very large animal. The castle seemed to breathe with remnants of life, phantoms echoing their lives through the ivory marrow that once encased their now-lost souls.

Or were the souls truly gone? Did they linger amid the walls, invisible, pining for their stolen existence?

Fate wondered how the necromancers chose their victims. Did they hunt and poach any wayward trespasser that dared set foot near Necrosia? Or was it planned out, strategically calculated and executed?

On the Surface, elephants were slaughtered unceremoniously for their tusks, a prestigious trophy for some khaki-wearing millionaire who'd never even set foot upon the arid sands of Africa. They merely paid for their prize, unconcerned for the fate of the calves left behind or the pack grieving their fallen companion. It was only for the glory, the selfish desire for pomp and prestige that drove those humans to murder the masses of the animal kingdom.

Were the necromancers so different? Didn't they prove their greed through their macabre art?

Fate could not ignore the obvious; it watched her from every corner, decorated every inch of the palace. And then there were the zombie races. How could she ignore the savagery of the competition that her dear, sweet Aura had endured, yet succeeded, in overcoming? Sure, she'd gotten a second chance at life, but what of the others? Were they summoned to race, with their decayed bodies covered in rotting flesh, for the simple entertainment of the citizens of Necrosia?

Or maybe the necromancers were being generous, giving new life to one who'd lost it so young. Offering immortality to the one who proved themselves worthy.

Maybe, but Fate wasn't convinced. The necromancers had secrets, dark ones, and she could feel it all around her. This place had hundreds of skeletons in the closet, literally.

A chill slid over her spine as she reached the bottom of stairs. Her palms were clammy as nerves spun in her stomach like a merry-go-round. It was ridiculous how troubled she was to try this power-training thing again. If something interesting didn't happen today, she was going to be convinced that she didn't have any special powers at all. Many of the shades in Necrosia didn't have unique abilities, just average powers, like strength, acute hearing and sight, and maybe even the occasional pyrotechnically enhanced acrobat.

Mind you, they weren't born like Vale, Sybil, and herself. They'd been born alone, left as orphans in an unforgiving realm. Most, if not all, were born in threes, the way the ritual on the Surface called for. They were an anomaly, their powers enhanced because of the circumstances of their Surface death, which had made them particularly appetizing to the queen. Previous to her demise, inhabiting a single-born shade could have made her more lethal than she already was. Possessing a shade like Fate would have made the queen a perfect killing machine for sure, capable of stealing souls and cheating death for all eternity.

Death, Fate considered as she looked upon one of her pale hands adorned with black needle-sharp nails. *I'm certainly not dead, but I'm not quite alive either, am I? Though...I feel very much alive, maybe even more so then when I was on the Surface.*

Or was that just because of Kane? Did he nurture some side of her that had been left dormant as a human? Was his love the catalyst of her happiness?

She smiled as she wandered the hall towards the descending staircase that would take her to the cavern of education. Kane was her soul mate, the source of her joy.

Suddenly a worm of self-doubt wriggled within her conscience. *But he's loved another. Deeply. How can I know he loves me the same? Or more?*

She paused, setting a hand on the cool, rocky wall, stabilizing herself. What if she were some kind of rebound relationship, a stepping stone to heal his broken heart? She couldn't endure losing him, not now, not when she'd fallen so hard for him, given her heart to him.

I wish I could give him my soul, she thought sadly as she looked down upon the ring he'd given her. '*Vosira mea anima*' he'd said when giving it to her: *I give you my soul.* Fate sat down on one of the stairs, gazing at the teardrop stone.

"I have no soul to give," she whispered, her lips downturned. At least Seren had offered him both her heart *and* her soul. They'd shared a bond that Fate couldn't compete with.

And Ever. A child.

Fate's stomach dropped. She hadn't considered the ramifications of their mixed races. Even if they stayed together for eternity, she could never offer him another baby, could she? Were they incompatible that way?

"If we did have a child, what would it be?" Fate said aloud, frowning.

"*Powerful,*" a voice answered as though whispering from inside the walls.

She shuddered, rubbing her shoulders as she glanced around. There was no one there. No one alive, that is.

Quickly standing, she continued her path to the basement, hoping Vrill was down there. This place, this bone palace, was more than just creepy, it was haunted.

30

A hazy glow from the streetlights filtered through the dark blue drapes, leaving only a narrow, ghostly strip of illumination painted upon the floor. The shadows clung to the corners like bats, motionlessly glaring from their sinister perches. Shelby knew she had to work quickly, she didn't know where Rory had gone and he could walk through his front door at any moment.

At the bottom of the duffel bag, Shelby noticed an ochre parchment, rolled into a cylinder and tied with crimson ribbon. She reached in and pulled it out. The page was very old, thin and worn around the edges. It reminded her of the images she'd seen of the Declaration of Independence.

An ancient document? She considered as she carefully removed the ribbon and unfurled the page.

Golden, swirling letters danced on the page in a language Shelby couldn't understand. It didn't look like any writing she'd ever seen before. It was beautiful and haunting at the same time.

But it was the tiny smatterings of red that caught her eye. The page was covered in what looked like…blood. There was even a fingerprint on one side of the page, a perfect imprint. And she'd bet anything that print belonged to Rory.

She had him. He was going to see the inside of a prison for what he'd done. And she hoped he'd be forced to bunk with some big, hairy guy named Carl. He wasn't going to get away with this.

Then a thought chilled her blood. What if Scarlet wasn't the only one? What if Rory was a serial killer? Many kids, not just Scarlet, had gone missing during that sinister night in October over the years.

No, she thought, *he couldn't have. He wouldn't have been old enough…would he?*

Maybe this was some kind of cult activity, carried on by member after member like some sort of initiation or rite of passage. Her stomach flipped, nauseating her. What had she fallen into?

What would happen to her if they found out?

Then the silence of the house was shattered by the slamming of a car door.

Her heart stopped mid-beat—he was home. Rory was back!

She knew it was too late to run to the basement and sneak out the way she'd broken in. She'd have to pass by the front door if she wanted to get to the stairs.

She'd have to hide—or fight her way out.

"Oh my God, oh my God," she whispered under her breath as she hurriedly stuffed the black cloth back into the duffle bag and zipped it up. Gently, but quickly, she rolled up the scroll and tucked it into the back pocket of her jeans. The knife, however, stayed firmly in her hands. She hated that she had to touch the handle, possibly ruining what evidence might be on it, but at this point it had become a life or death situation. The scroll had blood on it, hopefully Scarlet's or the other missing kids', and that should be proof enough.

When the front door slammed shut, reality settled in—she was trapped with a murderer.

Why didn't I just stay home? Shelby thought, her bottom lip quivering as she pressed her back against the bedroom wall. She took stock of his room, panning from left to right, then back again. His bed was just a couple of mattresses on the floor, so nothing to crawl under. There was a small closet, but it was full of boxes and crap, no way for her to wiggle in there and hide. There was a dresser and a night table.

There was nothing to work with. There was nowhere to hide from the monster—and his footsteps were getting closer.

This is it, Shelby, you're done for!

Fresh beads of sweat meandered over her brow, tickling her nose and lips. Her long red hair clung to the dampness, curling at the ends as though joyously oblivious to their imminent demise.

His steps slowed, then stopped right before his bedroom doorway. Shelby's heart slammed relentlessly in her chest, so loud she was worried he'd hear it. Never before had she been so afraid, so intimately close to her mortality.

Only one more step and he'll see me!

Her stomach twisted, launching a full-on revolt, threatening to expel all she'd eaten while waiting in the car. She swallowed hard, but quietly, knowing that her every movement was within earshot of a killer.

Eyes painfully wide, she watched as the edge of his boot appeared just outside the door. He was only a few feet away. She could hear his breath, almost smell his cologne.

This was it. He was going to turn the corner and see her in plain sight. There was nowhere to go. Nowhere to hide.

She was going to leave her own family in ruins, just like the Princes' were without Scarlet. Greg would be destroyed, even more so than he already was. At least, she hoped he'd be. What kind of boyfriend would he be if he wasn't?

Rory took one more step—then his cell phone rang. Shelby stifled a breath of relief. In that moment, she'd never loved technology more. If nothing else, it gave her a few more minutes to live—and to hide under his comforter.

She curled up on the floor, pulled the blanket over her entire body, making herself as small as possible as she clutched the knife and prayed.

After the second ring, he answered the phone.

"Yeah," Rory's voice resonated just outside the bedroom door. Shelby shuddered at the sound of his voice. Was he really a killer? Or was she completely delusional? She'd just broken into his house! Concluded that he murdered her best friend because he had a stupid knife in a bag!

Maybe she did deserve to be fitted for a straight jacket.

"What? They're at your house right now?" he said, irritated. Shelby slowed her breath and strained to hear over her heartbeat raging through her veins. "No Steve, I told you not to worry."

Worry? About what?

"Steve," Rory almost yelled into the phone. "I told you, Malus will protect us. She's always protected me. Just tell the cops the same story I told you to tell them and it will be fine."

Malus? Shelby frowned. *Who is Malus? Some old girlfriend of Rory's? What a stupid name.*

"Yeah, okay Steve, call me when they leave. Kay, bye," he said quickly, followed by a beep as he hung up. "Fucking idiot," he muttered under his breath as he stepped over the threshold of his bedroom door.

Shelby sipped short, shallow breaths as he rummaged through some things in his dresser drawer. He was so close, she was sure she could hear him breathing.

Just stay calm Shelby, she soothed. *It'll be okay.*

But no matter how much she told herself that, she just wasn't convinced.

31

The castle seemed eerily quiet; the usual hustle and bustle of necromancers seemingly at a standstill. Normally the silver-skinned race was abuzz with some sort of production or another. Always a ball to put on, a wedding, or their favorite: a funeral. They rarely sat still, and were hardly ever without plans of grandeur.

Kane wandered from room to room in search of the witchdoctor, or at the very least someone who knew of his whereabouts.

Portraits of various necromancers gazed down at him from the walls, their swirling star-like eyes filled with wisdom and unending patience. Some Kane recognized, like Vrill and the elders, others appeared to be part of the past, their clothing and style of another era. Kane wondered how death worked with the necromancers. Did they simply pass on like everyone else in Dark World? Or did they occupy a new body, carrying their knowledge with them into a new host? He knew they were immortal, but accidents happen, and no one is impervious to those. Perhaps some of these were the tributes of those fallen in battle?

A rug upon the floor caught his eye, its various shades, textures, and colors a seemingly perfect palette. He knelt down and touched it, the softness caressing his blue-black fingertips. It was familiar somehow, this material, but he couldn't quiet place it.

Then it struck him.

"Hair," he whispered with a shudder. "It's a rug made of hair."

Quickly standing, he walked away from the carpet as fast as he could. There were many a thing he could stomach, but the necromancers were proficient at finding his weaknesses.

Then, from the corner of his eye, he saw movement in the hall. Finally, someone to query as to the location of the odd necromancer.

"Petra," Kane called to Vrill's assistant, her long blue hair pulled into a conventional ponytail. "Do you the whereabouts of the witchdoctor? I wish to speak with him." Truthfully, he didn't want to see that weirdo again, nor have him do any kind of ritual on his daughter, but at this juncture he'd try just about anything to get Ever back—or just to make certain she wasn't his genocidal mother.

Petra smiled, responding, "I believe he's in the crypt." She nodded towards a darkened hallway and walked away.

"Crypt," Kane repeated with a shudder. Sounded like the last place he wanted to be alone with the half-naked head hunter. But, for Ever, he sighed and made his way downstairs to the place where the necromancers kept their dead.

His imagination took him to places he didn't want to go as he descended the dark stairwell. Fully aware of the necromancers' eerie fascination with death and bones, he couldn't even imagine what their crypt might hold. He pictured a dark cavern filled with decaying bodies, strewn about the room haphazardly, awaiting dismemberment and de-fleshing. There could be a mound of cleaned bones piled in one corner, a couple of artsy necromancers in another building chairs of marrow, a chandelier made of ribs, or creating decorative art from the tiny finger bones of an unfortunate pixie. Cobwebs draped the corners of his imaginary crypt; candlelight flickered ominously, creating dancing shadows on the wall.

Kane cringed as a cold shiver danced up his spine. As kind as the necromancers were, they held a darkness inside them, a particularly macabre shared soul.

The sound of his hooves clicking on the black marble stairs echoed all around him, the shadows enveloping him as a chill crawled across his skin.

He breathed deep, reminding himself of his status. A king's son should not show fear. Nothing could hurt him here; he was at least two feet taller than any citizen in Necrosia. Why should he be afraid of the dead? Nothing is more fearsome in Dark World than a shade, and he'd most certainly shown they could be tamed. He'd even faced his mother, the devil herself, and lived (barely) to tell the tale.

After all that, what could a crypt hold that should terrify him?

Nothing, he thought with a smile.

But then he heard the scraping.

32

"Powerful," the disembodied voices said all around her, their whispers laced with fear and urgency.

"Leave me alone!" Fate cried, covering her ears and running down the pitch-black stairwell, so dark that her infrared vision failed her. She ran blind and deaf, praying she'd reach the bottom soon, where Vrill was, where the voices would potentially cease.

Then she saw a light up ahead. Faint, but there, and she ran faster.

Just as she'd gained an ounce of confidence, however, the walls on either side of her grew arms. Dark, shadowy arms that reached for her from their rocky graves. They groped at her hair, grasped at her arms, legs, and ankles. She let out a shriek, trying to slap the hands away only to discover they were made of mist. Somehow they could touch her, but she couldn't touch them.

Suddenly, one on the left grabbed her hair, and another took hold of her ankle, and they began to pull her towards the wall. Then more hands joined in. She fought with all she had, but the disadvantage was just too great.

The whispers turned to laughter as they brought her crashing against the wall of rock, pulling her as though she was also made of smoke and could evaporate into the walls to join them.

Her fear suddenly turned to anger and something dark inside of her reared its head. "I said stop!" A burst of energy shot from her core, sending a tsunami of blue throughout the stairwell—and everything stopped. Silence. The hands were gone.

Shakily, she stood and smoothed back her hair, watching the walls for any sign of her offenders' return. Deciding she didn't want to give them another opportunity, she quickly descended the rest of the stairs and made her way for the illuminated doorway. Behind her she could hear groaning and scuffling, but she didn't look back. She needed to find safety—and sanity. It was no wonder that the necromancers had such a strange affinity with death; it was all around them, stalking them, haunting them.

Fate rounded the corner a little too fast, however, and nearly knocked Vrill over as she smacked into him.

"Fate," he stammered with a smile, catching his balance. "Whatever is wrong?"

She looked back at the darkened stairwell, the shadows leeching into the corners like ink pulling itself back into the bottle after it had spilled. "Um," she began nervously, trying to think of what to say. It seemed silly to be afraid of the unknown at this point. Everything in her new life was the unknown. What was she going to say? That she was afraid of some ghostly whispers that seemed to be coming from the walls? Of some phantoms arms groping her? She lived in a paranormal world now, she'd simply have to get used to extreme weirdness. Eventually, she replied, "Nothing, I'm so sorry."

"Are you certain?" he inquired, his swirling silver eyes bore into hers, concern welling within.

"I just...thought I heard something," she said with a cringe, certain he'd think she was nuts.

He smiled, then replied with a cryptic tone, "There are many ghosts in this palace, many indeed. Come," he turned on his heels, raising his arms to the side as though embracing the entire room. "It's time to train."

Fate grimaced, the disturbing incident with the ghosts evaporating in the midst of renewed frustrations. When was he going to let up? Didn't he see that she was no good at any of this? That she didn't have talent like Vale and Sybil? She could see it. Why couldn't he? There was the shockwave on the stairs, but that wasn't anything new to her, if anything it proved to her how menial her powers seemed to be. "Are you sure this is going to work?" she asked as she took her stance in the center of the room.

Vrill turned to her, buttoning an onyx, fire-retardant cloak to his neckline, and raised a non-existent brow at her, saying, "You humans, such faith in things outside yourself, yet you hold none within."

Fate debated whether or not she should be offended, then asked, "What do you mean?"

The necromancer took a step back, raising his hands and conjuring a brilliant orb of pure silver. He bounced it between both palms before stating, "You see this, no?"

Fate nodded. He then pulled his arm back and threw the pulsating sphere at her. She instinctively ducked, the orb narrowly missing her as it smashed into the cavern wall behind her, shattering in an explosion of light. "What the hell are you doing? Are you crazy!" she shouted.

He just smiled, tucking his hands into his velveteen robes. "You believed the orb to be real, why?"

Fate pushed her annoyance away, answering, "Because I could see it."

"How do you know it wasn't an illusion?" Vrill questioned.

She inhaled, frustrated. "I don't."

"Why then," he started, settling into a throne of bones, "do you have to see to believe?"

Fate folded her arms over her chest. She knew if she waited long enough, he'd answer his own question for her. She shrugged to urge him on.

"Fate, my rare flower, you are made of the very power you've seen with your own eyes. You cannot find the magic, you *are* the magic."

33

Shelby had to summon courage she didn't know she had to stay curled up on Rory's bedroom floor. Her fight or flight instincts were trying to claw their way out of her body, begging her to run, fight, do anything but stay where she was.

Why was it always her that was in trouble? Did she have some unknown death wish she desperately wanted to fulfill?

While there'd never been an instance quite this dire, she recalled several that could be considered *almost* as stupid. Like the time she climbed a pole to retrieve her tangled kite from a nearby tree—a fifty foot power pole, that is. Hey, it had little pegs on the side for climbing, what else was she going to do? In the end, she made the second page of the Edmonton Journal because someone called the fire department and the power had to be shut off for over an hour as they rescued her.

Then there was the time she ran over her brother—it was an accident. She was trying to save him, well, sort of. She was nine, Jason was six. He'd hit his head on the rock that she'd thrown at him, and he was bleeding. So, to help him, she told him to get into dad's truck and she'd drive him to the hospital. (Their mother was inside the house, but there was no need to bother her if Shelby could take him.) In her haste, she put the truck into neutral and it began rolling down the drive towards another vehicle. So, it made sense to jump from the moving truck, right? Heroically, (since he'd made it clear he wasn't going to jump on his own) she leaned way over and pushed Jason out the passenger side door, accidentally turning the steering wheel with her foot and, well, there was a big bump as the truck ran over something surprisingly solid.

He was fine, only a couple of broken arms.

Now this: trapped in a house of horrors with a potential serial killer. Perfect.

"Where is it?" Rory muttered to himself as he continued some frantic search through his room.

Is he looking for this? She clutched the serrated knife tighter in her hands. Panic eroded her senses, the air under the blanket felt like it was running out. What if she ran out of oxygen under there? What if she suffocated? How long would it take to use up all the air?

"Ahh, there you are," he said, puncturing the tension in Shelby's chest like a taut balloon. She had no idea what he'd found, but thank god he had, she was about to freak out and go all *Psycho* on his ass.

Could she though? Could she stab someone, kill them, if the situation required her to? And even if she did, if she was absolutely forced to, could she live with herself afterwards? How did people overcome that kind of guilt?

How did Rory live with himself? With the things he'd done?

For a split second, everything was still. Was this the calm before the storm? Had he sensed her there, in his room, only inches away?

She could hear his breathing, the creak of the floorboards as his weight shifted from one leg to another. Was he listening?

Why wasn't he leaving?

Please leave, please leave, Shelby pleaded within her thoughts. She had to get out of there, bring the knife and the bloody page to Constable Jack. This was the evidence she needed, she knew it.

After a few more moments, she heard him leave the room and while she didn't want to get her hopes up, she thought she heard him down in the landing—putting his shoes on. That would mean he was leaving again! She'd be free to get up and run, get the hell out of this place!

Her heart leaped for joy when she heard the front door squeak open. She held her breath, waiting for the telltale click of the lock.

Waiting.

Waiting.

Silence.

And then her cell phone started to vibrate from her back pocket—followed by a loud *ding* announcing a missed call. Frantic, she scrambled to pull her phone from her back pocket and silenced it by turning down the volume.

"Shit, shit, shit," she whispered under her breath, her heart thrashing in her chest. What if he'd heard? Had he already left by the time it went off?

She tried to silence her raging heartbeat, holding her breath as she listened for any movement, any sign he was still there.

Nothing but the ticking of a clock—until she heard the door click shut.

34

Kane cleared his throat and paused before rounding the last corner leading to the crypt. He hoped that whatever the scraping noise was would cease upon his arrival. The last thing he needed was to see a necromancer cleaning the meat off some bones or sawing up his latest masterpiece.

"Hello?" a voice called out and Kane recognized it as the witchdoctor.

"It is Kane, may I enter?"

The witchdoctor chuckled. "Of course, please, come."

Kane steeled himself for a macabre sight, but as he entered he was caught off guard. The crypt was nothing as he'd imagined. Golden candlelight warmed an impeccably clean cavern. Ivory sashes draped from corner to corner, creating a gauzy white ceiling rather than that of dark rock. Four gilded coffins were aligned on his left while statues of the fallen were being erected to the right. Two blue-skinned necromancers were shaving shapes from pure blocks of hematite, a smooth, shiny stone that resembles steel. The necromancers had delicate tools in their hands, carving the faces and bodies of what Kane guessed as the deceased into the rocks, hence the scraping noise.

Kane immediately felt foolish. Why was he one to readily jump to conclusions? Always doubting the other races, always so mistrustful. It was a trait he disliked in himself.

"Prince Kane, welcome," Kraton, the witchdoctor, stated. "What can I do for you?"

"I wish to inquire as to when the...ceremony...with Ever is to take place?" he stammered, attempting to be as polite as he could in regards to the upcoming ritual.

Kraton nodded, turning his attention to an odd placement of bones on the wall. "That would be..." his voice trailed off as he scanned the oddity, "the next full moon...tonight."

"Tonight! I see, thank you," Kane replied, narrowing his eyes at what he guessed was a calendar, though it simply looked like a pile of bones plastered to the wall. He hadn't expected the ceremony to be so soon. Nerves churned within. Would his daughter be alright? Was she still his daughter?

As he turned to leave, the witchdoctor spoke, "Sire, I understand your concern, but I assure you, if there is something to be found within your daughter, I will find it," then added cryptically, "And remove it."

35

Shelby stayed completely still, not surrendering a single breath. Was Rory still in the house? Did he hear her phone? She listened long and hard for the roar of his car's engine, willing it to start and drive away.

Tears of pure fear burned behind her eyes. If he truly was the killer she believed him to be, this was the very last place she should have been. What was she thinking? Why didn't she tell anyone? Greg, at the very least?

She dug deep into herself, summoning an ounce of courage as she prepared herself to peek around the blanket. Even if he wasn't in the house, she had to get out—now. She'd put herself in mortal danger. The dagger in her hands proved that. Why else would he have it stashed in the duffel bag? It's not your standard camping equipment.

And the blood on the weird scroll, she couldn't deny that was weird. Sure, it could be paint, but parked right beside a sharp knife, yeah, *no.*

Her entire body trembled as she pulled back a small section of blanket and peeked around it. His untidy room glared back at her, gratefully empty of its owner.

So far, so good.

Eyes wide and ears so fixated on the silence, she felt like a feral cat stalked by the animal catcher. Knees cracking in protest, she stood carefully and cautiously. If Rory was still in the house, he knew someone else was in it too.

Her heart beat so hard she thought it might burst out of her chest, the sound of her blood racing through her body pounded in her eardrums. Toe to heel like a ninja, she tread lightly out of Rory's bedroom and down the hall.

Every step was like a land mine. Every corner seemed to hold a dark demon, just waiting to leap from the shadows and pull her down into the depths of Hell.

She still hadn't decided her route of escape: back downstairs to the broken window or out the front door. The front door was closer, but that's where he might be waiting.

Nodding silently in decision, she chose to head for the basement.

The hardwood floor crackled beneath her feet with each step, the aging floorboards seemingly against her, heralding her every move like a squealing tattletale.

Sweat beaded on her brow as she met the end of the hallway. Even though she'd decided not to use the front door, she still had to pass by it to get to the basement steps.

Her mouth was sticky from dryness, her tongue stuck against the roof of her mouth. She couldn't recall a time when she'd been as scared. If Rory wasn't guilty, why did he terrify her so?

The serrated knife in her hands gave her a tiny boost in confidence, the blade glinting with the sparse light streaming in from the street lights. Why hadn't she come in the daytime? Why was hindsight so prevalent with her?

A streak of anger coursed through her, directed at her own foolishness. Did she really have to be so impatient? So reckless? She'd always been too spontaneous, too impetuous. Never thinking before she jumped. Never looking before she dove headlong into disaster. It was like she craved danger. Longed for an early death.

Well, she thought as she peered down the ever-darkening hallway with tears filling her eyes. *I may have gotten my wish.*

36

Fate pulled the power from her core, bringing energy to life around her. She'd managed, with Vrill's help, to manifest a ball of light that orbited her body. Tendrils of blue lightning snarled about the sphere as it pulsated round and round her torso. It was similar to the orb she'd created and fired at Kane's back when they'd first met, incapacitating him. But this one was much bigger, and harbored far more energy. It was a good thing she'd only been a newborn at the time, if she'd used this one against him, he'd likely be dead.

"Very good," Vrill whispered, his eyes wide with fascination. "Don't force it, be one with it."

Fate closed her eyes, surrendering to the unseen energy around her, simply allowing the magic to happen, not forcing it. She cleared her mind, freed it, letting the walls fall down.

For a moment, there was peace. A pause in time where everything was perfect—then something dark reared its head. Something deep inside crawled out of the shadows, black eyes glaring and brimming with evil. Her inner monster had made its presence known, it would not be ignored.

Fate's eyes flew open and she gasped. The orb in her hands spun out of control and shot sharply to the right—directly at Vrill. Without hesitation, he raised his hands and a shield of pure white erected around him, Fate's unstable creation exploding upon impact. Still, even protected, he was knocked off his feet and thrown onto his back.

"Vrill! I'm so sorry!" Fate exclaimed, running to his side.

He held up his hand, laughing. "Not to worry, I am fine."

She helped him to his feet. "I didn't mean to...it just..." she stammered, burying her face in her hands.

"Fate," Vrill reached for her hands and gently pulled them from her face. "We learn from our mistakes, they are a gift, not a sin. Understand?"

She nodded, though disagreed. He could have been killed, and it would have been her fault. More blood on her hands.

"Well, that's enough for today, you should go rest," Vrill said with a smile, though he limped away and settled slowly into his chair of bones.

"Okay," she said quietly as she started climbing the stairs, leaving the training cavern.

Darkness hugged the walls, the very walls that whispered to her and assaulted her earlier that day. Was this palace haunted? It would make perfect sense, considering how many bones held the place together. Or was it something haunting her? Maybe the souls she'd stolen—the unicorn's and the sphinx—maybe they'd come back to seek their revenge?

She shook her head and tried to laugh away her worries, but the sound came out strained. No, whatever she heard had spoken to her, spoken words. She doubted that unicorns and sphinxes, even dead, would torment her as though they harbored some newfound intelligence. They were just animals, right?

Light greeted her as she reached the top of the stairs, but in the same split second, a ripping sensation tore through her middle. Fate fell to her knees, overcome with pain.

She immediately knew what it was—the hunger, it wanted fed. Now.

Forcing herself to her feet, she staggered to the next set of stairs and willed her legs to climb them. She had to get to the Nexus.

Agony gouged her insides, her soulless body screaming, threatening to consume her if she didn't comply. Tears of pain and frustration rolled down her cheeks. Why? Why was this happening to her? Why couldn't she have just stayed Scarlet? Scarlet hadn't been plagued with this infliction, this damnation? She'd only had the perils of high school and puberty to contend with, and compared to this, that didn't seem so bad.

Finally reaching the top of the stairs, she turned into Vrill's private quarters. The Soul Nexus hovered above a pedestal at the far end of the room—but she'd have to pass by Ever in the process.

The scent of Ever's soul drifted under her nose like a dew-laden rose, the sweet smell called out to her, begged her. Fate put her hands over her face, tearing her lustful gaze from the sleeping princess.

She couldn't. She wouldn't harm Ever. It would destroy her. It would kill Kane.

The hunger raged within. A deep, roiling fury that clawed at her insides, demanding to be nourished. She raced toward the Nexus and slapped her hand on it. White electricity sparked beneath her palm, the power of the necromancers' creator surging through her.

But the pain didn't cease. The hunger didn't subside. The beast inside her rejected the Nexus' sustenance. The bright orb that had blessed the necromancers with their eternal souls, the sphere of power that fed the wayward shades of Necrosia, had failed her.

There was no more Bloodstone in her possession, and now, no satiation from the one source she was told could never fail her. What was she going to do? She couldn't surrender to the hunger, couldn't devour the innocent to feed her own sickness. She couldn't lose herself. Not again.

But the lust was winning.

The blackness was consuming her.

She had no choice but to obey.

There was only one thing left. The one thing she had desperately tried to avoid.

As she dropped her hands from the Nexus, her gaze fell on Ever.

37

Dark shadows held fast in every corner of the castle. Skulls of the long-since departed served as candy dishes and candle holders, gazing from sightless eyes, scrutinizing Kane as he searched each room for Vale.

During the day, this palace felt somewhat inviting; what with the necromancers' seemingly boundless energies, but at night it was a whole new ambiance. A creepy one. One filled with unseen monsters, restless phantoms trapped in purgatory, wandering the premises as though searching for their long-lost bodies.

Kane suppressed a shudder. As much as he didn't want to leave Ever and Fate behind, he was anxious to be away from the castle, at least during the nighttime hours when most everyone was sleeping.

Finally, Vale's cool and cocky voice emanated from a room on his left, one of the many dens. Kane turned into it, nodding a greeting to both Vale and Sybil.

"Good evening," he said to both, then turned to Sybil. "Oracle, I must speak with Vale in private, if you don't mind."

She smiled as she moved for the door. "Of course, I was just leaving."

Once she was gone, Kane sat across from the shade, who appeared quite comfortable sprawled across a ribcage loveseat.

"What can I do for you this fine evening?" Vale inquired, raising his glass of burgundy wine to the prince.

Kane cleared his throat, unsure as to where to begin, then asked, "Will you accompany me on a journey? I could use a shade of your…talent and expertise," Kane said with extreme seriousness, his cerulean eyes narrowed on the rogue.

"Maybe," Vale said with a smirk, clearly inebriated. "What kind of journey?"

The demon paused, uncertain as to how much to divulge. He needed the shade to come along, but there were things he didn't want him to know. "We need to retrieve the remaining scrolls."

The shade nodded, seemingly interested. "When would we leave?"

"Tomorrow morning."

His eyebrows rose slightly. "Who else is coming?" Vale inquired, folding his hands behind his head and nestling between two pillows made of sphinx hide.

Kane paced the room, his black tail swinging from side to side as he walked. "You and I, and Vrill has lent two of his best trackers."

Vale looked dismayed, likely upset that he'd have to leave Aura. But he eventually nodded, asking, "Where do we have to go?"

"To the banshees and wraiths, for certain. And I must check on Legion." He held back the rest of the destinations, knowing it would only cause problems. The wraiths were scary enough, but no one, not even Vale, would willingly go to the reapers' lair in the Nether Caves. But it was a necessity, if Vrill was correct. And Kane desperately hoped he was or all this would be for nothing, just a suicide mission.

"Banshees?" Vale looked confused. "Why would we need to go there?"

"Vrill has been studying the scrolls and believes that to open the fissure; we not only need the scrolls, but at least one of each of the races to be present," Kane replied, then added reluctantly, "And Fate."

"But she's not coming with us?" Vale looked confused.

"Not initially, we'll retrieve her afterwards, once we've gathered the races and scrolls."

Vale eyed the prince suspiciously. "Does Fate know any of this?"

Kane's jaw tightened. "No, not yet. She has enough on her mind with her training." Vale didn't need to know all the details. He didn't need to know that Kane had to stop in the Valley of Shadows. Why he had to see Seren—and why Fate couldn't know about it. Besides, he needed someone he could trust to stay with Ever. And there was no one he trusted more than Fate.

"Alright, whatever," Vale stated nonchalantly, but unease colored his glowing white eyes.

Kane disliked this shade, he found him arrogant and undependable. But he had no choice. Vale was a single-born; he had useful powers and was able to control his hunger for souls more than most, not to mention he could touch the scrolls without being cursed.

"So you're in then?" Kane asked.

Vale nodded with a grin pulling at the corners of his mouth. "Wouldn't miss it."

"It's set then," Kane said with a nod of appreciation as he exited the room. "We leave in the morning."

38

With knife in hand, Shelby traversed the long hall. Shadows seemed to breathe around her, as though Rory was hiding in one of them, just waiting to pounce.

What would he do to her if he caught her? Whatever he did to Scarlet? On one hand, Shelby found solace in that thought. She'd know what had happened to her best friend. She'd know Scarlet's fate. On the other hand, she wasn't ready for death. She had far too much to live for, far too many journeys planned for her life. If she had to, she'd fight to the death in order to live them.

Pausing before the last corner, she listened for any movement. Any breath or sound that would give Rory away. Was he even there? Maybe he didn't hear her phone. Maybe he did leave when she heard the door click. But then, she didn't hear his car leave. Maybe it was just quieter than she thought.

Or maybe he was around the next corner.

She inhaled a breath of courage and slid around the last junction. If he was here, this is where he'd be. He wouldn't know her plan to go out the way she came, rather than the easiest route, the front door. She had to believe that she was one step ahead, had to believe she had the upper hand. Because if she didn't, he had her right where he wanted her.

Part of her wanted to bolt, to run as fast as she could down the hall, flailing her arms and screaming like a little girl. Her instinct pleaded with her, begged her to simply get the hell out of there. But something else told her to be cautious, that she might get out of this if she was quiet, and patient.

The basement doorway was now in view, a gaping black passage that led to her freedom. She had no idea how she was going to get herself back up and out the window, but she figured she'd take one step at a time.

Sending off one last prayer to any angels that might be hovering nearby, she held her breath as she took the long walk past the front door, the short flight of stairs leading down tempting her.

Freedom was right there, only a few feet away—but then, he could be too.

Shelby hesitated, a bead of sweat trickling down her back. What if she'd chosen wrong? What if her plan to outsmart Rory backfired? What if she was making it easier for him?

She forced her paranoia aside, she'd come this far, she had to follow through with the plan.

Slowly, without any sound at all, she made it all the way to the basement door. Elated, she nearly ran down the stairs, but held back, still cautious until she reached the bottom.

I did it!

She scrunched up her eyes, searching the shadows for anything to climb up onto, anything to boost her up and out the window. Her heart soared when she saw the outline of a chair. Fate was on her side, she was going to get out of this!

Shelby tucked the serrated blade into the back of her pants and moved the chair beneath the window, then climbed atop and lifted herself almost effortlessly out the narrow passage.

The cool night air kissed her cheeks as though in greeting, street lights streamed down with angelic presence. Caution still raced through her blood as she scanned the quiet street, noticing his car was absent from the drive.

She shrugged. *Must not have heard it leave.*

Shelby smiled, smug satisfaction crawling through her as she strolled towards her mom's car.

After pulling the knife and scroll out of her pants, she opened the driver's side door and settled into the seat, placing the items on the passenger side.

She sucked in a few breaths, relaxing and releasing the anxiety. She'd done it. She had what she needed. Scarlet's death would not go unnoticed; her murderer would not go free.

Plugging the keys into the ignition and cranking the tunes, she started the car and with one last glance at Rory's darkened house, she drove away.

It wasn't until the first stop sign that she saw the shadow rise from the back seat.

39

Fate clutched her torso, her body moving against her will, pulling her towards the sleeping princess—pulling her to destroy Ever. The hunger had her; it had taken over, possessed her. Her body was no longer her own. Her soul was no longer in charge.

Ever's long silver-white hair cascaded over her shoulder, down the side of the bed, the ends reaching for the floor. Her face, pale skin like milk, soft, beautiful, unmoving as though made of marble. Long golden robes draped her petite yet feminine form, the neckline plunging to a point between her breasts, exposing her ivory chest. She glowed with an unearthly pallor, a heavenly hue illuminating a dark world creature.

Drawn, seduced, Fate found herself at Ever's side, the princess's soul whispering to her, calling to her. Haunting her. Like a hellish lullaby it sang a deadly song, drawing Fate closer. She drew in a long breath, savoring the scent, intoxicating herself with the demon girl's essence.

Soon, Ever's heart beat alongside her own, making it one.

Beat beat.

Closer.

Beat beat.

And closer.

She raised her hand, setting it upon Ever's chest, her demon skin like fire beneath Fate's palm. The soul inside pulsed with joy, racing with anticipation in conjunction with Fate's thrumming heart. Her mouth watered as her eyes changed from white to black, the monster stepping forward.

The bond, the blending of souls, a dance of death…

"What the hell are you doing?" A voice shouted from behind her, the fiend recoiling in an instant.

The malevolent aura that held her dissipated as she spun around. A necromancer guard glared at her, his sword drawn and in attack position. Several cloaked necromancers stood behind him holding what appeared to be black candles, their eyes filled with fear and concern.

Her eyes watered and she shook her head as she stole her hand from Ever's chest, staring at her palm as though it was the point of a dagger. What was she going to do? What had she almost done?

Fate stifled a sob as she buried her face in her hands and fled the room, the guard's expression a mixture of confusion and disgust.

She made it to her room without running into anyone, her heart pounding in her chest, torn in half with guilt. How could she? Was the beast inside so strong, so in control of her that she couldn't stop herself of ripping the essence out of her best friend?

Scarlet would never have done this. Scarlet had willpower, strength, dignity. This new being, this shade formerly known as Scarlet, was more monster than human. She knew that now.

And she had to put an end to it.

40

For once, Kane missed home. He longed for the unruffled existence beneath the red sands, the nearly predictable routine; the familiar faces—even the unpleasant ones.

While this adventure was exciting and forced him to cross the borders of new worlds and make new friends, he yearned for the quiet moments. For the times when his world made sense.

Legion, the buried Atlantian palace, embraced him, held him against its bosom in the moments of his greatest need. Raising Ever alone had been daunting, not because of her, of course, but he lacked the maternal instincts a young demon girl needed to flourish. He'd depended on many of his fellow, female demons to assist him—like Deme.

A rush of guilt overcame him with the thought of Legion's best tracker. He knew he'd hurt her when he left the demon city in pursuit of Fate. It wasn't lost to him that she harbored feelings for him, romantic feelings.

He pulled in a tense breath, his blazing blue eyes scanning the stairwell in which he descended. It was almost laughable how things had changed. One day, he loathed shades, the next, he loved one. By all rights he should have ended up with

Deme. He'd always cared for her, admired her—but never loved her like he loved Seren.

Fate was the only one to warm his broken heart after a century encased in ice. He wondered what the residents of Legion thought of him now. Did they despise him? Did they feel betrayed by his choice?

He knew the answer. They would never accept her, or him again for loving her. Shades were the dark abomination of Dark World, the evil incarnate—the work of the Devil.

But there were more pressing matters at hand.

Ever.

His baby.

What was he to do?

His head ached, his heart torn.

He needed to talk to someone. Someone who would not judge him.

And he was almost there.

Kane rounded the corner to the animal pens, the intense smell of the creatures preceding them. Not as offensive as he might have suspected, but potent nonetheless.

He passed several unicorns, whinnying softly as though whispering words to one another in a foreign language. To his left, a caged chupacabra snarled, his horse-like face and red eyes glowering as Kane walked by.

The pen he wanted was at the end, the largest of them all.

Arcanum raised his head the moment he saw Kane, almost as if he recognized him. The dragon's copper scales glimmered in the light, his great wings folded on his back.

Such a magnificent beast, Kane thought. *No wonder he was my father's favorite.*

Kane stood before the dragon's pen, his head lowered. He needed someone to talk to, someone who would listen. He realized that Arcanum was but a mute beast, but he was the only familiar shoulder that he could confide in at the moment. Fate was preoccupied, and frankly didn't need anymore stress. Kane considered Vrill a friend, but not necessarily a confidant. It took years and years for Kane to truly trust someone, Fate being a rare exception to that rule.

"I apologize for not visiting sooner," Kane muttered to the dragon whose large ochre eyes remained fixated on the prince, a quiet wisdom shining behind them. "There's been a lot going on." He sighed, leaning on the gate. "Ever has not yet awoken, Vrill feels she may indeed harbor Malus' soul. He has suggested…" he paused, looking up at the dragon, "that we terminate her life, just to be certain."

Arcanum's eyes widened and he huffed once as though he understood the prince's words. Kane frowned, wondering if it were possible for a dragon to comprehend language.

Shoving off the notion, Kane continued, "I don't know what to do, I cannot—I will not—allow anyone to hurt my daughter, but I don't want to be responsible for the demise of what remains of Dark World. If Malus is in there, and she takes over Ever, she'll be unstoppable." He lowered his eyes, shaking his head. "What am I to do?"

The dragon's scaly brow furrowed as he lowered his great head, long curved golden horns bowing before the prince, his talons scratching the surface of his pen.

A soft sound behind him drew Kane from his thoughts. It was Petra; her eyes did not meet his.

"Your Highness," Petra said with barely veiled trepidation, "it is time."

The prince nodded, uncertain if he could go through with this. Ever was his only child. His duty was to protect her—no matter what.

Slowly, he turned from Arcanum and began to walk away when the dragon huffed angrily behind him. Kane glanced back, brows furrowed, meeting the beast eye to eye.

There was something there, something so familiar, but Kane couldn't decipher it. The dragon stirred a memory within Kane's subconscious, buried so deep it lie just out of reach.

"I will keep her safe," Kane vowed to the dragon, not knowing why he'd made a promise to a mere beast.

Upstairs, Vrill's room was nearly unrecognizable. A haze of power lingered in the air like a storm cloud waiting to unleash its rains.

Ever lie as though made of marble, pale and angelic against the dark of the room. She looked so small, so helpless there.

All Kane wanted to do was scoop her up into his arms like when she was little and steal her away from all of this.

Kane's stomach fluttered with nerves as the last of the black candles were lit. His daughter's lifeless body lay in the center of light. Shadows danced upon the walls like ebony ghosts observing the ceremony.

The witchdoctor approached Ever, silver tattoos glimmering against the flames. Vrill stood silently in the corner, his hands folded in prayer. Hooded necromancers lined the walls, waves of lavender energy emanating from them as they charged the room with power. A power the witchdoctor would utilize to talk to his daughter's soul—or his mother's.

Vale hung back in the shadows, his glowing white eyes the only marker of his presence. The Oracle, Sybil, stood at the end of the bed near Ever's feet, smoke from burning black incense shrouding her in an eerie veil of mist. Her eyes closed and hands hovering over the princess, she seemed to be in a trance, humming quietly.

The entire scene was morbid, frightening even. Kane's instinct was to stop this warped séance, to end the madness. But he knew better. He knew this was the only way. The only way to know which soul owned that beautiful creature.

Even if his mother surfaced, he wouldn't let them hurt Ever's body. He'd find another way. He'd make his mother leave.

This he knew without a shadow of a doubt.

Fate would understand, she'd probably help him escape with her if he had to run away from Necrosia.

He frowned as he realized Fate's absence. Where was she anyways? He was sure she'd want to be here, or did she? He'd told her of it earlier in the day. Maybe it was too much for her. He could understand, this was almost too much for him.

He thought of Seren. What would she have done in the predicament? Would she approve of Kane's choice?

He'd have to remember to ask her when he saw her next.

"En sanctus animus, voisira mina soray," Kraton murmured as he waved his arms in the air, shaking some sort of rattle up and down the length of Ever's body.

The necromancers hummed alongside his words, deep, throaty sounds that echoed in the chamber. The eerie resonance wove through the room, changing the atmosphere, raising the frequency. Kane's heart rammed against his rib cage, his head swam, the power's vibration consuming the space, thickening the room as though it was filling with water.

"En sanctus animus, voisira mina soray," Kraton repeated over and over, louder and louder, his tone becoming shrill. "Come forth soul! Awaken!" he shouted.

Out of the corner of his eye, Kane saw Vrill take a step forward. Kane fired a warning glance in his direction, frowning as the necromancer neared the princess with slow calculated steps. Then the necromancer leader stopped a few feet from the ceremony, reaching into his left sleeve. Kane's blood froze when he recognized the hilt of a blade hidden in the leader's garment. Kane growled, low and baritone, gaining Vrill's full attention.

Acknowledging the prince's glare, Vrill dropped his hand and returned to his original station.

Kane turned back to the ritual, which was now reaching a terrifying peak.

"Come forth soul! Speak with us!" Kraton howled, shaking his whole body as he stood over Kane's daughter. Sybil seemed to mimic the witchdoctor's lunatic behavior, writhing and humming.

Kane could hardly breathe, his knees falling weak. The witchdoctor's rattle sounding in his ears combined with the necromancers' chant, Sybil's trance-like humming—he had to stop this.

He had to get out.

Just as he was about to grab Ever and run from the room, it all stopped.

Silence gripped the room, every breath was held as all gazes were fixated on the princess. Kane was afraid to move. He watched Ever's unmoving body, watched for any sign she'd returned.

Several moments passed, and just as Kane was about to drop his hopeful stare to the floor—Ever's eyes opened.

41

Fate locked the door, then walked to the dresser. She opened the top drawer and retrieved the small, violet bottle prescribed to her by the shaman. Cradling it in her palm, she eyed the liquid inside. What would it do to her? Would she be cured of this torture? Would it tame the fiend within?

Or would it kill her?

She'd almost taken her best friend's soul. Almost murdered her love's daughter. It had to be stopped, one way or another, it ended here, now, no matter what the consequence.

She couldn't say with all certainty that she trusted Shaman Goretus. He was a demon, and she, a shade. Two races born to hate one another, born to destroy each other. Whether she wanted to admit it or not, she was still a killer in their eyes. Part of a race that forced the demons into slavery, culling their kind with ruthless intent. The sins of her fellow shades ran thick through her undead body.

The vial was cool in her hand, the amethyst bottle glinting and gleaming with every movement.

This was it. She had to do it. There were no other choices left. The Bloodstone Vrill had given her was all gone, a source too scarce to keep her satiated for all eternity. The Soul Nexus had failed her, its power inexplicably extinguished.

Whatever was in this tiny bottle held her fate.

She pulled out the cork; it relinquished a tiny pop like a small bottle of wine. A wisp of white smoke escaped into the air, the scent of roses intermingled with mint drifted under her nose.

Fate took in a deep breath, whispered a prayer, and brought the bottle to her lips.

Part II

The Journey

1

The geysers spat high into the atmosphere, indicating the late hour. Crimson mist crawled over the desert, the heat blistering and unwelcoming. Mighty and terrifying beasts began their nightly hunts, their maws hungry for an easy kill.

The rider's glowing eyes panned the width of the Great Wall, anxiety climbing. The time was near. His quest was almost complete.

His black horse whinnied, ears twitching as though danger was near. The rider looked up, searching, but only a snarling sky glared back at him with judgment, as if it were about to impale him for his crimes.

His horse snorted again, agitated. "Silence, Exodus," the rider warned. "The time is almost at hand."

He would wait for the sign.

He'd waited this long.

2

"Ever!" Kane cried out as he rushed the podium to hold his only daughter. Her blue eyes were open, her glorious, shining eyes!

Kraton spun around in an instant, shaking his rattle at the prince, and hissed, "Not yet! I must speak with her first. The devil is full of tricks. She could be right in front of us and we'd never know it!"

Rage simmered beneath the surface of his demon skin as Kane ground his talons into his palms. But he understood that they had to know for sure, and he forced himself to be calm.

"What is your name?" Kraton asked as he hovered above Ever's ethereal face. When he received no response, he raised his voice, demanding, "Spirit, what is your name?"

Every soul in the room, the necromancers, Sybil, Vale, held their breath, daring not to move as they awaited the answer. Kane watched with fascination as Ever blinked, swallowed, and inhaled deeply, as if coming back into the world, and said, "Ever."

Her voice was like a chorus of angels to Kane's ears. He grinned like the day she was born. "It is Ever," he uttered, more to himself than anyone else.

Kraton's brow furrowed. "We must be sure," he stated, waving for Kane to approach the bedside. "Ask her a question that only your daughter would know the answer to."

Kane took in a breath, searching his memory for something only he and Ever would have knowledge of. Something Malus would not know.

Then he knew.

Leaning over, gazing into her stare, he asked, "Sweetheart, can you tell me why we named you Ever?"

Her brow furrowed and she seemed to search her thoughts.

Kane waited patiently, then asked again, "Can you remember why we called you Ever?"

Her long white lashes fluttered over her eyes for just a moment, then she smiled and replied, "Because the moment I was born, you told my mother that you had never seen anything so beautiful…ever." She paused a moment, then added, "Daddy, where am I?"

Kane fought the tears forming in his eyes.

She was back. His little girl was back.

"Don't get up too fast," Kane said softly as he helped his daughter to sitting, her ivory hand in his.

"I'm okay," Ever stated, her voice a little weak. "Just a little dizzy."

"Sire, I must insist that you give me some time with her," Kraton began, taking a step towards the prince and princess. "There's still more to…"

"No," Kane interjected firmly. "I am grateful that you have awoken my daughter, more than you know, but she is back, I see no need to continue with the ceremony."

Vrill stepped forward, extending his hands to help Ever from the podium. "Your highness, I understand your excitement, but if Kraton could be granted just few moments alone with the princess…to be certain," he said carefully.

"No," Kane growled, his blue eyes narrowing. "I will not allow anything further to be done to her. She has passed the test. She is Ever."

"Yes, sire," Vrill said with a nod but glanced apologetically to Kraton.

Kane's temper reignited. Hadn't they heard her? She knew the answer to his question. Malus would not have known the answer; she hadn't even known of Ever's existence, how would she have known why he and Seren had named her Ever? It wasn't a lucky guess. That is how he'd always told Ever of how she received her name, word for word.

He held Ever's arm as she crossed the room, her form even more delicate than before. She'd lost a substantial amount of weight over the weeks of unconsciousness.

Kane noticed Vale's eyes illuminating from the corner, his icy stare scanning his daughter distrustfully. The prince scoffed inside, what did that shade know of Ever? He'd never even spoken to her before.

Kane knew his daughter, and this was her. Not his mother. Not the devil.

There was no question whatsoever.

3

The liquid was as cold as ice, yet burned like fire down her throat. Fate threw the vial across the room, smashing it against the far wall. She fell to her knees, a scream rising into the back of her throat as the elixir meandered slowly, like lava, through her esophagus, eventually winding through her intestines. Her hands clutched at her neck, pain rippling over every inch of her body.

She felt a war ignite within, the hunger resisting. The monster would not die easily, would not let her go without a fight. Fate felt what remained of her soul fading, her life force slipping away like water through her fingers.

Oh no! This can't be happening! I don't want to die…again…like this!

Tears watered in her eyes, she'd made a mistake and she knew it. She should not have trusted the shaman. She was a fool to think there was a cure. He'd poisoned her. Murdered her.

Fate writhed on the floor, clawing at her stomach, praying for the pain to stop. At this point, she hoped she'd die; she couldn't endure this agony much longer. She thought of Kane. Ever. They'd be so disappointed in her. She'd given in to weakness, knelt before cowardice, too afraid to fight the beast.

Suddenly the pain changed, morphed, as if taking on its own consciousness. It converged in her core, pulling itself from every other area of her body, settling on her soul. She moaned as unbearable heat pulsed over her heart. She could do nothing but curl into a ball on the floor, hugging herself, hoping for the end to come soon.

Then, as quickly as it had begun, the pain dissipated, vanished. Fate lay there a moment in disbelief, amazed that she was still alive. She sat up, examined herself from head to toe, astonished that nothing had changed.

Well, almost nothing.

She rose from the floor, still a little shaky, and took a few steps towards the mirror. Warily, she inspected her face, afraid to see a change, yet hoping for one as well.

The same star-like eyes stared back at her, a hint of a smile playing upon her black lips. She looked exactly the same, but the hunger was gone. The ache that ripped at her insides was just…gone.

She gave her reflection a big grin, taking in a huge breath of relief.

"It worked," she whispered, her voice small, as though afraid she might awaken the beast again. "It really worked," she said, a little louder.

Fate sat down on the bed and closed her eyes, setting her hands on her legs and bowing her head as she let the feeling of peace flow throughout. The nightmare was over. The hunger, the monster was dead.

She smiled wide and opened her eyes.

Then she noticed her hands—and stopped smiling.

"What is this?" Fate said aloud, bringing the backs of her hands closer to her face and examining them.

Her veins, the thin forks that used to hold a bluish tinge, were now a network of black. She flipped her hands over and found the same, a roadmap of ebony. Beneath the skin, her veins were coursing with what appeared to be...black blood.

A flicker of panic ignited within. Was something wrong?

She quickly stood and ran to the mirror, scrutinizing her face, but there was nothing.

Fate frantically pulled off her top, then her pants—and gasped.

Everywhere but her face was painted with lines of black ink, down her arms, her legs, her back.

But the worst sight was her upper body.

Over her heart, in the center of her chest, was a hideous web of black lines. Like a crack in a windshield, it radiated outward, spreading like hundreds of spider's legs. It ran to everywhere on her body except her face. She was like the nightmare version of Davinci's *David.*

The shock overwhelmed her as she stood before the mirror, gaping. What was she going to do? Why was this happening? If this was the only side effect of the elixir, she was sure she could come to terms with it, but something didn't feel right about it. Something told her this wasn't a good side effect, that she should tell someone. But who? Kane would freak out for sure. Vale would probably laugh. Sybil would have some horrible precognition of doom.

Maybe Vrill, she thought, tracing a dark line down her hip.

After what felt like forever, she finally got dressed, covering herself completely from the neck down.

"At least I can hide this…for a little while," she said quietly.

A knock at the door frightened her.

"Just a second," she called out; scanning herself to make sure she was completely covered before opening the door. The lines in her neck still peeked out from beneath her collar so she grabbed a fashionable scarf from the drawer and draped it around herself, flipping a long end over her shoulder. It would pass on the Surface for sure, but here, she wasn't so sure.

The person knocked again. "Coming," she said, trying to sound calm as a flock of butterflies took flight in her stomach. How was she going to hide this? She couldn't stay covered up forever, especially in front of Kane.

Fate opened the door, crying out when she saw who was there. "Ever!"

Ever and Kane stood before her, huge grins decorating their glowing faces. "Hi," Ever said, jokingly nonchalant, then plunged herself into Fate's arms, hugging her very hard.

Fate squeezed her back, Ever's white hair like silk against her palms. "How…I mean…" she stammered as they drew apart.

"Kraton, the witchdoctor, he performed his voodoo...thing, and well," Kane said, beaming as he waved a hand in his daughter's direction.

"This is so wonderful," Fate exclaimed, then asked as a dark thought settled in, "So, no...you know who?"

Kane shook his head vehemently. "Ever was asked a question only she'd know the answer to, and she was correct." His eyes were so warm, so affectionate as he gazed at Ever, Fate had never seen him so happy, and it was easy to understand why.

He had his Ever back. They had their Ever back.

4

"Aren't you warm?" Kane asked of Fate as they head to the dining room for a celebratory dinner, eyeing the black gloves on her hands. The necromancers had whipped up an impromptu party, taking mere hours to decorate the entire hall, the very same hall that had been destroyed only weeks earlier. The necromancers had repaired the room in record time, even adding a new, elaborate ribcage chandelier overhead.

Fate fidgeted with the scarf, making sure it was secure around her neck. "No, I'm fine," she lied, flashing a smile at Kane who frowned back in concern. His worry was short-lived however, what with Ever on his other side.

"Where were you this afternoon?" Kane inquired under his breath. "You did not attend Ever's ritual."

Fate cringed as a flood of guilt washed through her. Not only did she miss an important event, now she had to lie about why she didn't go. "I...um...was just so tired, from Vrill's training," she started. "I...fell asleep. I'm so sorry." Fate dropped her gaze to the floor, feeling equally worse for lying as for missing the ceremony.

Kane smiled sweetly, setting his strong black hand beneath her chin, cupping it as he brought her face to his. "I understand. You've been working so hard, I'm proud of you."

Fate forced her lips into a pleasant curve, though inside she was tortured with shame and regret.

Thankfully, after a gentle kiss, he turned his attention to Ever.

"How are you feeling, sweetie?" he asked the princess, her emerald gown trailing long behind her. Fate glanced around Kane, awaiting her answer. Ever seemed distracted, distant. Her usually sparkling sapphire eyes carried a low flame, disturbed somehow. As though her thoughts were plagued with waking nightmares.

"Hmm?" she replied with a vague smile. "Oh, I'm fine, just a little…out of sorts."

"Do you want to go lie down?" Kane asked, already turning around to take her back upstairs.

Ever waved away his concern, stating, "No, no, let's go to dinner, I'm sure I just need food."

"And Bloodstone," Kane added. "Your body will be requiring a heavy dose."

Ever nodded politely, extending a gracious smile to her father, but the light did not reach her eyes.

Something is different about her, Fate thought, examining the princess, then shrugged it off. *She's probably just hungry.*

"Friends!" Vrill called out when he saw the trio, the entirety of the table rising from their seats to greet them. "Ever," he gushed, clasping his hands together, "so wonderful to have you with us."

Ever smiled warmly at Vrill and his guests, taking a seat next to her father at the head of the table. Fate followed suit, sitting on the other side of Kane, a plate of Bloodstone already set before her.

She fought back a grin. It was wonderful not to have that gaping, ravenous hole inside. The hunger had completely vanished, the monster seemingly dead within. The relief she felt was substantial, yet a new fear had begun to grow. What was this new side effect streaking through her body? This black blood? Should she be concerned, or simply take it in stride, accepting it as a mark of triumph over evil?

Self-conscious, she tried to look casual as she checked that her sleeves were adequately covering her wrists.

Thank goodness it didn't seep into my face; I'd have no way to hide that!

"So, Fate," Vrill piped up suddenly, sending a flash flood of nerves through her stomach. Could he tell? Was one of her new veins peeking over the scarf?

She took in a calming breath, meeting his eyes, replying, "Yes?"

"Shall we continue your training, say, tomorrow?" he asked as he brought a silver goblet to his lips, savoring a sip of burgundy wine.

Fate fought back a groan, forcing herself to smile. "Of course, tomorrow." She saw Kane shift in his seat, his cobalt eyes suddenly wrought with fresh concern. Leaning over, she whispered, "Are you okay?"

He nodded, his heavy black horns glistening against the flame of the chandelier. "Yes, but…I must speak to you later, in private."

Her stomach did an uncomfortable flip. What could he need to talk to her about?

Before she could ponder it further, Vrill stood suddenly, goblet in the air. "I'd like to perform a toast, in honor of the princess. To your return!"

Fate looked at Ever, expecting to see her blush, or any sign of gratitude, but instead saw a trickle of irritation flash through the princess's eyes. What was wrong with her?

For just a split second, Fate worried that Ever had somehow been compromised by the former devil of Dark World. Without trying to be obvious, she scanned Ever up and down, trying to see anything out of place, anything that would be inherently *not* Ever.

Vrill rattled on with his speech as Fate scrutinized every movement, every breath the princess took. There had to be something different, didn't there? If she truly was the princess, there'd be no doubt.

Suddenly Fate felt eyes on her, watched from the other end of the table. She followed the sensation and locked eyes with Vale. His glowing white eyes trailed from hers; landing on Ever, then back to Fate.

And he shook his head, as if to say, "*No, I don't believe it either.*"

5

Kane took Fate's gloved hand into his, leading her out onto a secluded balcony. His insides roiled, heart tortured with indecision. He hated leaving her, hated every moment he had to spend away from her.

And now Ever.

His baby was awake, though still out of sorts; he despised the thought of abandoning her in her hour of greatest need.

But he had no choice.

The sooner he gathered the races, the faster he collected the scrolls, and the earlier he spoke to his wife, the better. So much needed to be done. So many quests to be completed. He was overwhelmed, but ready. Dark World needed him.

"What did you want to speak to me about?" Fate asked, her voice shaky as she looked up at him with concerned eyes.

He took a big breath in before replying, "I am leaving tomorrow, there are many things that need to be done to save this world."

"I will go with you," she said quickly.

Kane sighed. "No, you cannot." She opened her mouth to protest, but he added quickly, silencing her, "I need you here, to be with Ever. There's no one in the world I trust more. Please, stay here, for me?"

Pain filled him as he saw glimmers of tears form in her luminescent eyes, how he hated upsetting her. But she nodded as she turned from him, wrapping her arms around her torso.

"Fate," he said softly, pressing his body against her back as she leaned against the railing. The scent of her hair caressed his face, lingered in his senses, driving him to distraction. He raised his hand, running his talons through her long white mane, then down the arch of her lower back. "You know it will be agony to be away from you."

She stood up straight, turning around slowly. Her chin still lowered, she whispered, "I don't want to be alone."

He cupped her face with his large black hands, saying, "You will not be alone, you will be with Ever, and I will always love you, no matter where I go. No matter how far. And I will be back as soon as I can."

She nodded, though was obviously unconvinced. "Who is going with you?" she asked quietly, a hint of jealousy in her tone.

"Vale, and two necromancers," Kane replied.

Fate's eyes narrowed almost imperceptibly. "And Sybil?"

He shook his head. "No, just Vale and two necromancers. Trackers. Vrill recommended them."

"I see," she said, seemingly relieved as she turned her back to him again, leaving him to wonder why she was worried who he would be alone with. He then remembered her youth, her innocence. She was but a teenager when she left the Surface, a baby in Dark World years. Though she'd been forced to grow up far too quickly in the underworld, her human inexperience was bound to test her.

"Fate," he whispered, taking her by the shoulders and urging her to face him. "There will only ever be you. There is no other that owns my heart…or my soul." He trailed a talon over her ring finger, hidden beneath a black glove, reminding her of the promise ring.

She shivered as she exhaled, relaxing a little. "I know, I just…worry," she said, lifting her face to his.

"Never doubt my love for you, ever," he stated as he brought his lips to hers.

She smiled, gazing up at him, then said, "I'll be here, waiting for you."

He grinned. "You'd better be."

"I promise," she whispered, hugging him tight.

6

Necrosia's courtyard was overflowing with well-wishers. A rainbow of streamers undulated in the hellish breeze as though waving their own silent goodbyes. Necromancers danced and sang while pyrotechnic shades shot fireballs into the air. Vrill, Sybil, Ever, and Fate all stood in a line to wish the men farewell and safe journey.

"Prince Kane, this is Mezza and Slater, they will assist you throughout your journey," Vrill said with one hand dabbing the corners of his eyes, and gesturing with the other at two very muscular necromancers, who in turn, nodded respectfully at the prince.

"Thank you," Kane replied, feeling surprisingly relieved. It was going to be a long and perilous journey, to have others accompany him was a welcome gift. He'd learned his lesson travelling alone in Dark World. The last excursion had nearly cost him his life. If it weren't for Ever and Arcanum, he'd have been torn to pieces by Ba'al's blood rain. There were far too many dangers that lay ahead for him to adhere to his foolish ego and his need to do everything alone. Besides, it was nice to have friends again, even if one of them was Vale.

"I packed you a lunch," Fate muttered with a somber expression as she handed him a large satchel, her solemn gaze locked onto the ground before her.

"And I packed you supper," Ever added, her tear-stained face evident as she offered him an even bigger bag.

Kane suppressed a bittersweet laugh. His girls, his beautiful girls. The way it looked, they would miss him even more than he would miss them...if that were possible. It could be weeks, maybe months, before he'd see their faces again. Disquiet reared inside of him. What if they were not safe here? Should he leave them? He could bring them along, but deep down he knew that Ever was in no condition to make such a demanding journey. She'd have to stay in Necrosia, and Fate with her.

He'd have to trust that destiny was on his side. That he'd be brought back to them soon, safe and sound.

"Thank you ladies, I shall enjoy every bite," Kane said as he accepted the girls' gifts, throwing them into his bag and heaving it over his shoulder alongside the sheath that held his black diamond sword. He then kissed both of them, Ever on the forehead and Fate on the lips. "Now, where is my trusty sidekick?" Kane inquired of Vale's whereabouts.

Ever giggled amidst her tears, saying, "Um, he and Aura are...saying goodbye." And she pointed to a far corner of the courtyard where Vale and Aura's faces were mashed together in passion.

Kane rolled his eyes. This was to be a long journey.

"Vale!" he bellowed across the courtyard with his hands cupped around his mouth. "It's time to go!"

Startled, the frisky couple pried themselves apart, blushed, then made their way through the gathered crowd.

"Finally," Kane teased as Vale picked up his satchel and flung it onto his back.

Vale just smirked, turning to Aura as she blew him a final kiss that manifested in the air as a misty butterfly, floated the distance between them and disappeared in a burst of sparkles on his cheek. He grinned, bowed in thanks, then wisped out of sight only to reappear next to his sister several feet away. He hugged her, but also whispered something into her ear. Kane noted this, but thought nothing more of it.

Fresh tears rolled down Ever's face as he gave one last squeeze goodbye, then turned to Fate and pulled her into his chest as well.

He prayed this would not be the last time he held them.

Upon releasing them to Vrill's open arms, he heard Vrill whisper, "Safe journey, Prince. We are depending on you."

As the drawbridge opened, the crowd cheered and the quartet made their way out into Dark World.

7

The world around her seemed hollow, empty without Kane close by. Just knowing he wasn't near made her heart sad, cold. Fate couldn't remember how she'd felt about the notion of soul mates when she was on the Surface, but she certainly believed in them now. It was hard to believe that destiny had chosen them to find one another, especially considering where she'd started.

As a human, she recalled feeling awkward, stumbling around a society of petty concerns and cruel intent. So many people on the Surface seemed to have a selfish agenda, an alternative plan devised only to feed their insatiable souls. Money, status, belongings, those were the items of insanity on the Surface. The more you had, the better you appeared to be. Dark World had long since suffered under a living, breathing devil, but the Surface owned a far more insidious fiend—greed.

Thankfully her family understood a greater calling, a far richer purpose than the ownership of mass materialism. They loved one another, deeply. Tears burned in Fate's eyes with the broken memories of her first home, her previous family. There'd been so many fun times, so much support.

And now, here, the one that loved her more than anyone, the one that held her the closest, was gone. Maybe not forever, but far enough away for her to feel the chill left by his absence.

"Hi," a soft voice said from behind, drawing her from her sorrows. Fate turned to see Ever's saddened expression, a mirror of her own she was sure.

"Hi, how are you feeling?" Fate asked, glad to have an excuse to think of something other than Kane.

Ever shrugged, her ivory horns nearly opalescent against the light of the dozens of candles illuminating the hall. "I'm okay, I guess. I wish my father could have stayed with me longer before he had to go."

Fate nodded, suddenly feeling guilty for thinking she was the only one affected by Kane's departure. "Hey, do you want to the market later? Shopping was something that I remember always cheering me up on the Surface."

Ever nodded with a smile, a glimmer of light returning to her sapphire eyes. "That sounds great," she started, then yawned. "But I think I need to rest a while first."

"Of course, let me take you upstairs."

They'd only made it a few steps when Vrill approached them from behind. "Come, come ladies, no need to be glum," he exclaimed in his usual candor. "The men will be back in no time, I'm certain of it." His words were cheerful, but Fate recognized a guarded sliver of concern behind the necromancer's swirling eyes. There were things that he and Kane were not telling her. Dangers they had not confessed.

After he was out of sight, Fate tugged at her sleeves and then checked the scarf at her neck. Were the black striations peeking out? She didn't know how long she could keep this up. How was she going to hide the black blood racing through her veins? Someone was bound to notice. At the very least, they'd inquire as to why she was obsessively pulling at her clothes or wearing turtlenecks, scarves, and gloves in the midst of an eternal heat wave.

A sudden weight against her side jarred her from her worries. It was Ever, leaning against her for support.

"Ever?" Fate asked, startled as she attempted to hold the princess upright. "What's wrong?"

"I...don't feel well," Ever said quietly draping her right hand across her pale forehead as though she had a headache.

"Are you alright?" Fate asked, suddenly feeling selfish, only worried about her own afflictions. Ever had just awakened from a lengthy coma, she was bound to be fatigued, even ill from lack of food, water, and Bloodstone. And here all Fate could think about was herself. "Come," Fate took Ever by the elbow, guiding her down the hall and into the main entrance. "Let's get you to bed."

"Okay," Ever complied as she allowed herself to be led up the staircase. "I'm sorry to be such a bother."

Fate shook her head vehemently. "No, you are nothing of the sort. I should have known better."

She steered Ever to her room, opened the door and helped her into bed. Instantly unconscious, Fate pulled the comforter up to Ever's neck, tucking her in.

Poor thing, Fate thought as she eyed the sleeping princess. *I wish there was more I could do.*

Fate examined the princess's contented face, her silver-white hair cushioning her ivory horns. The demon girl was so beautiful, inside and out. So gentle, so soft-spoken, how could Fate have thought her capable of deceit? It was obvious she wasn't the queen. Unless the queen was able to control Ever somehow, or pretend to be her.

Fate shook her head. The queen would not have known the answer to Kane's question. Or would she? Maybe the queen was able to unlock Ever's thoughts, taking them as her own.

The shade sighed as she gazed at the princess. She had to trust Kane's instinct. If he says this is Ever, she would believe it too.

Unless proven otherwise.

Slowly and quietly, she tiptoed out of the bedroom, closing the door behind her. As she made her way back to her own room, she suddenly had an unfamiliar sensation in her stomach. A pulling feeling followed by a gurgle.

She instantly smiled—she was hungry, but for real food this time. It had been a very long time since she'd felt the pang of culinary desire. It was refreshing to say the least, so foreign in comparison to the torturous ache of soul hunger.

Nearly skipping as she made her way to the kitchen, she savored the moment, the sense of normalcy, the return to her true self.

If only she could rid herself of these vile black lines, this roadmap of darkness. What was it? What had the antidote infused within her? Part of her didn't care, she was healthy, close to normal—almost human again.

Fate hummed as she rounded the corner into the kitchen, anxious to take her first bite of food since descending into Dark World.

What should I have first? She thought excitedly as she yanked off her gloves, ignoring her exposed network of shadowy veins.

Before her, a feast lay in waiting. There was a large bowl filled with various fruits, newly picked from the magical trees in the courtyard. In another sat a fresh chopped salad made with blue mushrooms, purple carrots, and boiled griffin eggs. Fresh baked muffins, cakes, and cookies. All this and more.

But while these choices looked fantastic, they didn't appeal to her as much as the huge plate of ribs she spied at the back of the room. Her mouth watered as she crossed the room, grabbing hold of a large rack and tearing into them with her sharp fangs.

She devoured them with the same frenzy she would have a soul. She licked her fingers, gnawed on the bones, stripping them of every ounce of meat. She couldn't get enough. Her stomach begged for more. More meat. More flesh.

She ate until there was no more.

It wasn't until after she was done, when the carnage had ceased, that reality set in.

The ribs had been raw.

8

The mountains stood as silent sentinels in the distance, the stony stalactites overhead nothing more than a blur of shadows, hidden by miasmic billows of smoke and ash. The landscape lay open to them, the backdrop a reddish haze of calm, peaceful even.

But Kane knew better. It was just a deceptive invitation to traverse the horizon of Hell. Dark World was nothing more than seductive mistress that tempted her victims with mystical wiles, whispering promises in the dark that she never intends to keep. All to lure one to their death upon her bosom of evil.

Kane scanned the desolate terrain with narrowed eyes; he had never been this far east before. His father had planned to show Kane the entire kingdom once he was of age, but of course that day never came. The world as Kane knew stopped the day his father died and he was thrown into the mines where he didn't see the light of day for almost one hundred years.

Then he and Seren escaped, along with a handful of others. They'd spent years, decades, on the run from his mother and her ruthless army of shades. Many were lost. Many were found. But all were on the brink of losing hope that'd they'd ever truly be free from the queen's tyranny.

Until Kane found Atlantis. Buried beneath the sands of the Crimson Desert, he'd chased the legend until he made it reality. A safe haven for his people. A home for his wife and unborn child. It was perfect, a gift from the gods.

Then, the day before they were to move to safety, a shade broke through their defenses, attacked Seren, stealing her soul and leaving their only child without a mother.

Kane's eyes burned over the scarred landscape before him, his thoughts painted dark with pain and loss. He had to end this torment, this once powerful world torn apart by greed and suffering. And the only way, he knew, was to relight the pyramid. To give the people back their magic, rekindle the flame of immortality within; only then could they begin to heal. To rebuild the kingdom.

"So boss, where to first?" Vale asked as he kicked a rock across the red sands of the Crimson Desert, watching as it skipped and rolled before disappearing under a parched shrub.

With a deep breath, Kane forced himself to the present situation, considering a moment before answering. The banshees lived in the west, quite close to the Valley of Shadows, where Seren was. If they went there first he could steal away unnoticed and hopefully find her without raising any suspicion. He wanted to confront her alone. He didn't know what state he'd find her in.

But the reapers lived in the north; on the way to Exile Island. He could collect the reapers' scroll and then retrieve the rest from Myth, then swing back around to the gather the races for the relighting of the pyramid.

There were just so many tasks to complete. His head swam with indecision. To make things even more complicated, he wished to visit Legion in the south, to see how his fellow demons were doing. They were likely concerned as to his well-being, well, he hoped so anyways. Maybe they were happier without him. Maybe Syphon and the elders were relieved to be in complete control without his presence to interfere.

Bitterness wound tight around his heart. He had tried his best. He had tried to serve his people well, but without the guidance of his father, his heart was just not in it.

"Well?" Vale inquired again, staring at Kane with a bored expression as he awaited instruction.

"We head for Sensua, to the banshees," he stated confidently, turning to face the west. Despite his reservations, he had to talk to Seren first. It was imperative.

"But I already took their scroll," Vale offered with sly grin.

Kane sighed. "Yes, but we still need to gather volunteers from each of the cities."

"Ahh, right," Vale said with a shrug. "Forgot."

Mezza and Slater nodded loyally, shifting their direction to the west immediately while Vale rolled his eyes slightly, ran a hand through his wild silver hair, and reluctantly followed behind.

9

"Oh! Gross!" Fate shouted, examining her grease-laden hands with horror. She'd eaten raw meat! Not that she was a vegetarian on the Surface, but she'd always had a bit of guilt when eating the flesh of animals—and that was when it was cooked! Never would she have considered eating *raw* meat! Yuck! "What is wrong with me?" she asked aloud.

"Is everything okay?" a concerned voice queried from the kitchen door. Fate looked up, startled and embarrassed to see Sybil there, her eyebrows drawn together in concern.

"Oh, um, yes…of course," Fate stammered, rushing to the sink to cleanse herself of her sins. She cranked the hot knob to full, washing away the clingy film of grease and remnants of stripped flesh. "I just…dropped a piece of food on the floor, I'm so clumsy," she said with a forced laugh, hoping Sybil would buy it. But she was a psychic, so Fate was pretty sure she was onto her.

"Fate," Sybil started, crossing her arms over her chest, adopting a patient-doctor air. "Do you need to talk?"

Fate turned off the water, steam dissipating around her face, and nodded as she tugged her sleeves over her hands. She may as well confide in someone. "I…think something's wrong with me."

Sybil tilted her head inquisitively. "Like what?"

Fate took a long breath in. Should she tell her? Could she trust Sybil? There was some history there, sort of. They'd both been from Edmonton on the Surface, suffered through the same indignant death at the hands of a killer. That gave them a bond, didn't it?

Maybe Sybil knew of a cure? She was, after all, the Oracle. She'd been up and down Dark World more than most over the last hundred years. She must have come across something like this before. Fate couldn't be the only one, could she?

She sucked in a breath and released it noisily, debating whether or not to expose her newfound scars. Was it the judgment she was so worried about? Would Sybil view her differently? Act differently around her?

Fate rolled her eyes at herself. This wasn't high school anymore. She couldn't assume that everyone around her was out to get her. Out to make her life a living hell. Sybil was an elder, despite her youthful appearance. She'd lived a century already, decades more than most on the Surface.

She had to know what this was. And had to be mature enough to understand why Fate chose to take the potion.

"Well," Fate started, shaky as she reached for her right sleeve in order to lift it and show Sybil the black blood running throughout her arm. "I drank this…"

"Hello ladies!" Vrill's cheerful voice suddenly boomed through the kitchen.

Fate hastily covered her wrist, her heart slamming in her chest, and turned to face him. "Vrill, um, hello," Fate stuttered, stealing a glance at Sybil who eyed the necromancer stonily, as though she was annoyed by the interruption.

"Vrill," Sybil greeted him without emotion, though Fate sensed a deep mistrust treading just beneath the surface of the prophetic shade. Did Sybil know something about Vrill that Fate did not? If there was anyone that would know something was awry, it would most likely be her.

"What on earth on you doing in here?" he asked, but continued without waiting for an answer. "Come, come, I must steal Fate away for her training."

Fate groaned internally. This was the last thing she wanted to deal with today. Then she thought of an excuse. "Oh, I have to check on Ever, she wasn't feeling well and…"

"Sybil can do that, can't you dear?" he stated, taking Fate by the elbow and guiding her out of the room, leaving Sybil alone in the kitchen with a scowl upon her face.

By the time they reached the stairs leading to the training cavern, Fate had surrendered to the idea that she wasn't going to get out of this one. Why was he so determined to train her? She hadn't shown any real potential. Any real talent. Did he simply have nothing else to do but attempt to force her to hone her skills? Skills she may not have?

"We're going to try something new today," Vrill said excitedly once they reached the training room.

"Oh," Fate replied, a serving of fresh anxiety coalescing with the raw meat in her stomach.

"Yes, we're going to try a whole new approach." He clapped his hands, then began conjuring something from thin air. The room began to fill with a green fog, thick and rolling, choking the room like a giant serpent.

"Oh goody." Fate cringed as she cradled her roiling stomach. What did he have planned for her now?

The ghost-like mists crawled across the floor, churning and writhing with purpose as it moved closer and closer to Fate, reaching for her with finger-like tendrils. Touching her, caressing her.

Vrill had fallen into some sort of trance, humming and whispering words she could not understand. His silver eyelids flickered, the stars in his eyes visible for only a split second at a time.

What is he doing? Fate's skin crawled with apprehension as the seemingly conscious vapor began to take form before her. Vrill said they were just going to take a new approach. What was that? Fear therapy?

Well, it was working.

The miasmic mass seemed to be at war with itself, dodging and avoiding cohesiveness until it finally appeared to decide on a shape. At first it just looked like a humanoid figure before her. A male physique, not overly tall, and definitely not foreboding.

But then color started filling in. Brown hair, sea-green eyes, sun-kissed skin. He was as beautiful as she remembered.

Fate's lips trembled as the words fell from her mouth, "*Rory Dean.*"

10

Crimson froth and plumes of silver smoke belched from the mouths of the miniature volcanoes that surrounded them. Only a few feet high, the lava fountains were but dwarves of their elderly siblings who shadowed the entirety of the southern horizon. While they appeared harmless, only spitting out the occasional stream of molten rock, they were all programmed by nature to explode faithfully once a day. At exactly midnight, every one of the hundred and four scorching craters would spew a rain of hot magma in near perfect unison.

While the field of volcanoes lay dormant for the duration of the day, it did not, however, leave the area at a comfortable temperature. Save for the volcanic ridge in the south, it was the hottest place in Dark World.

Kane, Vale, and the two Spartan necromancers navigated their way quickly through the mine field, not because midnight was near, but because of the scorching conditions.

"We're nearing the end," Kane announced, pointing to a clearing ahead.

Vale exhaled loudly. "Thank the gods," he stated as a fresh bead of sweat rolled over his forehead, joining the dozens of drops plummeting from his pale jaw. "I was beginning to feel well-done."

Kane laughed. The shade was probably very hot indeed. Kane's own heat-tolerant demon skin was beginning to feel a bit singed, so the shade was likely getting quite crispy around the edges. Mezza and Slater, on the other hand, appeared impervious to the heat. In fact, they seemed resistant to every inconvenience. They didn't appear to tire, get hungry, or even stop to use the washroom. They were beyond inhuman, to say the least.

Once they'd moved beyond the inferno and into the cool, open air, Kane called to his group, "Alright, let's rest here."

Mezza and Slater looked confused, but complied, seating themselves on the ground across from Kane. Vale raised his hands dramatically, as though praising the gods and then fell to his knees, pretending to kiss the ground. He then lay on his back and did a few sand angels before closing his eyes and resting.

"We've only been travelling for half the day, Vale—and we have many weeks ahead of us," Kane said, trying not to sound irritated. "Are you going to be able to finish this journey?"

Without opening his eyes, Vale replied, "I suppose I have no choice."

Kane swallowed the growl rising in his throat. "You are welcome to leave if you wish."

Vale opened his eyes, sighed, and sat up. He locked eyes with the prince. "Now, you and I both know that's not true."

Kane frowned. "I do not understand. You feel forced to be here?"

The shade shrugged, standing and wiping the sand from his black leather pants. "Well, the way I see it, you need me...and I owe you," he added with quiet reluctance.

"I need you?" Kane scoffed. "How is that?"

Vale laughed. "How do you propose to obtain the remaining scrolls without a shade's help?"

Kane grimaced. He had him there. His father's spell prevented anyone in Dark World from touching the scrolls or they'd age one thousand years in the blink of an eye—but shades hadn't originated in the underground world, therefore the spell was void upon them. Kane surrendered a nod, then asked, "And why do you...owe me?"

"Well," Vale started with a cocky tone. "I did steal your city's scroll."

"Yes, yes you did," Kane said with a chuckle, not holding it against him, but sensed the shade wasn't finished.

"And..." Vale's gaze turned to the ground, "your wife saved my sister."

"She did? When?"

"It was when Sybil was in hiding. She told me she saved her life...long ago," Vale offered quietly.

Kane searched his memory, but came up empty-handed. "I'm sorry, I did not hear of this."

Vale shrugged. "I don't know all the details. You'll have to get Sybil to tell you about it when we get back to Necrosia. But regardless, I feel I owe you, and your wife, a debt of gratitude."

"You are welcome," Kane replied despite the gap in his recollection. When had Seren come to Sybil's aid? Why had Seren never spoken of this?

Maybe Seren was ashamed to tell him she'd helped a shade? At that time, it would have been unheard of; shades were still very much the enemy. But Sybil was similar to Fate in many ways, strong-willed and independent, and very unwilling to serve the queen. Perhaps that was the link.

It made sense that the queen would have pursued Sybil in the same way she hunted Fate, she was also a single born. She would have been a suitable match for the queen to transfer her soul to. But the need, as it turned out, was not there. For many years, there was a rumor that the queen had touched one of the sacred scrolls, therefore aging one thousand years. The rumor was just that though, a rumor. She'd never needed an heir, for possession purposes anyways.

So why then was she after Sybil? Shortly before she was killed, Malus had admitted to Kane that Fate was the key to opening the Crystal Pyramid. Did Sybil have unknown abilities as well? One that the queen desired?

Kane decided to have a long chat with the oracle shade when he returned to Necrosia. He wished to uncover whatever secrets the seasoned psychic might harbor.

"Shall we?" Vale asked, spreading an arm over the impending horizon.

Kane sighed. "Yes, I suppose we must continue. We'll head for that group of mountains," He pointed into the distance, "and camp there tonight."

Mezza and Slater must have concurred with Kane's decision as they began marching in the chosen direction without delay. Vale, however, lagged behind, his normally mischievous eyes tainted with worry as he cased the posse's perimeter a little too often.

Kane fell back to speak with him privately. "Is everything okay? Do you need some Bloodstone?" He wasn't in abundance of the rare stones, but he'd rather share it than end up losing his soul to a ravenous shade sometime down the road.

The shade's eyes lit up a little. "Yes, I suppose I might just be hungry, but…don't you feel that?"

Alarmed, Kane glanced around. "Feel what?"

Vale looked behind him, his paranoia palpable, and said under his voice, "Like we're being followed."

11

A scream sat trapped in Fate's throat. Rory Dean! Why was he here? How?

"Vrill?" Fate squeaked, her eyes racing back and forth between her mentor and her murderer. Why would Vrill summon him? Was he real?

Rory's perfect twin grinned at her with the same malevolence as the night he'd killed her. His eyes burned with playful venom as he took a step towards her, and another.

"Vrill!" she screamed, backing away. "Help me!" She looked to the necromancer, but he simply stood there and watched the scene unfold, seemingly indifferent. "Vrill!"

Fate tripped over the leg of a chair, falling hard against the floor. She crawled away from Rory's slow, steady approach. He was so real. She could even smell his cologne.

"No! Please! No!" she cried. "I can't do this again!"

"*There is no death,*" Rory hissed as he closed in on her. "*Only transition.*"

She knew she should stand and fight, tear him limb from limb. She'd tangled with a herd of sphinxes and won! The power was there, cowering within, but she simply couldn't face him.

"*Sccarrlett...*" he taunted, edging ever closer.

Soon she had nowhere to go, her back was pressed against the rocky wall of the dark cavern; her worst nightmare only inches away. All she could do was curl into a ball and weep.

Several moments went by before she heard, "Fate?" Vrill's soft voice called to her. "Why don't you fight him?"

She shook her head, afraid to look up. "I can't."

"He has no power over you," Vrill stated, kneeling down beside her, his hand on her shoulder. "He's gone, Fate."

Warily, she looked up, the figment of Rory was gone. The room sat as benign as before. "Why?" she pleaded, looking into Vrill's swirling eyes. "Why would you do that to me?"

He surrendered a small smile. "I didn't."

"What do you mean you didn't? I was right here, you made that…thing," she shouted, now angry as she waved her arm over the space where Rory had been. Recalling her 'condition', she quickly checked to ensure her black veins were suitably hidden, then asked, "If you didn't make him, then who did?"

"You," he said quietly, standing as he tucked his hands into his oversized sleeves.

"Me?" Fate paced the room, her arms folded over her chest. "No, I would never do that."

"Your fear summoned him, *he* is your greatest fear," the necromancer explained in a guru-like tone.

"Yeah, no shit, I could have told you that." Fate stormed around the room, uncertain if she should stay or leave. What was Vrill thinking? Didn't he know she couldn't handle that? She tugged at her sleeves and checked her neckline again.

Vrill sighed. "I am sorry," he said as though reading her thoughts. "I'd hoped you were ready to face your fears."

Guilt wormed its way through her anger. "Why? Why would you think that?"

Vrill approached her, took her left hand firmly into his and pulled up the fabric, revealing her railroad of black scars, saying, "Because—we're running out of time."

12

"Followed?" Kane scanned the desolate landscape, his eyes narrowed. "I don't see anyone."

Vale rolled his glowing eyes. "I don't see them either. I just...sense it," he stated, glaring into the crimson oblivion.

"Well," Kane started, uncertain as to how much stock he put into the shade's sixth sense. After all, he wasn't his prophetic sister. "Let's move on then, maybe there's something in this area watching us from afar."

Vale nodded, moving forward, but continued to glance back every few minutes.

The mountain range Kane had chosen for camp was only a few hours away, hopefully whatever Vale was paranoid about would abandon its plight before then.

Sensua was at least two days walk to the west, if they didn't encounter any problems. The western realm of Dark World was home to substantially more dangerous predators than the south. The south harbored the sphinxes and death worms, which were both lethal to a small band of four, but the west held beasts of another nature: beasts that could wield magic. Dark magic.

Over the centuries, Kane had come across many books from the Surface. While he couldn't interpret the human's language, a great many were rich with illustrations. Before the great crevice opened countless millennia ago and swallowed the Atlantean palace, the ancient humans lived alongside gods and magical creatures. Many were benign, friendly even. Unicorns, pixies, griffins, all lived harmoniously with the humans. Others, like the sphinxes and dragons, simply caused a bit of havoc amongst the Surface dwellers.

But then there were the others, the darkest of monsters. Rare and fantastic creatures that were wise enough to steal their next meal in the dead of night, robbing babies from their cradles, escaping detection, stoking the fires of myths and legends.

The ancient books and their artwork depicted a vast variety of zoological oddities. The Atlanteans seemed to have made it their goal, their passion, to collect as many as these creatures as possible. As a demon child he was spellbound by these pictures, and how over the centuries these beasts had been reduced to nothing but mere myth.

Kane had always found it humorous that the humans believed these creatures, even the topic of magic, to be that of fiction. If only they knew.

How sad it would be to live without magic, Kane considered. *How do the humans live without the prospect of something so amazing, of becoming so much more than mortal? So much more than…average?* He was certain that they must live a purposeless, if not boring, existence without the glory of fulfilling their true, magical potential.

"Um, what is that?" Vale suddenly asked, pointing to the right, tearing Kane from his internal wanderings. The two necromancers were immediately still, eyes locked on that location, now on high alert.

Kane followed his finger and narrowed his eyes to focus. "What? I don't see anything." The horizon appeared as barren as before; just the same, flat, unyielding desert gazed back at him.

Vale stabbed his finger in the air as if that would help Kane see better. "That!"

Then he saw what the shade was looking at. "Oh no, that's bad news, that's what that is."

13

Fate snatched her arm away from the necromancer, pulling her sleeve down as far as it would go.

"When did this happen?" Vrill asked, pinching the bridge of his nose with thumb and forefinger as though plagued with a sudden headache.

"A few days ago," Fate admitted reluctantly. "Why? What is it?"

"Come with me," Vrill ordered almost impatiently and started for the doorway, only instead of heading back up the stairs, he led her down another dank and darkened hallway. It twisted and turned like a labyrinth before he finally stopped in front of a triple padlocked door, two heavily armed necromancer guards stationed on either side. Vrill produced a key from within his robes and unlocked each lock in turn. The heavy, iron door groaned in protest as he pulled it open.

What is so important that it needs so much protection? Or maybe it was something so frightening; it couldn't risk being let loose. Fate shuddered with the thought.

Vrill ushered her inside a small, circular room, igniting a candle overhead with just a flick of his finger. Pale yellow light illuminated the room but lent no warmth to the permanent chill in the air. There were no windows and no other way in or out—except down. In the center of the room was a hole, at least ten feet in diameter. The pit brimmed with pure darkness as no light seemed to penetrate the abyss.

Fate took a step forward, glaring into the pitch dark, trying to distinguish what could be down there. A foul stench rose from the void, teasing Fate's gag reflex. It was a familiar smell, like rotting meat on a hot summer's day. What creature was held here? What being deserved this treatment? She was momentarily both annoyed and concerned for the beast.

She took another step closer to the hole, leaning over as she peered in.

"Take care, don't get too close," Vrill said suddenly, his voice hollow in the cylindrical room. He put his hands together and conjured a sphere of light, then tossed it down into the hole.

The ball of illumination fell about fifteen feet before it landed on a sandy floor. Bones lay scattered all over the ground, it was as though a graveyard of skeletons had suddenly erupted and spat up all the remains of the dead after completely sucking all of the meat off the marrow.

"Who…or what…is in here?" Fate asked as she scanned the hole, looking for whatever she was to be cautious of.

Vrill just eyed her with a sad expression, then pointed into the hole. Fate followed his finger.

In one corner was a little girl, a shade, of about ten years old, huddled against the back wall, weeping, shivering, and afraid of Vrill's sphere of light. Her long silver hair ran the length of her back, wearing a once-white nightgown, torn and stained brown with remnants of dried blood.

Instantly angry, Fate shouted at Vrill, "What is this? Why do you keep her here?"

Vrill sighed. "Look closely," he whispered, his galactic eyes brimming with sadness.

Fate leaned in, inspecting the girl. Her sorrowing sobs echoed off the walls, tiny frame wracking with every breath. She appeared to be a normal little shade girl. What was she supposed to see?

Finally Fate called to the little girl, "Hello? Are you okay?"

The crying ceased, the child now still, her face still covered by her hands and hair.

Fate narrowed her eyes, trying to focus in the darkness. She leaned over even further, almost falling in.

Suddenly there was a growl from below, a low guttural, animalistic growl. Fate instinctively pulled back from the pit just as the little girl spun around. Her tiny face and neck were riddled with the same black veins that marred Fate's body, but her eyes were ink-black, gleaming with hatred and hunger. The child stood for a split second, eyeing Fate from her prison, then crouched like a feral cat and sprang. Narrowly missing the edge, the little girl fell back to the sandy earth, but immediately got up and began clawing the wall beneath Fate, snarling, spitting, and howling as she tried to climb the smooth rock wall.

Backing away from the hole, Fate exclaimed, "Vrill! What the hell is she?"

Vrill stood motionless on the other side of the pit, his gaze fastened on the little girl shade below, then said in a sad, hopeless voice, "She is your future."

14

The distant horizon darkened as a seemingly sentient black cloud rolled and writhed through the air, undulating quickly towards Kane and his group. A hissing, droning sound vibrated in the air, getting ever louder as the anomaly grew closer.

"Run!" Kane shouted as he turned from the oncoming slaughter and started sprinting. Vale, right beside him, kept up pace. The two necromancers, however, fell behind, their brawn lessening their speed.

"What is that?" Vale called out.

"Scarabs!" Kane shouted back. "Thousands of them, we need to find cover! Fast!"

Kane looked back at the lagging necromancers, concerned. He needed them as guides; they were Vrill's best trackers. Not to mention Vrill might be exceedingly upset if he were to return to Necrosia without them. "Hurry!" he urged them. But suddenly they stopped, and turned to look at one another. Kane knew they were communicating telepathically, but was beside himself as to why they would stop running from the looming cloud of killer insects.

Scarabs were vicious, horrific bugs that endeavored to crawl beneath their victim's skin and proceed to eat their prey from the inside out. It was usually a very slow and painful death. And that was just one scarab. At least being attacked by thousands, the death would be mercifully quicker.

"Mezza! Slater!" Kane's voice was nearing a scream. "Move!"

But they didn't budge; they just stood there, almost awaiting their demise.

"What do we do?" Vale shouted over the oncoming hum of the swarm.

Kane just shook his head. "We leave them," he said sadly, then asked the shade, "How far can you travel with your talent?"

Vale smiled coyly, answering, "Let's see." And with that, Vale took Kane by the arm and wisped him into oblivion, reappearing approximately fifty feet from their original position, the scarab storm still well within range.

"That's it?" Kane asked as they started running again. "That's as far as you could go?"

Vale scowled at the prince, his white eyes storming with annoyance. "Hey, you're not the smallest guy out there, and it takes a lot of energy to carry someone else!"

Kane glanced back, squinting, panning the landscape. Mezza and Slater were nowhere to be found. His heart fell heavy as it appeared the two trackers were gone, likely devoured by the storm of ravenous insects. He loathed the idea of informing Vrill that he'd failed to keep two of his citizens safe—if he lived through this himself, that is.

The scarabs swam through the air with such fluidity, such calculated continuity, that Kane wondered if they weren't joined in thought like the necromancers. Like an undulating eel, the mass dove and rolled as though riding the swell of an ocean wave.

It was then that the horde of carnivorous beetles seemed to notice the two running mates, and turned sharply in pursuit.

"Here they come!" Kane shouted over the earsplitting whir of wings. Thousands of black bugs, only the size of Kane's fist yet as deadly as any Dark World monster, descended on the pair.

"We're done for!" Vale yelled, his eyes wild with fear.

Kane wondered if his newfound power, the one that had exposed itself during his altercation with the wraiths, would manifest at this moment. Should he stop running, turn around, and fight this swarm head on? What if the power ignored his summons? He had no idea how it worked, or where it came from. Long ago, demons had a multitude of amazing powers, but that was due to the magical light of the Crystal Pyramid. Could he trust this mysterious magic now? In his moment of need?

The drone of the scarab wings vibrated inside his head. Their sound alone could drive a being mad.

I have no choice, Kane thought. *I have to use the power if I can; it's our only way out of this!*

With that, he stopped and swung about, facing the oncoming cloud. "*Ego sum legio!*" he shouted, raising his arms to air as he called to the elusive power. "*Ego sum legio!*" His baritone voice echoed for miles.

But nothing happened.

He waited, watching the locust-like insects descend on his location.

He would fall behind as a decoy, hopefully giving Vale a chance.

Kane closed his eyes.

15

"My…future?" Fate stammered, tears filling her eyes as she gazed down at the raging little girl, her tiny feet buried to the ankles by a graveyard of bones. "What happened to her?"

Vrill watched the feral shade, her eyes pure onyx with hate, and said, "She's what happens when the ritual on the Surface is performed wrong, very wrong indeed."

"Wrong? What do you mean?" Fate choked out, terror gripping her throat like an ice-cold hand.

"The ritual has to be with precision, as Malus designed it so long ago. On a certain day, by the light of a full moon, with three victims…those are the three unbreakable components…" his voice trailed off.

Hope rose inside of her as she realized he was wrong. "But the ritual is done wrong all the time! It's completed with only two victims, and," she pointed to herself, "one!" She adjusted her shoulders smugly, feeling vindicated. "And a full moon on the first of October is so rare; there must be thousands of shades who have been born otherwise!"

He shook his head. "Yes, the use of improper ingredients has induced much confusion in this world, indeed. But the worst is when the ritual is performed lacking in all *three* elements," he explained, then pointed to the little girl. "She was born using less than three victims, on the wrong day, with no full moon."

"How can you know that for sure?" she wondered, suspecting they had never been able to ask the girl directly.

Vrill just closed his eyes. "We've seen this many times before."

Fate exhaled, still confused. "Why do you say I'm to be like her?" She looked at the black veins running along her arms, then down to the little girl who bore the same markings.

"The marks do not lie," he explained, his expression grave.

"What will happen to her?" Fate asked quietly, uncertain if she really wanted to know considering it was likely her own destiny.

He paused, his brow furrowing. "She will have to be put to death…like all the others. They cannot be allowed to live."

Fate's black blood ran cold. "And me?" she forced her voice through a narrowing windpipe.

Vrill spun about, his face colored with renewed confidence. "You are unique. There must be something we can do. All of those in which we've found had already turned, already transformed into monsters,"

Looking down upon the girl, Fate asked, "What is she now?"

"She is what we call the *lamia,* an eater of the flesh," he said without meeting Fate's horrified stare.

"Eater of…the *flesh,*" she uttered as she recalled her raw meat session earlier that day. "How…long do I have before

I..." her voice trailed off as she gazed into the pit, into her future.

The necromancer closed his eyes, answering, "I do not know, weeks, days...there's no way to know."

"Why is this happening to me?" she asked, burying her face in her hands.

Vrill sighed, looking solemn. "I believe someone has betrayed you."

She looked up at him, tears rolling over her cheeks. "The blind shaman?"

"Possibly," he considered, watching the child-like fiend below as she gave up on her quest to climb the walls and crouched in a corner to gnaw on a meatless bone. "But I'm sure he did not work unaided."

Fate realized he meant the demons. "Why?" she asked with all hope and energy draining from her.

He shrugged, but offered, "Intolerance shadows the eyes of those not willing to see. For them, you represent pain, past grief and loss. They do not, and may never, see you as an equal, only a blemish in which they wish to have removed."

The necromancer moved gracefully along the edge of the abyss, meeting Fate on the other side and ushering her towards the door. She complied graciously, desperate to get as far away from the vicious girl as she could. It just didn't seem possible that she would eventually become this creature. How could she? Just from one stupid potion? What the heck was it made of?

With that thought, Fate inquired, "What do you think was in the elixir that did…*this*?" She held up her arms, cringing at the marks.

Vrill locked the door as the guards scrutinized Fate and her black veins from the corners of their eyes. Self-conscious, she tugged on her sleeves and pulled up the neck of her sweater as she and Vrill walked back down the hall from which they'd come.

Finally he answered, "I'm not positive of all the ingredients, but one is for certain—the blood of Legend."

"What's that?" Fate's head spun as though Vrill was speaking in riddles.

He paused, turning to face her. "Not *what*, but *who*," he clarified.

She frowned, suddenly very tired. "Who is Legend?"

The necromancer folded his hands together, saying, "You know him as the Night Mare."

"The Night Mare," Fate repeated. "The horse in the garden at Legion?"

"Ahh, so the demons do have him." Vrill nodded with a self-satisfactory smile, like he'd just learned some clandestine information.

For a moment, Fate felt as though she was betraying a secret; that the horse's whereabouts were privy only to those living in the underground palace. She tried to change the subject quickly.

"Okay, even if the demons did do this to me, what do I have to do to cure it—or is there one?" Her voice trembled a bit at the end, her undead body feeling colder than normal.

What if there was no way to fix her? What if she was to become a ravenous flesh eater? Before this, she thought nothing could be worse than being a soul eater, but this topped that for sure. Being a cannibal would be far more devastating to her already fragile psyche.

Vrill inhaled, the silver skin on his forehead creasing with deep thought. "The only thing I can surmise…because you will soon lose what remains of your soul…is…no, that won't work, well," he muttered to himself, tapping his temple as though provoking the answer.

Fate paced the training cavern, arms wrapped around her torso. She wished Kane was here. She wished she'd told him the truth before he left. Maybe he would have known what to do. Especially considering it was his own people that did this, perhaps he'd know a treatment.

She felt sick. Worse, she was getting hungry—and she only wanted one thing: meat. And not just any old meat, it had to be raw, and fresh. The fresher and bloodier, the better. She gagged at the thought. For once, she actually missed the idea of only wanting to consume souls.

Vrill continued to hum and haw over the options while her patience climbed to a critical end. "Well," she asked finally, chewing on the outside of her black fingernail. "What do you think?"

He shook his head. "I think we need to speak with Kraton."

Her insides cringed. *Great, we're bringing in the voodoo dude.*

"Let's go talk to him," Vrill suggested as he moved towards the door, Fate following reluctantly behind.

She trailed him up the winding stairwell, through the darkness, her thoughts glued to her future. Why had she tampered with things she did not understand? Why hadn't she left well enough alone? But it hadn't been well enough, the shade in her was killing what remained of Scarlet, she'd had no choice—and she knew it. But now the lamia blood coursing throughout her body threatened to extinguish everything she was.

As they topped the stairs, Petra met them, anxiety clouding her star-spun eyes. She gazed at Vrill, obviously telling him something telepathically. It kind of annoyed Fate. It was like those people on the Surface that purposely spoke another language in front of you even though they knew English, but didn't want you to know what they were talking about.

Fate observed them a moment, as curious as she was irritated. When his steely skin paled to light blue, she knew it wasn't good.

16

The power did not come. It did not manifest in his time of need. Why had he been able to wield it before? Why had it failed him again?

As the insects wove through the air with the grace of a flock of birds, taking aim at the now motionless prince, he thought of Fate and Ever. What would they do without him? He didn't want to think that they'd mourn him forever, but he knew the void left in their lives would be fathomless. He shouldn't have left them. He shouldn't have gone.

Again, he closed his eyes, awaiting the death that seemed inevitable. It was in these moments that he knew Death hunted him, sought to restrain him and drag him into submission. There had been so many close calls. So many attempts on his life.

Life had always been in his favor, always found a way—until now.

Then he heard a growl.

He opened his eyes, prepared to see more bad news.

Before him was a colossal cat, lean, lithe, and silver with an assortment of black spots. If his memory served him correctly, the ancient humans called this beast…a cheetah.

With its swirling eyes of stars, it nodded its head, inviting him to climb aboard. Not wasting any more time, Kane grabbed the beast by the scruff of its neck and yanked himself onto its back. The silver cat sprang forth, muscles rippling beneath a coat of steel fur. Kane brought his chest close to the animal's neck, further reducing any wind resistance.

The scarabs, seemingly aware that their meal was now getting away, gained speed, diving and darting about the dark atmosphere like a malevolent cyclone. But to Kane's surprise, the cheetah was faster. A lot faster.

Soon they were approaching Vale's fleeing figure. With only a quick glance over his shoulder, the shade grasped the situation and soon vanished into a wisp, reappearing on the cheetah's back behind Kane.

"So," Vale said loudly, his voice competing with both the wind and waning beat of insect wings. "I suppose I owe you one. . . again."

Kane laughed. "No, I think we both owe Mezza—or Slater—one." He had the urge to pat the massive cat on the head, but thought of better of it, leaving the necromancer to concentrate on his sprinting.

"Which one is this? Mezza or Slater?" Vale asked, his tone back to normal as the scarabs had ceased pursuit and the silver cheetah slowed its pace, panting.

The demon frowned, his blue eyes examining the beast as it came to a stop, allowing its riders to dismount. "Mezza?" Kane asked of the creature, then scanned the landscape, searching for the other necromancer. He desperately hoped the other was uninjured. It disheartened him greatly to think they'd lost a comrade so soon in the journey.

As Kane looked back, however, the silver cheetah had melted away, forming a large puddle of molten metal on the ground—from which *two* figures started to emerge.

"Whoa, I didn't know you guys could do that!" Vale exclaimed, watching the two beings regain their true forms.

Mezza just grinned.

"Well done, my friends," Kane stated. "And thank you, I am in your debt."

As the four resumed their trek to the south, Vale kicked at a stone, muttering, "Why couldn't *I* have been a necromancer?"

17

Vrill and Petra walked briskly ahead of Fate, so fast that she was certain they'd break into a run soon. She followed closely behind, both curious and concerned with whatever the emergency was.

I hope Ever's okay, she worried. It was her duty to watch over her, at Kane's request. She couldn't let him down, regardless of her new affliction.

The two necromancers climbed the marble staircase, heading in the direction of Vrill's quarters. Once at the top, he burst through the French doors and instantly threw his hand over his mouth, gasping.

"How?" he uttered, staring at the corner of the room with an expression of disbelief. "Why?"

Fate followed his distraught gaze, relinquishing a strangled cry of her own once she laid eyes upon the cause of his distress. The Soul Nexus, the source of both power and soul for the necromancers, had been destroyed. Pieces of glass lay shattered about the floor, a pool of thick silvery liquid congealed at the base of the podium that once displayed the orb.

"No!" Vrill cried, falling to his knees before the atrocity. "Noooo!"

"How could this happen?" Fate asked of Petra, who was sniffling and wiping away an endless stream of silver-blue tears. "I thought it was indestructible."

Petra shook her head with an incredulous expression. "I did too," she replied quietly.

"Why? Why?" Vrill wailed, his hands shaking as he tried in vain to pick up the pieces of his shattered world.

"What does this mean?" Fate wondered aloud, her mind spinning with the possible outcomes. What would happen to the shades of Necrosia? They depended on the Nexus to satiate their need for souls. Would they have to leave? Forced to forage for food outside the walls? Cast out into Dark World's unforgiving arms where they'd turn feral and uncontrollable?

And what about the necromancers? The Nexus was their reason for existence, their power. What would become of them?

Suddenly composed, Vrill stood, wiped his hands on his robes and turned to face her.

"It means," Vrill stated in a calm voice, "that we necromancers are now mortal—and the end is near."

The trio stood in dumbfounded silence, grasping the gravity of the situation. What did this mean for Myth? Was the creator of the necromancers dead? How long did the creatures of Dark World have?

"Who would do this?" Fate asked when she finally found her voice, then added, "Who *could* do this?"

"Only one had the power to do this," he said, voice trembling.

"Who?" asked Fate; though she wasn't sure she wanted to hear the answer.

His head lowered and eyes closed, he whispered, "The Devil."

18

The geysers spat high into the air, indicating the late hour. The westerly skies of Dark World filled with steam as hundreds of hot springs let loose their blistering waters.

"We must hurry," Kane announced, his thoughts turning to the imminent threat of death worms, a hazardous encounter he'd rather not repeat. Though they were uncommon in these parts, the battle between himself and a half-dozen giant sandworms still lay far too fresh in his memory for comfort.

Kane led them as quickly as he could to the nearest mountain range, hoping there would be caves in which they could camp in for the night. As they reached the rocky mounds, they scrambled up a winding well-worn path that seemed to lead them with purpose to the top.

"I see something," Vale said, squinting as he focused upward. "I'll go check it out." With that, he wisped from sight, enveloped in a nearly transparent black mist.

Kane scanned the rocky cliffs above them, keeping an eye out for the shade's reemergence. Then he saw him about fifty feet up.

"Keep coming!" Vale called down, waving his arms. "There's a great cave up here!"

The three ascended as quickly as they could, Kane's belly snarled and his soul ached with the need for Bloodstone. Even more, his heart yearned to be back with his loved ones, with Fate and Ever. He knew they were protected within the walls of Necrosia, safe under Vrill's watchful silver eyes, but a hint of something he couldn't name crawled beneath the surface of his consciousness. Was it simply paranoia that drove him to worry, or was it something else? Something instinctual?

"Shall we start a fire?" Vale asked of Kane, already gathering rocks and setting them into a ring formation.

Kane considered it a moment, glancing out the mouth of the cave. They were quite a ways up, and the cavern was deep. Surely they wouldn't gain the attention of anything at this height. With that thought, he nodded, giving Vale the okay to proceed.

Vale continued, pulling tufts of fire moss from the corners of the cave and placing it in the center of the ring of rocks. Red and wiry, the native plant could keep a fire lit for an entire night, especially if kept warm over a bed of stones.

Soon, Vale grabbed two flint rocks, squatted near the fire pit, and began clacking the rocks together in search of a spark. Kane watched for a few seconds, amused, curious as to how long it might take Vale to birth a spark worthy of flame. He was tenacious, Kane would give him that. After several failed attempts, Kane stood and took pity on the shade.

"If I may," Kane said as he held his hand over the crimson moss. "*Lucem ferre,*" he uttered softly, calling forth the ancient power that raced through his royal veins. A tendril of flame flickered in the center of his palm, dancing as it reached for the plant, tenderly kissing the delicate fronds, coaxing them into ignition. Heat enveloped the cave, instantly chasing the dampness to the far corners.

"Thanks," Vale muttered, unceremoniously tossing the flint stones aside.

Kane shrugged with a grin. "Thought it might speed things up a little."

Mezza and Slater rolled four large boulders to the fireside, then sat upon two of them and gazed into the flame's waltz. Their silver skin mirrored the orange illumination, making them appear as though made of fire.

Calm embraced the cave and, other than the crackle of the blaze, the four sat in weary silence.

The journey was to be very long. Kane knew this when he left Necrosia. Dark World's harsh terrain was not only dangerous, but physically taxing as many of the regions took days to traverse.

He considered asking the two necromancers if they could transform into beasts in which they could carry himself and Vale upon, but he suspected they could not hold their shape shifting forms for lengthy times. Besides, it wouldn't be fair to request of them.

Kane's fiery blue gaze settled on the shade on the other side of the fire. While he was grateful for Vale's participation, unwilling as it may be, he couldn't help but wonder if he had other, more nefarious, reasons for tagging along. Kane tried to shrug away his suspicion, hoping it was merely his inherited paranoia creeping in, but something about the shade didn't sit well with him. He was far too cunning, too sly in nature, to be completely trusted.

Kane sincerely hoped the shade would prove him wrong.

In the midst of the calm, both Slater and Mezza inhaled sharply like they'd been struck by a sudden pain, cradling their foreheads within their silver palms.

"Mezza? Slater?" Kane inquired, alarmed. "Are you alright?"

The two necromancers turned their heads to one another, eyes locked in quiet communication. Slater shook his head as if to imply 'no'.

After a moment, Mezza answered for both of them, "Nothing your highness, it is nothing."

19

Upon the branches of an ancient, magical willow, silver and gold leaves glittered in the haunting glow of Dark World's infernal, reddish hue. Ivory lilies drifted upon sea-green pads atop the Pools of Eternity while tendrils of trailing crimson roses curled and wound around the courtyard like the wild locks of some unseen goddess.

"Can you believe this?" Sybil said, her glowing white eyes narrowed in concern as she sidled herself next to Fate. "Without the Nexus, the necromancers are helpless against the outside world."

Fate asked the renowned prophetess, "Did you sense this coming?"

The oracle shade shook her head. "Not specifically, but I did warn Vrill of an impending darkness, a coldness I have been feeling for a long time."

Slightly annoyed, Fate wondered why Sybil, with all her power, couldn't have seen something like this on the horizon. She wondered if the oracle's abilities had been exaggerated over the years.

As if Sybil had read her thoughts, she added, "I wish I could have helped them, but my powers are limited by destiny."

Fate scrunched up her face, asking, "What do you mean 'limited by destiny'?"

The oracle shifted from one foot to the other. "What's meant to be is meant to be, I cannot interfere with fate. For whatever reason," she explained as she panned over the gathering crowd, "this has to happen."

"So your powers failed because they thought that if you knew—if the necromancers knew—that it could be prevented?"

"Exactly." She nodded, then turned her attention to the center of the courtyard.

Soon the square was packed with concerned necromancers, all summoned telepathically by their loving leader. A few random shades even showed up to see what was going on.

"Calm, please, be calm," Vrill said aloud, his hands wringing together uncharacteristically. "I understand you are all very afraid."

Fate's stomach churned. This was a terrible blow to their community. Not to mention, it appeared that the devil was still alive. But how? Ever was in the clear, Kane had said so himself. She'd passed the test. The witchdoctor had brought her back. Hadn't he?

Vale's image popped into her thoughts. That last night, at supper, he'd shaken his head, implying that Ever was not really Ever. Was he right?

She had to find out.

Fate turned to leave the courtyard, to make her way to Ever's room. She'd left her resting there only hours before. She'd just ask her some questions, talk to her, see if she could sense anything different about the princess. Fate had no idea what she was going to do if it turned out that Ever's soul was contaminated with the devil's essence, but she'd figure that out later.

Maybe she'd take her back to her people, the demons within the underground city. They'd know what to do. If nothing else, she hoped they could keep her safe from harm, and safe from harming others if it turned out she was indeed harboring Malus's soul.

Just as she reached the gate, she heard Vrill say in voice laden with ice-cold conviction, "I have the suspect here, she will be tried, and if found guilty…put to death."

"Oh no," Fate's heart slammed inside her chest as she spun about, knowing exactly who she was going to see in the center of the yard.

20

The further they walked, the more the western horizon gave way to a brilliant vision. Sensua, home of the banshees, revealed itself little by little with every step closer. A grand city with ivory, bulbous crowns topping their tallest towers marveled pictures Kane had seen in the ancient human documents of a building called the *Taj Mahal.*

Long, sheer lavender flags wavered and danced from a dozen or more tall, white pillars stationed outside a golden gate. Two nearly naked Amazonian banshees, both armed with a long bamboo staff topped with a very sharp, curved blade, approached them.

"State your business," one said, her voice strong, yet feminine as she took a defensive stance before the four male strangers. Her eyes blazed indigo, fearless and determined, bronze-brown skin gleaming like she'd been bathed in crushed diamonds. Her burgundy hair trailed long over her silk-soft shoulder, falling into perfect ringlets over her naked breasts, shielding *just* enough from curious eyes. Voluptuous, yet muscular, her physique was impressive, and profoundly alluring.

Banshees had a power over men, all men. Whether it was their sweet smelling pheromones or intoxicating beauty, they lured their select prey with little effort. And, as if they needed more venom, they could sing a haunting, angelic song, poisoning a man's mind, owning him. It made Kane wonder why they even needed weapons when the power of their voice was enough to bring a man to his knees.

While this particular banshee seemed disinterested in seducing Kane, she still had the upper hand in this situation—and he knew it.

Kane stepped forward, bowing chivalrously before the exceptionally tall female warrior, saying, "I am Prince Kane, son of Lucifer. I wish to speak with your leader about a pressing matter."

She eyed him suspiciously, the muscles in her soft, angled jaw flexing as she considered each of the visitors carefully, pausing long and hard on Vale before stating, "You travel with a shade?"

"Yes, he is our friend," Kane explained cautiously. It surprised him how he'd almost forgotten the ferocity in which Vale's kind had slaughtered the innocent and the impact that had left in its wake. It was a wonder she hadn't killed them on sight, based on Vale's race alone.

"Wait here," she said in an acidic tone as she conferred with the other banshee guard, nearly an identical twin of herself apart from the white-blonde hair.

Kane stepped back to join the others as the women discussed their fate. He glanced at Vale and the two necromancers, bemused at their lustful gazes.

"Careful boys, those girls are trouble," Kane warned playfully.

Vale smiled. "I'm only allowed to look, but those two," he pointed his thumb towards Mezza and Slater, "are smitten, I think."

Both necromancers' eyes were locked on the two banshees before them, their silver lips threatening to break into a silly grin. Kane smothered a laugh as they two women broke their huddle and waved them forward.

"Alright, we'll let you in," the redhead said as the men took a step forward, but she instantly blocked Vale, Mezza and Slater with her staff. "But only you." She glared, nodding at Kane.

Vale smiled thinly at her, a flicker of annoyance behind his eyes while Mezza and Slater turned away with expressions of pure heartbreak.

"Very well," Kane complied. "You guys stay out here, I'll be back as soon as I can."

The banshee led Kane to the looming golden gate, opened it and guided him through while the other banshee stayed behind at her post.

"This way," she said icily.

The entirety of the kingdom was built with white marble, walls, ceilings, chairs, floors; everything was comprised of the opaque stone. Not a speck of dirt could be seen in any corner, nor dust apparently allowed to settle on the furniture. From what he knew of women and their tidy nature, it was not surprising that this city was rumored to be female dominant. No one had ever seen a male banshee, and if not for the fact that they are required for breeding purposes, Kane would have guessed they didn't exist at all.

Kane's hooves clicked noisily upon the albino limestone flooring as the comely banshee guard led him down a long hall adorned with gold sconces and lavender sashes. She paused before a set of oversized French doors before turning to him and ordering, "Stay here."

She disappeared behind the doors, and Kane could hear soft mutterings emitting from the other side. He wondered what their leader was like. Was she as, or more, beautiful than the guard? Was she going to be difficult as he assumed she might be?

All he needed was a volunteer to accompany them to the Crystal Pyramid so he could open the fissure to the Surface. He scoffed silently at his optimism. He was certain that none of the races would comply so easily with his requests. If nothing else, Dark World's residents had survived because they'd been scrupulous with whom they'd trusted. Only the cunning and suspicious had made it through the Apocalypse alive. The weak had perished, leaving only the fittest of each species to move forward.

Reluctantly, he wished Vale had been allowed to accompany him. Facing this alone suddenly seemed remarkably unwise. Whoever lay beyond these doors made it through Hell for a reason. Kane knew he had to be on his guard. He had to be wary of every word, every negotiation, or he might not live to regret it.

Then both of the French doors opened and Kane was told to step forward, the doors sealing shut behind him.

Part III

Beauties and Beasts

1

She wasn't sure if it was the warm line of drool that escaped her lips and ran back into her hair that woke her, or if it was the blast of frigid November air rushing over her naked body. Either way, Shelby had been unconscious one moment and frightfully aware the next.

Flat on her back, she tried to assess her surroundings, turning her head slowly to the right, then left. Trees, snow, and a ceiling of cloud-covered night sky was all she could decipher before the pain hit her.

Her entire head throbbed, pulsated with excruciating pain. It was like she'd been hit in the back of the head with a bat or something. She tried to recall what had happened.

A car.

She remembered her mother's car. Had she been in a car accident? If so, how the hell did she wind up naked?

Shelby groaned as she tried to sit up, but her arms and legs wouldn't move. Even as she struggled with all her strength, she couldn't raise them. Some kind of thin rope raked her wrists and ankles with every movement. She was tied down somehow, tethered to the ground.

A sick feeling slithered through her psyche as she remembered what she'd been doing before she blacked out.

"Rory," she whispered the realization through trembling lips. She'd been at Rory's house, searching for evidence of his involvement with Scarlet's disappearance.

The moment she spoke his name she heard the shuffle of frozen leaves beside her.

"Ahh, you're awake!" Rory exclaimed with far too much enthusiasm. He knelt down beside her, his face only inches from hers. "So sorry I couldn't give you the same muscle relaxants I gave Scarlet, I ran out." He pushed his bottom lip out, feigning a pout.

Shelby's entire body shook with a culmination of rage and onset hypothermia. "You untie me, right now!" she shouted as uninvited tears spilled from her eyes. Her head screamed in pain with every word she spoke, every tiny motion she made. But she didn't care, she was going to fight him with everything she had.

Rory laughed, a maniacal, evil cackle, and said, "Oh, you are a spirited one, aren't you." He smiled as he produced the serrated blade Shelby had taken from his bedroom, and began polishing it with a rag. "Aren't you excited to see your friend?"

Shelby scowled at him, confused.

"You know, *Scarlet*," he explained in a patronizing, kindergarten-teacher kind of way. "I'm sending you where I sent her."

"What did you…do to her, you…bastard!" Shelby's teeth chattered so hard she could hardly get the words out.

"Oh, you'll see," he said, then raised his eyes to the sky, adding, "At least I hope so, there's no full moon tonight, and it's not October 1st, and well, it's supposed to be three victims. But oh well, I'm sure Malus appreciates all sacrifices."

"Mm..Malus?" Shelby managed, but she knew her body was shutting down. The subzero temperatures were assaulting her, slowing the blood in her system, cooling it down. She could see her clothes in a pile to her right—and her cell phone. If only she wasn't tied down, she could fight her way to it and call for help.

Rory didn't pause his obsessive knife polishing, answering, "Yes, the devil."

Shelby's mouth fell open. This guy was seriously crazy, and not a little bit crazy, he was like bat shit loony! Despite the sting of frost biting every inch of her body, her mind was suddenly crystal clear.

She had to get out of there.

Now.

2

The witch hunt had begun. The only thing the necromancers needed for a proper mob lynching were lit torches and pitchforks. Fate had to come up with a plan to save Ever. And fast!

Ever stood in the center of the square, her head lowered, white silken hair draping long around her face. Every necromancer in the crowd, including Vrill, glared vengefully at the demon princess.

How quickly they've turned on those they've sworn to protect, Fate thought sadly. It shouldn't have surprised her really, the Surface was just as fickle, just as quick to jump to conclusions and blame the easiest target. She'd had high hopes for this race, these peaceable necromancers that she thought had wielded the Zen-like powers of Dark World.

Fate lowered her gaze, sighing. The heart of man, it would seem, did not reside only in humans, but all conscious beings. Maybe everyone, Surface humans and Dark World beings, were created with the same energies after all. Same souls, different realms.

Soon, the air around her crackled with malevolence. A red haze began forming overhead, like a storm cloud filled with blood—and settled over Ever's motionless form.

"What's going on?" Fate whispered to Sybil.

Sybil lowered her eyes. "They're going to break into Ever's mind, to see if she's guilty or not."

Fate frowned. "Well, that's a good thing, right? I mean, if she's innocent."

The oracle shade shrugged. "I guess."

Fate scowled at her, asking, "What do you mean."

"Guilty or innocent, she might not live through it."

Panic took hold of Fate. She couldn't let them do this! It could kill Ever, even if she didn't do anything wrong!

"Stop!" Fate shouted, pushing her way through the throng of necromancers. "Stop this, right now!"

As she made her way to Ever, she placed her body between Ever and the crowd, creating a shield. She lowered her chin and glowered, stating, "If you want her, you'll have to go through me first!"

They ignored her, the crimson tempest continuing its formation overhead, growling and pulsating as snarls of lightning flashed within.

Behind her, Ever whimpered as the miasmic storm began to descend, reaching for her, probing her head with fingerlike tentacles.

"I said stop!" Fate bellowed. "I'm not going to warn you again!"

With that, she tore the black gloves from her hands and manifested an orb within her ebony-streaked hands. But instead of the cool, icy blue she'd always pulled from her core in her training sessions with Vrill, this one was pure black—and very large. Shrouded in dark mist, the sphere swirled and pulsed, as though excited to break free from her grasp and cause some serious damage.

Power raged beneath her skin, raced through her veins, pumped through her heart. She'd never felt anything like it. For the first time, she owned the power, it didn't own her. Every cell in her body exploded with this newfound energy. It was born of all her emotions: love, hate, empathy, and lust.

She never wanted it to end.

Vrill promptly raised his hand, giving the order to cease the assault, and the red cloud overhead pulled away from Ever. Fate meant business, and Vrill knew it.

The crowd of necromancers, now focused on Fate, waited with fear hidden behind their cosmic eyes.

"Okay, Fate, calm down," Vrill said through the barely veiled terror shading his voice. "Put it away."

Fate glared at him, her mentor, and whispered with an evil smile, "I don't want to."

3

The room writhed with half-naked banshees. Some belly-danced while others sang haunting tunes, plucking harps and jangling bells. Most of the females, their nude bodies visible through gowns of sheer fabric, were lounging about the floor on pillows. Many turned their lavender eyes to the demon as he entered, though few showed any interest that he was even there.

All Kane could do was scan the room with his mouth wide open. He was more appalled than aroused. Did these women have no pride in themselves? Or too much? He just wasn't sure of anything at the present moment.

In the center of the room sat a throne made entirely of silver, and on it, what Kane assumed to be the leader of the banshees.

And possibly the only male banshee in existence.

Profoundly obese, to the point of gelatinous, he looked like the females in shade of skin and hair only. Bronze and glistening, his complexion was that of his harem. His hair, a deep red, wound around his head several times forming what resembled a pointed hat.

The female guard who had led Kane into the room turned to him, stating, "This is our leader, Lord Lythos." With that she took her station next to the large aristocrat and stared straight forward, staff set firmly beside her like a true soldier.

"Prince Kane," he said, his double chin wobbling as he spoke. "Please, come in, come in! To what do I owe the pleasure?"

Forcing aside his shock, Kane uttered, "I...am here to request...a volunteer. To accompany us on a mission."

With one wave of his plump hand, the music and singing ceased. "Leave us," he commanded and the banshee women scattered, fleeing the room at his order. The female guard, however, remained at his side.

Lythos's indigo eyes narrowed on Kane, his fat face pursing in suspicion. "And why, pray tell, would you need one of *my* girls?"

Kane proceeded to tell him about his father's scrolls, the Crystal Pyramid, and Myth. The large banshee nodded a lot as the demon spoke, but never indicated his cooperation or rejection of the idea.

Finally, after Kane's speech was completed, he asked, "So, may we bring one of your citizens along to save Dark World?"

Without so much as a thought, Lord Lythos told the prince, "No." Lythos glared at the demon prince, clarifying, "I will not allow it. This is not our war."

Kane relinquished a frustrated sigh. He had suspected the banshee leader would not be eager to lend a volunteer to his quest. Banshees were known to be selfish, unwilling to join forces with anyone. They lacked compassion and despised cooperation with other races. Not unlike most of the races in Dark World, unfortunately.

Long ago, when Lucifer was king, the races were far more cooperative with one another, friendly even. Kane was certain that all of them would have gladly complied with his father's requests, no questions asked. What had changed? Why didn't Kane receive the same favor? What had he done wrong?

But he knew the truth. Until now, Kane had never made the effort to seek out the other races. Content to hide within his secret palace, he pretended the outside world didn't exist. That the problems didn't exist. Why would the banshees assist him? He hadn't come out of his hole to help them in any way over the last three hundred years.

His father had kept up the relations, erected the foundations of trust and amicability between the peoples of Dark World. And they obviously adored him for it.

Kane forced his thoughts to the present, to the banshee leader. He could not complete his mission without each of the races in attendance. The scroll required all of them to be there. It was the only way to open the fissure. Kane appealed the decision immediately. "Lord Lythos, I understand your hesitancy to join our plight, but if you only knew the urgency of the matter, maybe you'd understand, you see…"

"I understand the urgency completely," the portly leader explained, his face reddening with building anger. "I simply don't care to have one of my daughters traipsing about Dark

World with a..a *shade*." He spat the final word as though he'd eaten something disgusting.

Suddenly Kane understood. Inhaling a calm breath, he replied, "I sympathize with your concern, but Vale is a close comrade of mine, one who has proven himself trustworthy. If you would only meet him, I…"

Again, Lythos interrupted him. "Never!" he shouted, spittle flying from his fat lips. The rolls on his belly jiggled as he pounded the armrest of his silver throne. "I will not be associated with those, those—murderers—in any way!"

Kane exhaled, nodding. He should have expected this. What made him think the rest of the realm would change their thinking simply because he had. If it weren't for Fate, Vale wouldn't be on this mission, accepted as an equal. She'd altered Kane's reality, shown him that you do not have to become the expectations of others. She was marked as evil from the moment she was born into Dark World, but it didn't mean she had to agree with it. Demons had once been considered malevolent, pure wickedness, labeled as sin in sentient form, but they'd overcome that stereotype. Evolved from the empathy that pain had built.

It was unfortunate, but Kane understood all too well the misconceptions and racism of Lord Lythos. He only knew shades as ruthless killers. He did not know Fate. He did not know Vale. He only knew shades.

Kane centered himself, then tried again, saying, "If you would only meet my friend, maybe…"

Lythos' face pinched and swelled suddenly as a wheezing gathered deep in his chest. The guard ran to his side, kneeling as she patted his arm. "Father, please, calm down!"

"What's happening?" Kane rushed to the other side of the throne. "Is he unwell?"

She nodded. "He has been growing ill over the last few months." She paused, adding quietly, "We all have."

Kane looked her in the eyes. "Dark World is dying. Without the light of the Crystal Pyramid, we won't last much longer. Won't you please convince him?"

At this, Lythos thrashed harder, his face and arms purple with both anger and angst at not being able to catch his breath. Thick streams of sweat flowed from his plump brow, his once manicured red hair now unwound, damp with sweat, and hanging over his eyes.

"Father!" the guard yelled, tears welling in her eyes. "He's dying!"

Suddenly the French doors burst open and a team of six beautiful banshees raced in. They carried in their hands an odd-looking contraption, a bag of some sort attached to a long hose. Quickly, they attached the end of the hose to Lythos mouth and began squeezing the bag, filling his lungs with air. Within moments, the male banshee began to breathe better, gaining some of the bronze back into his skin.

"Alright," he whispered when he could speak. "Alright, you...win."

Kane brightened. "I do?"

"If you…can find…one that wants to go, she…may help you," he fought to expel every word.

The guard beside him stood immediately, her eyes fierce with determination. "I will go."

Kane nodded in gratitude, then asked, "And you are?"

Her indigo eyes flared proudly, thrusting her plentiful chest out like a peacock. "I am Sorcia, princess of banshees."

4

Rory hummed a happy little tune as he finished polishing the blade and proceeded to unfurl the blood-smattered scroll. Shelby's heart slammed against the inside of her chest. Was this how Scarlet died? Were these her last moments as well?

Poor Scarlet, Shelby thought, despite the fact she was about to meet the same fate. *Murdered at the hands of this…monster! This madman!*

Suddenly Rory was quiet as he stood before her at the base of the pentagram. He grinned at her, a wide, sincere smile set beneath a pair of wildly insane eyes.

"Rory, please, don't," Shelby pleaded. It disgusted her to do so, but at this point, she felt she had no other options. She was helpless with her hands and feet tied to the ground. She only had her voice and mind to work with. "Rory, you don't want to do this."

He looked shocked, stating, "Oh yes, I really do."

"Why?" she asked, trying to buy time, for what she didn't know.

"In exchange for sacrifices, Malus gives me power…and immortality." He moved to her right, kicking her small pile of clothes uncaringly, adding, "It's fascinating, really, the pentagram is activated by blood. As soon as even a little bit is spilled, it starts to open, pulling you under. Isn't that cool?" He smiled as though he were telling her a story about a cute kitten he saw.

Shelby frowned, her insides churning with disgust. "You don't really believe that, do you?"

His eyes darkened as he knelt beside her, the cold blade of the knife now at her throat. "Do you know how old I am?" he whispered into her ear.

"Nn…no," she stuttered from both terror and cold.

"One hundred and seventeen years young," he said proudly as though today were his birthday.

Shelby's memory drifted back to Rory's house and how it was decorated with a century's worth of antiques and collectables.

Could it be true? Was this kind of dark magic possible?

If so, then maybe Scarlet was still alive.

Somewhere. Somehow.

"Okay, enough talking," Rory straddled her torso, unfolding the scroll and reading words that Shelby thought sounded like gibberish.

She tried to struggle. She swore and screamed as loud as she could, calling for help, begging for her life.

But her cries fell on deaf ears. Insane ears. Rory was wild with lunacy, lost in his own psychotic world. Like a vampire in the midst of a frenzied bloodbath, Rory shouted the words, calling to some underworld monster to feed him his power and immortality.

"Take her Malus! Take her! I give her to you!" Rory hollered into the night, his voice echoing through the trees. "Take her!" He then reached for the knife and with both hands, held it over her, readying to plunge it into her chest.

Just as he sucked in a final, savoring breath, Rory swung his hands forward.

Shelby screwed her eyes shut tight. She couldn't watch anymore. This was it anyways; she didn't want to know what happened next.

She waited for her death. Waited for that last moment.

But it never came.

Instead, she cracked her eyes open just in time to see Rory get a hard kick to the face and go flying off of her, landing unconscious only a few feet away.

Shelby's eyes were so wide open they actually hurt. Who? What just happened?

"Hey babe," said Greg as he knelt down beside her, kissing her softly on her trembling lips. His usually mischievous eyes turned uncharacteristically serious as he asked, "Are you…okay? Did he…you know?" He winced, wondering if she'd been raped.

She shook her head, answering, "No, nothing like that."

Relief washed over his face. Then he scanned her naked body up and down, raising his eyebrows with an impish grin, saying, "This is a good look for you."

Shelby rolled her eyes, smiling. "Shut up and untie me."

5

The pulsing black orb in Fate's hands spun and growled with power, growing as it infused itself with fury, begging to be released so it could do its worst to the crowd of necromancers.

"Now Fate," Vrill started, taking a hesitant step towards the storming shade. "Be calm, we can talk this through."

Fate hissed at him through pointed fangs, her black eyes murderous and locked on him. "I won't let you hurt Ever!" The ebony blood beneath her skin pumped harder, faster, stretching beyond her neck and leeching into her face.

Vrill raised his hands in surrender. "I promise I won't."

Her body shook with rage and seething hatred. She wanted to kill them all. Punish them. Before taking the potion, it was as though there was two of her, opposing sides warring for control over her body. Now, whatever she was, owned her completely. But she owned it as well. It was the perfect marriage of monsters, the shade and the lamia.

Suddenly, Fate felt a gentle hand upon her shoulder. "Fate," Ever said as soft as satin. "It's okay now. Please stop."

Something small, deep inside of Fate, called from corners of her soul. It told her to stop. That these were her friends, her new family. It took everything she had to dim the dark light that possessed her. So much of her wanted to continue, to kill.

But that voice, Scarlet's voice, still whispered, still existed, though fragile and frighteningly diminished.

The orb within her palms began to weaken, growing smaller and smaller with every calming breath Fate took in.

Finally, the sphere vanished into a phantom-like mist.

Vrill exhaled, bending at the waist with his hands on his knees. Everyone stood motionless, watching Fate with terrified interest. As if she was an undetonated bomb, her finger still on the trigger.

After a few moments of fearful tension, Vrill stood tall and forced a feeble smile, saying, "Well, that was truly exciting. But we still have some business to attend to." He paused, measuring his words carefully. "Fate, if you will allow, I must ask that Kraton, the witchdoctor, be allowed to examine Ever again…to test her."

Fate eyed him warily, her body now shaky and weak. "You promise not to harm her?"

"I swear," he pledged, pressing his palms together and bowing gently to the shade.

Fate tuned to face Ever. "Are you alright with that?"

Ever nodded, a glimmer of fear nestled behind her sapphire eyes. "I think so."

"Let's do this then," Fate said, then added, "But know this, whatever the outcome, Malus or no Malus, I'm taking her home to the demons as soon as possible."

Vrill frowned, gazing into the eyes of his peers, speaking to them privately. Then he spoke, "Very well, follow me."

6

A nefarious wind snaked through the trees, rattling the skeletal branches of the forest surrounding them. Billowy clouds shaded the night sky, blocking out entire quadrants of stars. Their only light, a hazy glow from Edmonton's million-strong population, shone from over five miles away. But somehow it was just enough to see the love and relief on Greg's face.

"How did you find me?" Shelby inquired as Greg untied her hands.

He chuckled. "I've been stalking you."

"What do you mean?" she asked, sitting up and rubbing her wrists.

After undoing her ankles, he nodded towards her cell phone. "GPS locater, linked your iPhone to my iPhone…there's an App for that." He shoved his hands in his pockets, looking sheepish as she proceeded to get dressed. "I just wanted to make sure you were okay…and if you ever…went missing, I could find you." He looked at the ground and suddenly Shelby understood.

He felt somewhat responsible for Scarlet's disappearance.

"Oh Greg," Shelby said, crossing over the pentagram to hug him. "I'm so glad you did."

Shelby tossed a wary eye in Rory's direction, his motionless body only a few feet away. "So what do we do with him?"

"Well," Greg began nonchalant, exhaling. "I'm torn between dragging him behind my car by his testicles and burying him ass-up in my front yard so I can use him as a bike stand."

"We could do both," Shelby offered with a grin, then said with a shiver, "Well, whatever we decide, we'd better do it quick, it's freezing out here!"

Snowflakes landed on her face, disintegrating upon impact. If she listened close enough, she could almost hear them as they sparkled in the faint light. It would have been mildly romantic if it weren't for the dark, incapacitated lump of serial killer dampening the mood.

"Okay, in all seriousness," Greg said. "I say we drag his ass to my car, stick him in the trunk and deliver him to the cops."

Shelby considered this a moment, then nodded. "Yeah, I think that would work. Hopefully they'll have enough evidence to... Greg! What's wrong?"

Suddenly doubled over, Greg hollered in pain and clutched his thigh. Shelby strained her eyes to adjust to the darkness, to see what had happened.

Then she saw it. The serrated knife submerged to the hilt in Greg's leg—and Rory standing right beside him.

Dark blood soaked through his jeans as Shelby frantically looked around for something to beat Rory over the head with, hitting him with just her bare hands was probably not going to be too effective. But before she could even locate a stick or rock, Rory laced his fingers together and swinging his arms like a pendulum, smashed Greg in the face full force with both fists. Greg flew at least three feet in the air before landing hard on the frozen ground.

"Greg!" Shelby screamed as she launched herself at Rory, clawing and hitting him with all her might. "You bastard!"

Rory just laughed. "Feisty one, aren't you?" he taunted through the veil of darkness. "I like that in a woman."

Furious, Shelby kicked and punched without even knowing where she was striking him. Never before had she wanted to tear someone apart like this. She dug her nails into any skin she could find, hoping to find his face and rip out an eye or something.

Finally she got hold of something warm, his hand, and bringing to her mouth, bit him as hard as she could. Hearing his screams brought her such delicious delight. His howls of pain excited her to the core.

Then came her own pain as he punched her hard in the temple. Her mind bordered on unconsciousness, but she fought to stay awake. Blood trickled down her cheeks as she staggered blindly through the darkness, hands in front of her, groping the blanket of night.

She heard Greg moan. "Greg!" she shouted as fresh, hot tears ran down her cool cheeks. "Greg! Where are you?"

She stood still, waiting for an answer from him. Anything. Any sign he was conscious—and still alive.

"Greg?" she uttered through trembling lips.

Nothing.

Shelby stifled a sob, turning off her emotions as she strained her hearing, listening for any movement from Greg—or Rory.

Branches snapped sadistically in the distance, speeding up her heart and sending her adrenaline racing. Arid leaves rustled and crackled all around her. Was it a footstep? Rory's?

She waited, unmoving in the dark.

Then it occurred to her.

If I can't see him…he can't see me.

It was a game of cat and mouse, mortal hide and go seek, and she knew exactly who the prey was.

Maybe he took off?

But she knew better. Rory wanted her dead, to sacrifice her to some false goddess that he'd probably conjured up during some boring night when he felt lonely and insignificant. What was his deal anyways? Was he the leader of a Satanic cult? Or just a wannabe with no followers? Then she remembered the phone call when she was hiding in his room. He told some guy named Steve that Malus would protect him.

So there are others, Shelby thought, making a note. They would need to be found and prosecuted as well. She'd make sure that *all* of Scarlet's killers would not go unpunished.

If she lived through this, that is.

Seconds felt like hours as she stood shivering in the cold, awaiting any sign that she was not alone.

Just when she didn't think she could stand another moment lost in the darkness, Greg's cell phone lit up and dinged with a fresh notification. The faint light was enough to illuminate her immediate surroundings.

Her eyes scanned the perimeter quickly, assessing her whereabouts. She was only a foot or so from the pentagram, and about ten feet from Greg's lifeless body. A pool of blood stained the ground around his shadowy form. She had to hurry and get him some help.

That's when she realized that the knife in his thigh was gone. She narrowed her eyes, peering around the curtain of darkness. Nope, no knife.

Her heartbeat fluttered faster and ice rushed through her veins. That meant Rory had it again.

She whipped her head left and right, searching for Rory before the light on his phone died away. Her pulse raced so hard she thought she might faint. Where was he? Did he run off into the woods?

"Where are you, you asshole?" she whispered into the night as the cell phone light died away, plunging her into the pitch of shadows once again.

"Right here," Rory announced from behind her as he brought the blade to her throat.

7

White petals fell from a flowering cherry tree, drifting from the branches onto the courtyard, landing before Ever's feet as though weeping for her troubles.

"This way," Vrill said quietly, taking Ever by the elbow and leading her towards the castle. The once cheery streets had suddenly become darker, ominous. Both saddened and suspicious stares burned into their backs as they made their way through the city avenues, the procession felt more like the last walk to the gas chamber than an inquiry.

Despite Fate's confidence in Ever's innocence, she could not disregard the facts: the Soul Nexus had been destroyed, and only the devil could do it.

No matter how she fit the puzzle pieces together, it always formed the same picture—the devil was among them. But if it wasn't Ever, who could it be? During that fateful night, at Aura's inauguration, Malus had begun a transfer of her essence into Ever right before their eyes. No one else had even been close by. But Vale had killed the queen before the transfer could be completed. Hadn't he?

Fate couldn't deny it, all signs pointed to Ever as the culprit. As much as she hated to admit it, there was no other explanation. Ever must be the host for the queen's soul. Malus must live inside the demon girl, tethered to her granddaughter's soul, manipulating her.

Then Fate had a thought. What if Ever herself didn't know? What if the queen was able to take hold of Ever without being detected, like a subconscious parasite, wielding Ever like a weapon as she sleeps? Could she hide inside someone like that? Like a virus, pestilent and waiting to awaken to its full potential?

While she held a bittersweet triumph for her theory, it still did not bode well for the circumstances. If Malus was indeed inside Ever, the necromancers were going to discover it eventually. Paranoia crept up onto her shoulders, glaring down at the silver entourage.

"What are you going to do to her?" Fate asked suddenly, eyeing the necromancers nervously. They'd shown her that they couldn't be trusted, which was sad as she'd grown to love and respect them so much. She wondered if even Aura had been compromised. The sweet little zombie girl she so admired and adored, had she been swept into the sea of collective thoughts? Was she, too, now an enemy?

"She must pass a series of tests," Vrill responded icily, his gaze imprisoning the demon girl as he held her by the elbow, herding her.

Ever's eyes stayed locked on the floor as they traversed the windings halls of the castle. Sadness colored her once glowing blue stare with a longing for the past, a simpler, happier time. Fate was certain that the demon princess wished she'd never left the safety of Legion. There, she'd been sheltered from all the evils and betrayals of Dark World. True, she'd nearly been a prisoner of the underground palace; locked beneath a turbulent land for her own protection, but at least there she had been unreachable, protected from predators.

Here, she'd learned the truths of the world. The twisted nature of Dark World's inhabitants. Had any of them truly changed? Hadn't the tribulations of Dark World taught them anything?

Fate eyed Vrill, torn between an earned reverence and growing distrust. How had things changed so quickly? Wasn't he her mentor? Her guru? His eyes, his swirling silver eyes of wisdom, were suddenly wrought with malevolence, anger, and primeval judgment. She'd thought him above all that.

But he'd proven himself otherwise. Now who was she to trust?

"Tests?" Fate inquired. She felt like a coward. She should have wiped everyone out outside. Kane wouldn't have stood for any of this. He'd have painted the palace silver with their blood before allowing them to perform any more tests on his daughter. Fate suddenly felt like a failure. She'd failed her prince. She'd failed Ever. The necromancers weren't going to simply let them leave.

Vrill spun about, the entourage of necromancers pausing as their leader spoke. "Fate, it is imperative that you allow this. Just as it is imperative that you speak with Kraton for your own needs," he said, eyeing the blackened veins on her hands.

Fate brought her hands up, scrutinizing them. He was right. There was no time to mess around. If what he said before was true, that she'd soon transform into a flesh-eating lamia like the little girl in the pit, she'd have to figure out how to stop it—and soon.

They rounded the last corner, Vrill and Ever in the lead while Fate fell behind with Sybil.

"Do you know what they intend to do with her?" she whispered to Sybil.

Sybil shook her head, then said, "There's never been anything like this in the underworld."

"What if she is Malus?" Fate hated the fearful shiver that crawled up her spine with the mention of the belated devil.

Sybil sighed, her black lips twisting into a grimace, and said, "They'll have no choice but to kill her."

8

Kane and Sorcia exited the golden gates of Sensua, leaving behind a crowd of saddened banshees. They watched with their glowing eyes of lavender as their sister embarked on a dark journey, from which she might not return.

Mezza and Slater, however, looked positively ecstatic when they saw that the banshee princess was to accompany them. Flanking her on either side as they moved ahead of Kane and Vale, they appeared smitten with the notion of being her personal protectors.

Vale, on the other hand, seemed both annoyed and displeased with the new recruit. "What's with Cleopatra?" he inquired, scanning Sorcia up and down.

"Who?" Kane replied irritably. Vale's attitude was less than impressive. While he was grateful the shade had offered his hand in the quest, his ambition could have used some revamping.

"Never mind, Surface thing," Vale remarked, smirking as though he knew something Kane did not.

Kane sucked in a long breath in attempts to summon patience. It would take all he had not to beat the shade into submission. Straightening his shoulders, Kane forced himself to maintain calm, stating in a voice loud enough for the entire group to hear, "We'll travel until nightfall, camping at Shiver Falls."

"Shiver Falls?" Vale's eyes widened. "Are you sure that's wise?"

Kane paused, then asked, "Why?"

Vale shuddered as though in recollection. "It's just…it's so close to the Valley of Shadows."

Internally, Kane winced. He'd hoped he could steal away from the group unnoticed and find Seren. But if Vale already knew the area—and it's secrets—Kane was sure to be caught.

Sorcia and her necromancer entourage also paused, glancing back with worry in their eyes.

Kane cleared his throat, ready to divulge his secret mission, when suddenly there was a disturbance overhead—and then beneath them.

"What's going on?" Vale's voice quavered as the ground shook violently under his feet, a roiling cloud of silver and black churning above.

The demon frowned, tilting his heavily horned head back, inspecting the rock-covered sky. "I don't know, but we should find some shelter."

"We could return to the palace," Sorcia offered, her amethyst eyes narrowing and crimson hair whipping about as gale-force winds assaulted her.

"Yes, maybe we should…" Kane began but was soon silenced as the earth under him rocked and groaned, sending his entire posse flying in all directions.

"Run for the palace!" Kane shouted, his hooves digging into the dirt as he tried in vain to gather enough traction to move forward.

Mezza and Slater each held tight to Sorcia with one hand, clawing at the ground with the other, desperate to get her back to safety.

Angry red lightning forked through the blackening clouds, crackling and then bellowing violent thunder.

Is this Ba'al? Kane wondered, recalling the elemental's attack on him. Squinting through the squall, the demon witnessed Vale struggling to hold onto a nearby boulder. Slighter and weaker than the others, the human-turned shade clung for his life.

Kane knew he had to do something, he had to try. Despite his failure at last attempt to summon the mysterious power, he tried again.

Reaching his black talons to the covered sky, he shouted, *"Ego sum legio!"*

The ground heaved violently, splitting into two as a crevice opened up. The widening crack raced over the terrain, opening like the mouth of a giant beast, ready to swallow its prey—and heading right for Sensua.

9

Shelby tried to scream but Rory tightened the blade against her windpipe, silencing her. Fresh tears gathered in her eyes. Just when she thought she was going to get away, a new nightmare had begun. Only, this time, she was certain it was the end. Rory wasn't going to let her get away this time. He was going to finish what he'd started.

"Lay down!" he roared, thrusting her towards the center of the pentagram.

Her legs wobbled in fear as she fell to her knees and then lay down onto her back. A sob escaped her lips as she closed her eyes. As much as she wanted to fight back, as much as she hated him, she knew he'd won. He had the knife. Greg was probably dead. No one could lose that much blood and survive. She may as well join him in death. Or if Rory was telling the truth, she'd see Scarlet soon as well.

It's not fair that the villain will win again, Shelby pondered in attempts to distract herself from the terror welling within as Rory straddled her again, pinning her hands down with his knees. *He should be punished. He should experience the same pain and suffering that he's inflicted on those he's hurt.*

Rory muttered his incantation, eyes rolling into the back of his head as he raised the serrated blade over his head with both hands, preparing to plunge it into her heart.

Scarlet was a good person, a great person! Shelby thought as a powerful rage swept over her. "And so am I!" she screamed. She swung her right leg up, toe leading, and kicked him in the back of the head hard enough to make his teeth rattle. Stunned, the knife slipped from his hands and landed right beside Shelby. Letting her instinct take over, she wriggled one arm free from under his knee, grabbed the knife and thrust it into the center of his chest.

Rory shrieked like a little girl, his surprised echo resonating throughout the darkened forest. Stunned, eyes wild with confusion, he rolled off of her with his hands clawing at the hilt of the knife embedded in his heart. Shelby crawled away from the pentagram as fast as she could, leaving Rory to writhe and groan as thick, dark blood poured from his chest, forming a puddle on the ground.

"Why?" he whimpered through a blood-laden gurgle building in his throat, pulling himself towards Shelby at the edge of the circle. "Malus, please help me!"

Shelby stood at the perimeter, hands on her hips, glaring down at him as he attempted to leave the pentagram.

"Oh Rory," Shelby said in a sugar-laced voice, then snarled. "Give my regards to Malus!" And she kicked him hard in the face, sending him sprawling onto his back, where he remained, whining, but unmoving as he waited to die.

"Greg!" Shelby ran to his side, praying she wasn't too late. "Greg, baby?" She searched his neck for a pulse. His skin was cold. The fresh-fallen snow surrounding him painted pure red.

For a few moments, there was nothing. Only the hush of night breathed around her, soundless snow flakes descending, spiraling as though dancing in a light breeze. The trees stood quietly, steadfast against the winds. Even Rory's jagged breathing had given way to silence.

She was alone. With death all around her.

Amidst the quiet, Shelby began to cry. Her weeping resonated throughout the silent woods.

"Shh...baby, please don't cry," Greg said suddenly, struggling to sit up.

"Greg!" Shelby shouted. "You're alive!"

He laughed softly. "It would appear so."

"How? I mean, all the blood you lost!" She was dumbfounded as she kissed every inch of his face.

He shrugged. "My guess...Heaven and Hell discussed it, and decided that neither of them wanted me. So here I am." Then he looked alarmed, his eyes searching. "Where's the shithead?"

Shelby nodded towards the pentagram. "I got him."

"Way to go!" Greg smiled. "Help me up."

"Shouldn't we tie off your leg first? Slow the bleeding?"

He didn't stop; he just continued to rise to standing, leaning on Shelby for support. "Nah, just a flesh wound. I'd rather make sure that little asshole is really dead."

Making their way to the pentagram, Greg hobbling beside her, they inspected the circle.

But Rory wasn't there.

Shelby gasped. "He's gone! But that's impossible! I stabbed him in the heart!"

Greg peered into the darkness. "Well, wherever he is, let's hope he's going to suffer."

10

Vrill's private quarters, empty of the once radiant Soul Nexus, held a somber tone. Sybil stood stoic in a far corner while Vrill, with just a flick of his wrist, magically lit hundreds of black candles. In the center of the room, Fate recognized the twelve necromancers from the zombie races, the ones that had transformed Aura. She concluded that they must be some sort of council, ones that were older, wiser, and had more power than the rest of the necromancers. Clad in crimson cloaks, they stood around the shivering princess, hands pressed together in prayer, chanting under their breath.

Fate felt a chill crawl across her pale skin. This was like some sort of séance, some witchy ritual she'd only seen on the scariest of horror movies. Magic on the Surface was only pretend, at least that's what she'd always believed until she was sent to this place. She considered all the Surface legends she'd read about, all the stories she'd grown up with, and now wondered if they didn't hold an ounce of truth. With all she'd witnessed since her arrival, she found it difficult to dismiss what was always deemed fantasy. Like spells, curses, ghosts, and demonic possessions, all things she'd been taught was silly, was now a reality. Magic was commonplace here, accepted. Normal.

In fact, to be without magic here was practically blasphemous. She could see how the demons disregarded the humans before they became shades so many centuries ago. Something as frail and powerless as a human being would be considered a sub-creature, lesser than. Gods dwelt in Dark World, gods with powers greater than anything seen on the Surface.

Then Malus changed the game. She gave the humans that had fallen from above a fighting chance, she offered them a taste of magic. In exchange for their human soul, she gave them power, strength, and immortality, a tempting offer for any weak and mortal being. And, of course, they'd accepted.

Now, centuries later, the new world order hung in the balance. Demons had grown empathetic, many shades tired of the hunger, Dark World yearned for change and longed to evolve. Change that could only come with the death of the queen. The underworld was on the brink of a new dawn—and it all came down to this moment.

"Let us begin," Vrill announced, the red-cloaked necromancers closing in around Ever at his command. He then turned to Ever, saying, "Lie down, please."

While he was cordial, Fate sensed barely suppressed resentment simmering behind his galaxy-like eyes. How was it that she hadn't seen this side of him before? Does everyone harbor some dark side, one that remains buried deep within until some unfortunate test forces it to surface? She'd considered him wise, all-knowing. But now he was just like the demons within Legion, judgmental and intolerant, fueled by fear and preconceived notions. It saddened her to know that he was just like many of the others in Dark World, easily tempted to a darker nature. Easily swayed towards evil.

Ever's sky-blue eyes were doe-like as she complied with Vrill's orders, settling back onto the same podium from which she'd awakened only days before. Her white, knee-length hair swung long like a silky drape as it cascaded over the side of the makeshift bed, pooling on the cool marble floor like a patch of ice.

Mistrust and indecision curdled inside of Fate. What if this was all a ploy? What if Vrill was going to kill her despite his promise in the courtyard?

Fate couldn't hold back, inquiring with a narrowed gaze, "What *exactly* are you going to do to her?"

Vrill inhaled deeply, as though drawing patience from thin air, explaining, "We are going to probe her thoughts, search for any sign of the queen."

Fate eyed him warily, then each of the necromancers, unsure if she should allow this 'mind-reading' session to proceed. Kane wouldn't allow it, that she knew for certain. He would have given each and every one of the necromancers a good pounding just for eyeballing his daughter the wrong way. Maybe she should put a stop to this. Maybe Kane's testosterone-rich instinct was onto something.

Before she could voice her concerns, however, Vrill added, "Fate, my dear, it is imperative that you seek out Master

Kraton and discuss the remedy for your…ailment." He glanced down at the black, web-like marks tattooing her hands.

She brought her hands up, scrutinizing them. In all the excitement, she'd forgotten about her own problems. According to Vrill, she didn't have long to cure this before she'd be transformed into an even fouler beast than before.

Fate stood in the center of the room, wracked with indecision. Should she leave Ever alone with them? Or should she try to save herself?

If she didn't try to heal herself, she'd be no good to Ever, regardless of the outcome of this psychic trial.

Then Ever's velvet voice called to her, "Fate?"

The shade pushed through the horde of silver-skinned beings, arriving at Ever's side. "Yes?"

Ever forced a weak smile, speaking quietly, "I need you to do me a favor."

"Of course, anything," Fate replied, suddenly feeling as though she was consenting to aid in a last wish for a terminally ill patient. A sick feeling twisted inside. She hoped this would not be the last time she spoke with the beautiful young demon.

"Please," Ever started, reaching into a small pocket on her gown. "Give this to my father when you see him." She handed Fate a small envelope sealed with a melted red emblem made of wax.

Fate shook her head. "No, you'll see him soon. You'll be able to give it to him yourself." Uninvited tears gathered in her eyes as she lightly pushed the note away.

Ever's blue eyes pleaded with hers. "Fate, please…just in case," she said as though she knew something Fate didn't know. Did she suspect Malus was inside of her too? Had she known all along? Vale had been suspicious. Vrill was convinced. Maybe Fate had been in denial all this time.

Hesitantly, Fate took the letter, promising, "Alright, I'll take it for now. But I'm sure you'll be fine. In fact, I *know* you will." With that statement, Fate sent a glare at Vrill, a silent death threat warning him that Ever had better come out of this room as perfect as she'd come in.

"Thank you, my friend," Ever whispered, closing her eyes and looking profoundly more peaceful than she had a few moments before.

Vrill cleared his throat nervously, then said, "Okay, let us continue. Fate, will you go to Kraton then?" He searched her face.

She sucked in a breath, answering, "Yes, I will go, but Sybil must remain here." Fate tossed a pleading glance in Sybil's direction and was met with a nod. Fate felt a small sense of relief wash over her, at least Ever would remain among someone she trusted.

Vrill appeared perturbed but agreed. Fate then moved for the doorway, casting one last look at the vulnerable princess before she left.

11

The crevice raced with seemingly sentient purpose towards the helpless city, which likely felt the earthquake but were completely unaware of the dangers descending upon them.

Kane had no time to think. No time to contemplate how or why this was happening, he only knew he had to try and stop it. He only hoped the powers that had served him before would honor him once again.

"*Ego sum legio!*" Kane summoned the mysterious magic, praying it would come in time to save Sensua. Sorcia shrieked loudly, so high-pitched it pierced Kane's eardrums like a lance.

"My people!" she shouted, tears streaming from her lavender eyes. "Help them! Please!"

The fissure continued its charge towards the banshee city, ever widening as it neared, like the gaping maw of a ravenous beast it tore through the hardened earth like paper. Lightning flashed overhead, thunder roared, tornadic winds whipped wildly about them. This was no ordinary storm. No ordinary earthquake. Kane had his suspicions as to who the perpetrators were. This was their territory.

And he doubted that his unpredictable powers were enough to stop them.

Kane searched the covered sky, panning the horizon as he waited. Why was the magic not working? Why had he been saved by it before, and not now? His heart deflated. Whatever the magic was that had saved Fate from the clutches of the wraiths, had chosen to ignore his pleas for assistance.

And now it was too late.

"No!" Sorcia screamed as the crevice reached the golden gates of Sensua. Terrified voices emanated from within the structure as it rocked and heaved, thousands of banshees wailed all at once, their cries echoing across the desert.

Then silence.

The city was enveloped by the earth, swallowed whole, the soil sucking them under. Great towers fell, toppling upon themselves. The tall, sentinel pillars that had stood so stoic before the gate fell from grace; cracking in two as they hit the hardened desert floor, then disappeared into an abyss beneath the sands.

Sensua was no more.

The clouds overhead dissipated as quickly as they'd formed, the sands settling on the ground as though they'd never been disturbed. Sorcia fell to her hands and knees, sobbing inconsolably. She was the last of her kind now. The last of her race.

"Sorcia," Kane began, "I'm…so very sorry."

Mezza and Slater knelt on either side of her, each setting a soothing silver hand upon her back. Vale only stood, gaping at the destruction before him.

“What the hell just happened?” the shade asked, shaking his head.

Kane exhaled before responding, “I think we’re being followed.”

“By whom?” Vale raised a brow.

“I’m not certain yet, but if I’m correct, they’re trying to stop us from relighting the pyramid.”

Sorcia raised her head at this, her indigo eyes blazing. “So, this is your fault?” she spat, voice laced with venom.

“No,” Kane said. “I’m attempting to save this world, but someone else, it would seem, would rather see its demise.”

“Who?” she asked through gritted seat, rising from ground with the help of the two necromancers.

Kane panned the horizon. “I have my suspicions, and I’m sure they’ll reveal themselves soon enough. Come, let’s keep moving. There’s nothing we can do here.” He looked at empty space where Sensua once stood, realizing the journey had just taken a violent turn for the worst.

“Where do we go from here?” Vale asked.

He’d wanted to keep it private, but considering what had just transpired, Kane didn’t feel right withholding information. Finally, he surrendered, “I have some personal business to attend to, in the Valley of Shadows.”

12

Despite the scent of black roses hanging in the air, the smell of death still lingered. Fate swallowed, hesitant to commit to entering the lair of the dead. But this had to be done. She had to find a way to stop the transformation. If she waited too long, she'd become one of the lamia and have to be destroyed. She'd want it that way. She didn't want to live as a cannibal. With that thought, her stomach rumbled and images of raw meat flashed through her thoughts. Fresh, bloody, raw meat. At first, it didn't startle her. She'd seen the inside of a butcher shop many times as Scarlet, but then the thoughts turned darker. They showed her biting into an arm, a leg, a stomach, tearing through the tissue like a half-starved lion, red staining her mouth and cheeks.

She gagged, forcing the images away.

This new development both disgusted and angered her at the same time. Just as she'd apparently *cured* herself of one affliction, a new one took its place. Now she didn't want to rip open a creature's chests and steal their souls, she just wanted to eat the flesh around it.

She wondered how Kane would feel about this. How he'd react if he knew. Would he be disgusted with her? Turned off?

Honestly, she didn't think so. He loved her as a shade, knowing full well her dark side. Would her desire for flesh really be any different than souls? Maybe she could stay this way. Maybe she could control her desires for blood as well as she'd controlled her need for souls.

Then the image of the little girl in the pit flickered within her thoughts. The clawing, the snarling, the rabid, animalistic behavior. What if she couldn't control it? What if she became this untamable beast, forced to dwell in an abyss until Kane could find the strength to put her out of her misery?

She set aside her fears and entered the domain of the witchdoctor. Hundreds of lit candles cast long, dancing shadows upon the jagged walls of the hollowed-out cavern. Silvery, polished statues stared at her from one corner, their eyes void of color and pupils, yet she felt watched all the same. The room was clean and organized, sterile as a hospital, but the eerie ambiance still held ghosts, invisible to the naked eye, but there all the same.

"Fate," a voice called from a dark corner. "Welcome." Kraton stepped into the light, his tone friendly despite the disquiet lurking in his eyes. Was he afraid of her? Or worried she couldn't be cured?

Fate nodded, dropping her gaze to the floor. She didn't want to see it anymore. The uncertain stares, the freak-show ogling. She was tired of it all. Quietly, she asked him, "Vrill sent me. He said you might be able to fix…this." she held up her hands, showing him the railroad of black markings.

"Of course, but I must hurry, I have to go upstairs to assist with…other things." He cleared his throat, avoiding the topic of Ever as he approached Fate, taking her hands into his own, inspecting them.

At least he doesn't appear disgusted, Fate thought with a touch of relief.

For several moments he just examined her markings, following them up her arms, tracing them down her neck. Finally, he said, "Yes, I believe I know how to heal you, but you must hurry, your transformation is nearly complete."

"How?" Fate asked as a smile graced her lips, fresh hope ascending to the surface. "How do I stop this? What do I need?"

Kraton closed his eyes as though in meditation, then said in a creepy tone, "Your soul."

Fate's brow curled in confusion. "My soul? How? I thought it was gone for good." The very thought of her soul still existing somewhere made her heart skip a beat with excitement. Why hadn't anyone told her that it still lived? Was it nearby? Could she just call to it like a long lost pet and have it come to her?

Kraton smiled. "A soul cannot be destroyed, it simply moves on. Except when held against its will, as with the case of your kind devouring souls."

Overwhelming guilt shadowed her. "What happens to those souls?"

"They are cursed by the shade, unable to be freed until the shade who stole it is…killed."

Fate's eyes widened. "Is that the only way?"

The necromancer smiled thinly. "Yes, unfortunately. But yours is not cursed, it's only gone home."

She clasped her hands together, asking, "Where is it?"

Kraton turned from her, moving towards a marble countertop where jars filled with miscellaneous items sat. Not unlike the demon shaman's lair, the items carried with them a mystical tone, similar to a witch's stash of cauldron-filling ingredients. "Your soul has returned to the Guf."

"The Guf? Where is that?" Fate asked, excited as she sidled next to him while he prepared a concoction in an obsidian flask.

Kraton responded quietly, as though the words caught in his throat. "Beyond the Blood Palace."

"The Blood Palace," she repeated, her undead blood running cold.

He nodded, elaborating, "The house of the devil."

Fate tried to shrug it off but couldn't quite still the quiver in her voice. "Well, Malus isn't there anymore, so I guess there's nothing to be afraid of."

The odd necromancer paused his mixing and turned to look her in the eyes, saying, "Evil is an energy, it cannot be created nor destroyed, only transferred."

Fate shuddered as she looked into Kraton's swirling silver eyes, uncertainty nestling into her core. "Then how do I get my soul back?"

He placed a cork in the mouth of the vial, shook it once, then handed it to Fate. "Take this," he said, "once you have left Necrosia."

"What is it?" she asked, recalling the last brew she'd swallowed, the one that got her into this mess in the first place.

"It is a map, memories of our ancestors, they will guide you."

She cradled the potion in her hands a moment before asking, "So, if I get my soul back, I'll be cured of this." She flashed him her blackened wrist.

Kraton looked away. "I cannot be certain of the outcome."

Fate reeled. "What? What do you mean? You don't know what will happen?"

"You have been without your soul a very long time," he explained. "If you had retrieved it within hours of being damned to Dark World, things may have been different."

She closed her eyes, suddenly exhausted. "You're not making any sense. If my soul is in this Guf place, why can't I just go get it and…stick it back inside of me?"

Kraton sighed. "It may reject you."

"Reject me?" Fate felt like crying. It was *her* soul, *her* essence, how could it reject her?

"It may have forgotten you; it may be lost to you."

She pulled in a centering breath. "How do I make it remember me?"

He looked her in the eye, despair gathering in his cosmic eyes, "I wish I knew, my dear, I sincerely wish I knew."

13

"Why do we need to go to the Valley of Shadows?" Vale asked as they trekked through ash-laden sands. Sorcia and her male entourage perked up, eavesdropping on the answer.

Kane gathered his thoughts. Should he tell the inquisitive shade his motives for seeing Seren? It was really none of his business. But he was being forced to come along, so Kane relented.

"I'm going to find my wife," he said through gritted teeth, hoping Vale would leave it alone.

"Your wife?" The shade's brows furled. "But, she's dead. Isn't she?"

Kane's large black chest expanded as he took in a frustrated breath, explaining, "Yes, but she was murdered by a shade."

"Ah, I understand," Vale replied, quieted by guilty association.

Suddenly Sorcia interjected, "I don't. What do you mean? How can you go see her if she's dead?"

Kane stopped in his tracks, looking the banshee in the eye, saying, "You must know this." How could she not know about shades and their victims? Had she truly been so sheltered from the outside world?

She shook her head, lavender hair moving elegantly over her bronze shoulders. "No, I do not. Our father would not speak of the shades; we only knew that they were evil. Other than standing outside, guarding the palace, I had never been outside those walls."

"I see," Kane said as they walked. "When a shade kills, it takes the soul, using it for energy," he explained. "But since a soul cannot be destroyed, it remains inside the shade, trapped. Without its soul, however, the victim's body is left cursed, damned by the shade that stole its soul. It must live out eternity as a phantom until…" He stopped as he thought of Seren enduring centuries of loneliness, wandering purgatory without him. Without anyone.

"Until?" Sorcia urged him on.

"Until the shade that stole its soul is killed, releasing the soul from damnation. Then the soul is free, and it goes home to the Guf."

"The Guf?" Sorcia asked, her eyes as wide and innocent as a child.

Kane smiled at her. "The place where souls are born."

The princess smiled. "It sounds beautiful."

Kane nodded. "Yes, I imagine it would be."

"You've never seen it?" Sorcia asked.

"No," he said. "Very few have." She looked puzzled so he explained. "It is…very difficult to get to. It lies within the realm of the Blood Palace, the home of the devil."

"But she is dead, no?"

He paused. It was true, without the queen the shades of the Blood Palace might have abandoned their home, gone in search of souls to eat. He shuddered with the thought. They'd nearly decimated the population of Dark World the first time they'd been allowed roam free, he couldn't imagine what they could do to it now. "Yes, but there are many…obstacles, shall we say, preventing smooth travel to the Guf."

This time Vale perked up. "Obstacles?"

Kane took in a breath, he'd hoped he wouldn't have to discuss this with anyone in his lifetime. The guardians of the Guf were most terrifying, and almost no one knew of their existence. The only reason Kane knew of them was because his father felt it imperative that Kane was aware of the dangers. Finally, he answered, "Yes, there are many safeguards in place to ensure the protection of the souls within the Guf, that is all I can say."

Everyone shifted their gaze away from the prince, and for that he was thankful. He didn't want to have to explain the horrors before the Guf, he hoped that he, nor anyone he loved, would ever have to face them.

After what felt like several hours of travel, Kane saw a sign that they'd arrived at their destination.

The Valley of Shadows lie burrowed amidst a ridge of obsidian mountains, sleek and reflective as mirrors, the steep cliffs echoed the pains of those it held below. Hundreds, thousands, of soulless phantoms wandered the fields of purgatory, their ebony mist-like bodies churning with anger, sorrow, and loss.

Their very souls, their selves, had been stolen from them. Violently and selfishly. These beings only knew the torment of a life lost, in a dark world where light could never be found.

And many were angry about it.

While some wept unending tears, many lashed out with the fury and power of a poltergeist, determined to take out as many of the living as it could before it faded once more into soulless oblivion. They saved up their energies, hiding amongst the wailing ones, charging themselves until their chosen prey arrived—the living.

"Are you sure about this?" Vale asked, biting the cuticle around his long black fingernail.

"You don't have to come," Kane replied as he drew his sword from its sheath on his back. "In fact, you can stay behind with Sorcia."

The shade appeared visibly torn. To admit his fears aloud was obviously torture, but to go down into the valley was suicide. The dark ones would most certainly go after him first.

Mezza and Slater, however, looked eager to enter the den of lions. Their star-like eyes spun with excitement as they gazed into the core of the valley. Frankly, Kane was far keener to have the two necromancers on either side of him than an inexperienced banshee and a jumpy shade.

After a few moments, Kane simply decided for him. "I would like you to stay with the princess, if you don't mind; she is the last of her kind and needs to remain safe." He tried to make the job sound a lot more courageous and endearing than it really was.

With a reluctant nod, Vale agreed. He sidled next to the banshee and watched as the demon and the necromancers readied their weapons. Mezza's hands melted away, his metallic-like skin reforming into two long blades. Slater's hands became two sharp axes, blades on both sides.

"Ready?" Kane asked the silver beings.

With two quick nods in reply, the three moved forward down the slippery obsidian slopes. Slowly and carefully they traversed the angled paths, every other step threatening to give way. Like black ice, the rock face glittered and gleamed with adversity, its sharp peaks reaching high into the covered sky as though it were the bottom jaw to the ceiling of teeth.

Despite his intense concentration on the descent, Kane's thoughts drifted to Seren. She was there, somewhere, below them. True, it was only her phantom he was seeking, her soul imprisoned within some ravenous shade, but her nonetheless. He hoped she could answer his questions. Hoped there was enough of her left that he could put his heart at ease.

Time was lost to him until they reached the bottom. It might have been hours since he and the necromancers left the safety of the top, he wasn't sure. All he knew was that he was now inside a land from which many do not return.

Cradled within the dark mountains was a dystopian hell. Wailing, crying, weeping, bombarded them from every direction. Screaming and shouting pierced his ears. It was both heart-wrenching and frightening. To see what others had become, what they'd been reduced to, was altogether disturbing.

Wraith-like bodies undulated past, many with their faces buried in their vaporous hands, others groping and clawing at some invisible sight before them. Many had gone mad in the desperation of losing their lives and their loved ones; it was simply too much for them. Others were simply suffering in sadness, an unending stream of tears for their lost souls, the violent end to their existence.

As profoundly distraught as these made Kane feel, it was the ones who'd turned to evil for comfort that raised his hackles. The ones who sought revenge on the living for their eternal demise.

"The white ones are of no threat to us; it is the ones who radiate red that we need to be careful of. Remember, they cannot be killed, they are already dead, but they can be slowed by disrupting their form," Kane explained to the necromancers. "Hack them in two if you have to, upset their cohesion…it will buy you some time to get away."

Slowly, steadily, the trio walked amongst the phantoms, largely unnoticed. Kane eyed each of the ghosts he passed. There were so many, so very many. And all races: wraiths, banshees, necromancers…but especially demons. Thousands of them. Their vaporous bodies gathered in sorrow, all trapped within this miniature version of Hell.

A knot twisted in his stomach. What if his father was here? What if he were to come face to face with the deceased king? He, too, was murdered by a shade, his chest torn open, soul missing. What if he were here amongst the pitiful? Seeing Seren was going to be hard enough, if he had to see his father in this state as well, he didn't know if he could stomach it.

Mezza and Slater walked cautiously ahead of him, taking care as to not disturb any of the phantoms despite the fact that they were shoulder to shoulder with them. They cut a slow and steady path through the throng of apparitions. Kane tried not to look at them, not to make eye contact, even though he should have been more vigilant about whether or not he was going to be attacked. He just couldn't take witnessing the pain in their eyes, the vacant stares, or the anger and loathing. At least all of them were still white, their vaporous bodies had not given way to complete madness.

So many of these demons were his family, his kin, his blood. Their cries, screams, and keening were wearing his strength thin. He needed to find Seren quickly. He needed to get this done and over with.

Suddenly Mezza and Slater stopped in their tracks, crouching into attack position. Kane's heart sped up. What did they see ahead?

Kane peered around them, and immediately understood.

14

Fate packed her clothes into one side of the large pack, reserving a hefty section for the pounds of raw meat she knew she'd have to take long just to make the long trip. Nausea overwhelmed her for a moment. The intermingling of hunger and disgust swirled inside her stomach. Why did this have to happen? Why now, when Ever needed her? When Kane needed her? She was supposed to stay here, take care of Ever, protect her. But now she had to leave.

Fate gazed around the room. Was this the last time she'd see Necrosia? The one place she'd felt closest to a home since she'd landed in this crazy underworld?

She then walked to the bureau, retrieving Ever's sealed letter for her father. Clutching it within her hand, it burned a hole of curiosity into her palm. What did it say? Was it a goodbye letter? Did Ever know of Malus's presence? Or was it simply a note professing her love and worries? Perhaps it was some devastating secret, some clandestine knowledge that the princess had held deep inside for many years and now felt it vital to communicate.

Fate might never know, but she'd have to trust the princess and deliver the message as soon as she next saw Kane.

Spark zipped around her room, singing the corners and leaving trails of smoke in his wake. The tiny phoenix was trying to convey a message; apparently he was excited to be going on a trip. She'd decided to take him along; it was agony to think of doing this alone. True, it was a risk, considering her new penchant for fresh meat and all, but she trusted herself enough to bring him. She wouldn't hurt him, would she? Maybe this new lust would prove her wrong? What if she tried to eat him in a moment of weakness? Or what if she lost him like she'd lost…Ick.

Her heart ripped inside of her. Ick, with his shiny, green, moon-like eyes. His cashmere fur of snow white. She'd forced him along one of her journeys—and she'd paid the dearest price of all for it. Her luminescent eyes tracked Spark at he displayed his joy of soon being free to fly within the airs of freedom. How could she say no to him now?

"So, you all packed?" a voice asked quietly from the doorway, startling Fate from her thoughts.

Fate shifted her gaze to Aura, who leaned against the frame, eyes cast to the floor. "Yeah, just about."

Aura took in a deep breath, sighing as she exhaled. "So, I guess you're really leaving us, huh?"

Fate nodded, a brand new pain twisting in her core. She'd hoped to sneak out without saying goodbye. Cowardly, maybe, but far less traumatic for everyone.

The lithe necromancer took several slow steps into the room before saying, "I want to come with you."

Fate shook her head. "It's too dangerous. I can't ask that of you."

Aura raised her eyes to meet Fate's and grinned. "You didn't. I offered."

Fate considered it a moment. It would be wonderful to have company, but could she restrain herself from…eating…the beautiful necromancer? Not only that, but if the journey was to be wrought with peril, and the young girl was hurt or even killed, how was she going to live with herself? How would she tell Vale his love was wounded, or worse, dead?

"No," Fate said decidedly. "I need to do this alone." She really did. She'd gotten herself into this mess, she had to get herself out.

Aura's face fell, pain and rejection colored her eyes. "But…I can help you. I know I can! If you just give me a chance, I…"

"Aura," Fate interjected. "I love you, and I would love to have you come with me, more than you know. But I couldn't live with myself if anything happened to you. I owe it to you…and Vale…to keep you safe. Besides, I need someone I trust to look after Ever." It was the truest statement she'd ever made. Not that she didn't trust Sybil, but she needed more on her team, now more than ever. If she had to leave Ever, she had to be certain there'd be people looking out for her well-being.

The necromancer stood before her. "Are you sure?"

Fate nodded, though still uncertain. Could she really do this alone? Could she face Dark World again? If she hadn't met Vale along the way, and he'd taken her to the shelter of Necrosia, what would have happened to her?

Frankly, she was more afraid this time than before. She might be a cannibal shade now, but Dark World was probably going to eat her alive.

15

Before them stood a sea of red, hundreds of infuriated phantoms, their eyes seething and locked upon the three who'd wandered onto their territory. Mezza and Slater glanced back at Kane, their expressions a mixture of fear and anticipation. They needed to know what to do, only, Kane had no idea. This was the worst case scenario come true. These ghosts, these furious poltergeists who'd lost their lives and blamed the world, eyed the intruders with a vengeance that could only be described as murderous.

Most of the crowd was of demon descent. Maybe the fact that they were his own kind would appeal to what might remain of their sympathetic side. Clearing his voice, Kane stepped forward, hoping to avoid a massacre with a verbal approach. "Hello, my name is Kane, son of Lucifer; I am searching for a female demon that goes by the name, Seren. Can anyone help me?"

The group, their crimson eyes raging and glowering at Kane, parted in the center like a red sea. They seemed to be waiting for him, inviting him to move onward. Tentatively, he took a few steps forward, glancing back at Mezza and Slater as the phantoms closed the circle behind him, separating him from the necromancers.

I don't like this…not at all, he thought as he moved slowly past the mob of glares. Where were they taking him? Did they actually know Seren? Maybe they were just doing the old 'divide and conquer' scheme, where they separate him from his posse and slaughter him individually, hence less of a fight for them to contend with.

He took in a deep breath as he moved ever further through the throng, sadness forming in his heart as he looked at every face. *There's just so many!*

So many loved ones stolen, so many souls, so many lives ripped apart. He could understand why the remaining races were unwilling to accept Vale and his kind. The shades had all but desecrated Dark World.

Faces. Hundreds of them watched as he walked by. Old, young, all races, colors and creeds, the shades had not shown sympathy to anyone in their savagery.

Which would Seren be? Would she be one of the wailing? One of those who'd lost their minds with grief and sorrow? To be without one's soul for too long would destroy a person; bring them to brink of existence without any hope of a future. Would she have, after so long, given up on finding peace? Would she even remember him?

He suddenly felt guilty for not coming to find Seren sooner. He'd known where she might be, all this time, but hadn't had the courage to face her. It wasn't that he didn't love her, quite the contrary, but to see someone suffer so, and not know if he could help.

But now he knew he had to try. He had to find her and ask her the one thing he'd been meaning to for all these years since her death.

Suddenly the phantom crowd around him cast their gaze to the front, toward a single form, glowing hotter and redder than all the rest. Kane followed their line of sight, and his cerulean eyes landed on a very familiar face.

"Seren?" His voice was but a whisper as he stared at the face he'd not seen for almost one hundred years. She was almost as he remembered, despite the crimson hue surrounding her, her ebony hair ran long and swimming over her shoulders, cheekbones high and proud beneath a pair of curled, black horns. But it was her eyes he did not recognize. Her once ochre eyes that radiated joy, emitted sun-like rays of patience and happiness, now blazed with anger, hatred, and revenge.

"Kane," she said, her voice hollow and sarcastic. "How nice of you to come."

His eyes widened, surprise holding his words captive. She remembered him. She was coherent.

And she was a poltergeist.

16

Dark World lay open before her, the torrential storms of winter roiling in the distance, marring the horizon and devouring the view of her journey. Ahead of her lie her future, paved with danger and new fears, behind her sat her present life, filled with uncertainty and mixed emotions of comfort and concern.

Fate stood there amid the ruins of the dark world, tormented, not knowing which way to go. If she stayed in Necrosia, she'd become a new kind of monster, worse than the one she was before. If she left, embarked on this new quest to find her soul, she could fail, or worse, face more change, more upheaval in this already messed up afterlife.

With all she'd encountered down here, it made her human life seem almost boring. It made her want to go home to the Surface even more. But she couldn't go back. Not like this. Not a monster.

"Well," she said aloud. "I guess I have to do what I have to do." Spark, nestled on her shoulder, peeped encouragingly into her ear.

She walked across the bridge that separated Necrosia from the rest of the realm, walked away from security and into the unknown. A glance over her shoulder sent ripples of doubt racing through her body. Should she leave Ever? Was she safe with Sybil and the necromancers? Did she even have a choice?

Fate sighed, looking down at her hands, branded by the ebony blood of the lamia. If only she hadn't taken the potion, none of this would be happening. She wouldn't have to break her promise to Kane, she'd be able to stay and protect Ever.

But was she really Ever? What if the queen was inside of her like some invisible parasite? Living off her granddaughter? Biding her time until she could step forward, push Ever aside and take over?

Fate stopped in her tracks, red dust raining on her black boots. This wasn't right, she should stay. Stay for Ever.

As she spun about, the image of the little girl in the pit surfaced in her mind. The snarling, the ravenous hunger behind her eyes, the total and complete possession of the lamia. Fate couldn't allow herself to become that…thing. It was bad enough when she salivated for souls, but for flesh, raw, warm flesh; that was disgusting.

On the surface she'd be considered a cannibal. One of those half-humans that preyed upon their fellow man, ripping the skin so identical to their own. She didn't want to be that either, nor did she want Kane to see her that way.

With a heavy heart, she turned again to the gate and forced herself through it. She would make it. She would get her soul back.

She didn't know what awaited her at the Guf, but she was almost excited to get it over and done with.

Almost.

Part IV

The Devil Inside

1

Ever's ocean blue eyes flickered open, taking in her surroundings. She couldn't recall how she'd gotten there, but she recognized the crypt that resided deep within the underbelly of Necrosia's palace. A bright light shone onto her face, blocking her view of the shadows that encircled her. Voices murmured around her, low and conspiring, voices she knew were discussing her destiny.

She tried to sit up, but immediately sensed she was restrained, they were tight and unyielding—and invisible.

Enchanted, she thought as panic climbed into her chest, restricting her ability to breathe.

"Vrill?" she said over the dryness in her mouth. "Vrill?"

The mutterings around her stopped, but there was no response to her query. She knew he was amongst them, she could feel his judgmental eyes upon her. Scrutinizing her. Waiting for her to say the wrong thing, make one false move.

What were they going to do with her? Did they really believe Malus was inside of her? If she was, why couldn't Ever feel her there?

But then there were the unexplained blackouts. The moments of complete unawareness that had Ever tethered to darkness. Confusion. Bad things had happened when she was under those spells. Like the destruction of the Nexus. Things she'd only known had happened after she'd awoken from the…whatever it was. A trance, perhaps.

Was Malus in control at those moments? Was her grandmother using her body as a vehicle when she least expected it?

Ever had no idea. All she knew right now was that she was alone—and in danger. Fate trusted the necromancers, especially Vrill. But Ever sensed her dear friend was wrong. Vrill had ulterior motives, dark ones, but Ever couldn't quite put her finger on what it was.

Had Fate known what Ever already suspected, she'd never have left for the Guf. But she had to go, had to be healed. Ever knew this. She also knew she couldn't go along. Her destiny was here.

And by the looks of it, it wouldn't be long.

2

Volcanoes growled in the far south, streams of bright orange sprayed unsympathetically into the air from their gaping mouths. Streams of copper slithered down the sloped walls of the unsettled mountains, flowing as caramel would over a heap of ice cream. Carelessly, without rhyme or reason. Only nothing was cold, or sweet, about this world. Nothing was calm, relaxed. Just simmering anger, rage barely contained beneath the surface.

Fate's white stare scanned the horizon, scrutinizing her path. Debating. Part of her wanted to stay and fight the new disease coursing through her veins. It could be like a cancer on the Surface, where the odds of one's survival depended on the urgency and ardency with which it was treated. Could she beat this? Could she ward off the cravings, the desire, the lust for blood?

Something deep inside told her the answer: *No.* That little girl in the pit was proof, proof that this new monster was stronger than she was. That it could possess her, own her, and destroy what was good in her.

And even then, there wasn't much left.

The shade within had nearly crushed what remained of her soul. Had nearly driven out what made her whole, stolen her memories as Scarlet. She couldn't allow that. If there was a way to see her family again, even if just to remember them from the fragments of her shattered recollection, she had to try.

Fate sighed, glaring out at the long journey ahead. She had no choice, and she knew it.

Kraton had told her to head south towards the Blood Palace, then to take the potion and his ancestors would provide her with the memories she'd need to find the Guf.

Great, another potion, Fate thought, cringing. Then she shrugged. It couldn't get much worse than it was; she was already a worse monster than before. She had to admit though, while the hunger was almost uncontrollable when it hit, she didn't get hungry for meat as often as she did when she craved souls.

On that note, she thought she'd warn Spark. "Hey," she called to the adolescent phoenix as he soared a few feet overhead. "Come here for a sec." He complied, fluttering gracefully onto her shoulder and then nuzzling her cheek, heating her cool skin ever so gently like a warm summer wind.

"I just need you to know that if anything happens where…I start to look, well, hungry, you need to fly away as fast as you can, okay?" she spoke clearly and seriously. "Don't take any chances; I don't want to find out after I've had one of my little episodes that I've eaten one of my best friends, okay?"

Spark observed her with his beady eyes, firing off a burst of flame through his orange-red feathers as though in agreement.

"Great," she said as she began trudging southward through the ash-laden sands, the Great Wall that cocooned Necrosia getting smaller and smaller behind them.

While she wished Kane was there, walking alongside her, carrying her through this next journey, she was also grateful he didn't know about her newest affliction. Would he think her silly for taking the potion in the first place? No, but he'd be inconsolably distraught that his fellow demons had harmed her, thus betraying him in the process.

He might also, however, be disappointed beyond words that Fate had chosen to leave Ever behind. Had she done the right thing? Should she have dragged the princess along on this harrowing quest?

Then Fate realized the gravity of her concerns. It would have been impossible no matter how she stacked it. Bringing Ever along would have been selfish, not to mention dangerous. What if the hunger were to occur with the princess present? Then it would appear less like she was bringing Ever along to keep her safe and more like Fate had brought along a snack!

No, it was better this way. She'd had no choice. She had to trust that Vrill would keep his word and not harm the princess; even if Malus was found to be inside of her.

And Sybil. She didn't know her well, but there was an unspoken bond there, a trust between two former humans. Two people who'd been raised in the same Surface city. Fate had to trust her.

Her confidence building, she pressed on, hoping all the while that she'd be lucky enough to bump into Kane along this journey.

Kane. An involuntary smile pulled at the corners of her mouth as she summoned the image of her love into her thoughts. His long blue hair, hulking shoulders, and intense sapphire stare sent shivers of yearning throughout her body. She despised being away from him. Her palms ached to slide against his black velvet skin, to glide along his chiseled muscles and countless battle scars.

And his eyes. The longing behind them, the sadness that dwelt there; the hidden vulnerability that made her want to care for him, love him. He'd seen such sorrow, known so much pain. All she wanted to do was make him happy, help him find what was lost.

Fate shuddered suddenly, a prickling sensation pulled at the back of her neck. She spun about, expecting to see someone there. She'd felt their presence behind her, their eyes upon her. But no one was there.

She panned the length of the Great Wall, scrutinized the terrain. No one.

Shrugging, but rubbing her shoulders as though chilled, she moved on. She could have sworn she'd sensed someone—something—there.

"Relax," Fate told herself. "You're not completely alone." She looked to Spark who was happily dodging and playing amongst the billows of steam high in the canopy.

She knew to be very wary though. Despite the fact that she hadn't yet met all of the monsters this world held, she'd heard enough tales of terror to keep her eyes and ears open. Kane spoke of the death worms, enormous snake-like creatures that tunneled beneath the sands and came up under their victim to swallow them whole. He'd also mentioned others, like scarabs and gargons. She'd already encountered the sphinxes, and she had to admit that wasn't a pleasant experience.

But for some reason, it wasn't the animals and beasties she was afraid of—it was the sentient ones she feared. The demons, the wraiths, the banshees, and any other race that hated her just because she was a shade.

She couldn't blame them, really. On the Surface, every race had endured some kind of persecution from another. All had been named terrorists at some level for their actions. It depended on the point of view. Someone was always the bully, and someone was the victim. It was sad, really, that her own species couldn't get along, so it didn't surprise her that the races couldn't get along down here either.

Her luminescent eyes penetrated the gloom, the darkness only broken by the distant volcanic disruption. It would have been a beautiful world, down here, even without a sun to enlighten it. But Dark World had chosen chaos, dissention, and a discorded society.

She sighed. Maybe this really was Hell. Maybe it was supposed to be this way. Again she wondered what Heaven would be like. Was it the complete opposite of here? Colored with golden light, a perfect wind, and shatterproof peace?

Suddenly Spark sounded overhead, arching his body and diving straight for her. Fate frowned, wrapping her arms over her head protectively.

What was he doing? She quickly scanned her perimeter, had he seen something she didn't?

"What? What is it?" she called out to Spark who would not land but circled above her, chirping and panicked.

He's trying to warn me! But of what? Should I run?

Her heart pounded in her chest, eyes wide in anticipation. What should she do?

Then the noise came—and she understood.

3

Surrounded in a brilliant crimson aura, his former wife glared down upon him with a new darkness, an evil, residing within her once kind and loving stare.

"Seren?" Kane choked out, a vice of emotions seizing his throat. "Is that really you?"

Her eyes remained cold, uncaring, fixed on him as though he were prey instead of the love he once was to her. Hatred filled her aura, blood-red and radiating pure malevolence. This was not the wife he'd known, the loving demon he'd spent nearly a century with. Not the woman who'd bore his only daughter. This creature was possessed with rage, blame, and concentrated hate.

"Seren, it is I, Kane," he spoke softly, her bloody aura flickering like a lit candle with his every word as though agitated by his very presence.

"I know who you are," she spat, her every word laced with icy venom. "What are you doing here?"

Kane glanced back toward the two necromancers he'd been separated from, wondering if they were okay. Then he considered himself. Poltergeists were unstable, creatures of pure, unadulterated energy. Negative energy. Explosive and volatile, they could rip someone apart, shredding their flesh like paper.

Kane had heard horror stories over the years. Witnesses who claimed to see the violent outbursts of the phantoms. Without their soul, their means of compassion, understanding, and emotional comprehension were absent. They were simply the remnant, the shell, of who they used to be. Trapped within a world they didn't belong to anymore, existing as an echo of the voice that once was. All that remained of Seren now was raw emotion, so whatever she'd experienced as her last moments were amplified.

And she didn't appear to have found peace in those final minutes before her passing.

"I need to speak with you," he said, taking a cautious step closer to her.

She sneered, glowering down at him from her perch upon a large boulder. The other poltergeists seemed enamored with her, as though she were their leader. They gazed up at her atop her makeshift throne, enthralled with her every word. "*Now*? You've come *now* to speak with me?" she asked of Kane. "And what of the last hundred years? Where were you then?"

Her words bit at him, stung the soft, guilt-ridden spots in his heart. He'd known he should have come sooner. Known she'd be angry for his absence. It was just so hard. It was easier to remember her the way she'd been. He hadn't wanted to see her this way, or any other way than the way she was the last time he saw her. "I'm…so sorry, my love," he whispered, closing his eyes in shame.

She snorted. "Love? What do you know of love? You left me."

He frowned, asking, "Left you?"

Seren's aura suddenly shifted from a tempered simmer to a raging blaze, shouting, "You left me that day! Left me to die by the hands of that…monster!"

Her minions started to close in on him; Kane raised his hands in submission and they paused. He shook his head. Did she think he wasn't coming back that day? He'd only gone to see to the last details of their relocation to the underground palace. He'd tried to make it perfect, make it a real home for her and Ever. "I don't…understand," he stammered. "I was coming back for you, for Ever, don't you remember?"

"You were always gone!" she shrieked, the ribbons of flame surrounding her flickered aggressively, rippling a rainbow of burgundy, black, and violet. "All you cared about was the palace, and finding a new home for the demons! You didn't care about me! About us!"

He shook his head. "I was finding us a home, a safe place from Malus, from the shades!" With the mention of the word *shades*, the entire crowd wailed, a deep soulful cry from the depths of their existence. Kane cupped his hands over his ears, unable to endure the intensity of their keening.

"No!" Seren's shrill voice pierced the air. "All you cared about was *them*…the other demons! Not me!"

Kane stared at her, confounded. This was not the Seren he remembered. Not the patient, loving wife and mother he'd loved for so long. This being was wrought with rage, consumed by grief and anger. To continue with his quest would be pointless. She was beyond comprehension, unable to understand and listen to him.

He turned to walk away, to leave behind the one person he'd failed the most in this wretched underworld. There was no choice; he'd have to abandon his mission. If he couldn't speak with her rationally, he might as well leave and continue on with more pressing matters.

Head lowered, disgraced and broken, he willed himself in the opposite direction. Away from Seren, away from the pain and shame that would likely haunt him for the rest of his life.

But the poltergeists surrounded him, edging ever closer with their arms raised like mummies. They weren't about to let him leave, allow him to return to land of the living.

Kane could hear Seren's voice, velvet as it carried over the crowd, speak, "Oh no, you can't leave…not again," she called out. "Now you're going to stay with me…forever."

4

A bead of silver sweat gathered above Ever's brow as the necromancers, metallic faces buried ominously beneath their crimson cowls, surrounded the makeshift bed she lay upon. She desperately wanted to ask yet again what they were going to do to her, but she'd exhausted herself asking over and over with no response.

Where was her father right then? If he only knew what was happening to her. If only he were there, beside her. He wouldn't allow this; he'd slaughter them all before he'd permit this to continue.

She wished she were home, with the demons, safe inside Legion where she'd always existed. True, it was a prison with no walls for her. A place where she was kept hidden, away from her grandmother, but it also had held her captive for as long as she could remember.

But now that she'd experienced the outside world and its cold, cruel nature, she was a willing prisoner ready to return to her cell.

The necromancers hummed and chanted around her, calling forth some sort of energy as it entered the room, swirling and writhing amid the dark airs. It morphed from white to green, then green to purple, ever changing, ever moving.

Whatever it was, it moved gradually towards Ever, slowly, with purpose. What was it going to do? Was this another ritual to call forth the devil inside?

Was the devil inside of her?

"Ever," Vrill's voice sounded from somewhere amongst the collection of elders. "You are hereby convicted of harboring the soul of Malus, the Devil."

Her eyes widened, instantly burning with tears. "But…no!" she cried, fighting against the invisible restraints that held her tight to the bed. "You have no proof!"

"We have proof enough," Vrill said coldly, his tone hollow and uncaring. "We cannot allow you to live, cannot allow *her* to live."

"Please!" Ever begged. "I deserve a chance to…"

Vrill silenced her pleas with a wave of his hand, an enchantment sealing her lips shut.

Panic gripped her as she fought against the vice-like magic, trying with all her might to speak, to scream, anything. Nothing worked. She was trapped.

The hovering energy began to descend upon her like a fog, falling onto her, embracing her—and everything faded to black.

5

A deep, throaty growl sounded before her and a beast stepped forward. It must have been very good at tracking her so stealthily, not even Spark had noticed it sooner. It wasted no time in its pursuit as it lurched forward at full charge, snarling and licking its lips.

"Oh crap," Fate said, spinning about to run from the incoming slaughter. "Why now?"

Her lithe body, though riddled with a new disease, was still sleek and powerful as the new predator closed in on her. Spark spun wildly overhead, frantic flames shooting from his body.

Fate took a quick glance over her shoulder, processing her newest hunter. *What is that thing?*

It was hairy, whatever it was. From her quick glance, she could decipher a shaggy, rusty mane around a creature that appeared to have three heads. All of the heads reminded her of dogs, but each had a set of curled horns like a demon sprouting from their temples. While it had three heads, it only had one, very large body, then three tails pointed at the tips like a spade.

"A three-headed demon dog, wonderful," she muttered as she pushed her body to run faster, harder. Slobbering and snarling only steps behind her, she was certain she could feel the beast's hot breath on her neck.

He was gaining on her, and by the rapacious look in all six of his blazing red eyes, she was supper.

Inwardly, she sighed, realizing she was going to have to fight. She hated violence, despised destroying an innocent creature simply because it didn't understand enough to abandon its plight and leave her be. Then there was the prospect of being injured or killed herself. She didn't relish the idea of dragging her broken body miles upon miles to reach the Guf.

But with a fresh, warm line of slobber rolling down the back of her neck, she came to the grim conclusion it wasn't going to be an option.

In a spur of the moment decision, she stopped dead in her tracks and hugged her knees, curling into a tight ball. The mutated canine promptly tripped over her and tumbled several feet ahead of her, stirring up a formidable cloud of dust in its wake. While it gathered itself up for another run, Fate pulled power from her core and began forming an energy sphere. Fingers of blue and white light crackled and sparked around the ball, building in size and power as the dog charged her as furious as a bull. Shark-like teeth gleamed from each of its maws as it launched its enormous body in her direction. There was no stopping it now; it was as angry as it was hungry now.

"Sorry," she whispered as she fired off the orb, wincing as it raced towards its target. The poor thing wouldn't stand a chance. If her power didn't kill immediately kill it, it would be injured beyond saving for certain.

Fate closed her eyes as the ball was within range, unwilling to see the beast obliterated.

At least I'll have something fresh to eat, she thought, her mouth watering against her will.

Suddenly there was an ear-splitting crack and Fate's eyes were jarred open. "What the…?" she uttered in amazement.

Each of the heads had summoned some sort of fireball, the three balls of flame merged, racing as one through the air to meet Fate's projectile. Her orb shattered into a million, sparkling pieces, drifting harmlessly upon the tepid breeze as though it were merely a sprinkling of rain.

Her mouth agape, she watched in horror as the beast scuffed the copper sands beneath his massive paws and lowering his trio of heads, glowered at her as though inviting her to run again. She felt like she was the red cape wavering before the bull, simply bait for the shark. A mouse trying to run from the lion. And there was no escape.

Swallowing hard, she stole her gaze from the waiting monster, panning the potential of her surroundings. Where could she go? Where could she run to? The nearest straggly tree for her to climb was over one hundred feet away. Her one weapon, the power she'd once considered formidable, was mere child's play for this fiend.

She was in trouble—and she knew it.

6

The rage and hurt in Seren's soulless eyes tore at his heart, ripping it to shreds and leaving it with fresh scars. "Seren, please…" Kane began.

"No!" she shrieked, clutching her long black hair at the roots and pulling as though she couldn't bear to hear his pleas. "I will not let you live without me, not again!"

His massive chest rose and fell. Maybe he should stay with her, he owed it to her. She obviously blamed him for her situation. All she wanted was for him to be the husband he apparently hadn't been when she was alive. Maybe this was his penance. His punishment.

He lowered his head, closed his eyes, ready to surrender, sacrifice his life, his own happiness. Ready to accept his destiny, leave Fate behind, leave Ever, when he suddenly felt a chill devour the blistering airs around him.

His eyes widened. "Vale?" he uttered in disbelief, the shade had appeared from nowhere, and now flanked his right side.

"Hey," he said with a shrug. "You looked like you could use a little help. Need a lift?" he asked, tilting his head back to where he'd left Sorcia, and where he himself had been only moments before.

"The princess?" Kane's worried gaze climbed the mountain where the last banshee stood.

"She's okay," Vale said, pointing to two large silver birds circling overhead. "Let's go."

Before Kane could accept, the phantom mob wailed, screaming in unison as their sights locked on the shade in their midst. The reason for their pain, their soulless existence. Every poltergeist seemed impaired by their sorrow, holding their heads in their hands, sobbing.

Every soul there had had their soul stolen by a shade. Their lives shattered by a vicious, selfish act of lust. Only one thing could give them peace now, just one thing: the shade that stole their soul had to die. Only then could they be freed from their prison.

"We'd better go," Vale said urgently, taking Kane by the elbow.

"No, wait," Kane replied. "I have to ask Seren something, it's why I came."

The shade's eyes grew wide. "What? Now?"

Kane stepped forward, closing the distance between himself and Seren. Only inches from her, wanting desperately to take her into his arms, to stop the pain, stop the mourning, he whispered the words he'd waited nearly a century to say, "Seren, who did this to you?"

Amid her tears and torment, she raised her head, peering between the drapes of her long, once-silken black hair; and pointed her finger through the crowd. It landed on but one target.

Vale.

Kane stared in disbelief, gathering words from disjointed thoughts, uttering, "Vale…Vale killed you?"

He suddenly felt empty, hollow, dead inside like he never had before. How could he have allowed himself to trust Vale? A shade? Had he lost his mind?

Vale looked just as surprised, shaking his head in protest. "I can guarantee you, it was not me." He raised his hands, proclaiming innocence.

Kane saw red, and for the first time in his life, rage, pure rage, consumed him. "You! You stole her soul?" he shouted, reaching for the blade upon his back, drawing it and placing the tip against Vale's throat.

A rare anger rose within the shade's luminescent stare. "I told you I didn't kill her. That is a fact."

"How?" Kane bellowed, now oblivious to the wailing phantoms surrounding them. "How do you know? Your kind devours any its path! Kills! Destroys without prejudice! You are the beast! The monster! The plague of this world!"

His heart shrouded with cold blackness, fury consumed him. How could he have trusted the enemy? How could he have been so blind? Seren had named Vale as her killer. Kane had to kill him in order to free her.

And suddenly, that seemed like an easy task.

7

The three-headed dog launched at her, his enormous body sailing through the air and gravity pulling it down upon her. He landed atop her torso with horrific thud, Fate's body immediately pinned upon the crimson sands. Lord this thing was heavy! She struggled for every breath as she held the center head at bay, the two remaining snapping at her from both sides. For the moment, she was happy she could barely breath, all three mouths stunk of rotted meat!

This was not the way she thought she'd go out. Not the way she envisioned dying in this underworld. Death by slobbering dog. So undignified. So inglorious.

Fate grunted as she held the middle head only inches away, every moment getting weaker, her arms giving way. Where was this elusive lamia now? The one who'd conjured the black sphere in the courtyard when Ever was in danger? She could sure use that power now.

Not to mention the mysterious power Vrill had promised she'd uncover. Where was that when she needed it? Maybe she'd already found it? Maybe it was the black orb?

An unwanted thought forced its way through her mind. She wished she could still devour souls. It was right here, his chest, her hands. It would have been easy. But no, now she was a different breed of monster.

And that revelation sucked at the moment. That she'd prefer being a shade to a lamia. What was she now exactly? A tainted shade? A newborn lamia with limited and unpredictable powers? There was nothing worse than not knowing what she was. At least when she was human, as insignificant as that was, what with no powers or magic, she knew what she was and what she could and couldn't do.

A string of hot drool ran from the dog's mouth and landed on her cheek. She suppressed a gag, wishing she could wipe it away.

His heavy body was becoming too much for her ribcage to bear. His razor-sharp claws flexed, ripping through her clothes and piercing her pale skin, blood seeping through the fresh punctures. She was going to have admit defeat—and she knew it.

Okay Dark World…you win, she thought, readying herself to release her arms. *I wonder where my soul will end up next?*

And she closed her eyes for the last time—and let go.

Suddenly she felt lighter, like all the weight was gone. She hadn't expected for it to be such a painless death.

Hmm, she creaked an eye open, realizing she wasn't dead, then uttered in disbelief as she witnessed the three-headed dog hovering several feet above her as though suspended by invisible wires, "What the hell?"

Something had the mutant dog, something completely unseen, and it was carrying him away. She could see that something with talons had the dog by the fur. But whatever this thing was had at least twelve hands—claws—she wasn't sure. The mangy beast whined as it was carted away. Higher and higher it rose before it was released onto the sands with a thud. Fate cringed, strangely worried for the mutt, but relinquished a sigh of relief as it gathered itself up and ran off into the distance, whimpering and whining in confusion.

Fate herself was more than confused, she was confounded. What invisible creature was this that not only saved her, but could fly and had at least twelve hands?

Cautiously, she rose from what she thought would be her deathbed and looked around. Was this thing still here? Had it come back for her?

Something touched her shoulder suddenly and she let out a girlish scream. "Spark!" she said with a scolding tone. "Don't ever do that again!"

The tiny bird chirped happily, flames of joy rippled over his body, singing flyaway strands of Fate's silver hair.

Then she asked the bird rhetorically, "Do you know what's going on? What saved me?"

Paranoia crept up on her as the sound of wings fluttered around her. Then came the whispers. Another language. Many voices.

Oh, Fate thought. *It's not one invisible creature with many hands, it's more than one.*

She wasn't sure this made her feel any better.

"Who's there?" Fate demanded of the unseen creatures that surrounded her. She could hear their movements, their mutterings, and strangely, their giggles. "I said who's there? Make yourself known!"

Suddenly there was silence, unnerving silence.

"Hello?" she asked aloud, her voice shaky. Despite the fact that these things had saved her from the tri-headed dog, she wasn't sure if they simply didn't want her for their own meal. Nothing surprised her anymore in this realm, nothing. But she knew better than to take anything for granted. They'd saved her—but why?

Spark, however, didn't appear the least bit concerned. He continued his gentle nuzzling against her cheek, streams of flames rolling contentedly over his feathery breast.

Then she noticed the footprints upon the reddish sands, created entirely in front of her awestruck eyes. Tiny, clawed footprints. Like cats. Invisible cats?

What were these things?

Suddenly she felt them climbing all over her body, they pushed her to the ground, gently, yet firmly. Still invisible, they cuddled her, purred, and licked her face.

One in particular sat on her lap, its weight light but noticeable.

"Who…are you?" Fate asked of the concealed creature.

It paused, then leaned forward and licked the tip of her nose, saying in a cute, growly kind of voice, "Ick."

8

"Kane, please," Vale pleaded, though his eyes churned with anger. "I'm your friend, you know this." The shade was backing away with his hands raised in submission, but Kane knew better. This was just a trick.

Kane thrust his sword at the shade, but the wily shade simply vanished into thin air, leaving only a trail of black mist behind.

"Where are you, you coward! Come face your destiny!" Kane yelled, rage owning him, the crowd of poltergeists fuelling him. He couldn't think straight. Couldn't see beyond the anger. Vale had stolen his life. Seren's life. How could he allow him to live?

Vale appeared a few feet away and Kane lunged for him, sword leading, and he disappeared again. Furious, Kane spun around, looking for the shade. He had to find him. Had to revenge Seren's death and free her from this damnation.

"Kane," Vale's voice sounded through the crowd. "Look at yourself. This isn't you."

"Where are you, you white-haired freak?" Kane growled, his head spinning with rage. "Come out where I can see you!"

"Look at yourself," Vale repeated. "The crowd is controlling you…you're turning."

What? Kane stopped, looking at his arms, his legs, then a slow dawning came over him. He was covered in red. His aura had shifted to some supernatural possession.

He was becoming a poltergeist.

Then he heard Seren's laughter. He spun about to face her, the crowd parting as she approached him.

"Seren?" Kane said quietly, his anger dimming alongside the red flame that surrounded his body.

She snickered, her face contorted into a playful sneer. "So quick to judge your *friend*, aren't you? So quick to abandon your comrade? How fickle you are *Prince* Kane," she spat. "How terribly disloyal you are in moments of dire need."

Kane lowered his head. She was right. Only moments before, he'd been willing to abandon Ever and Fate to succumb to his guilt. And now, he was seconds away from destroying Vale without proof or admission of fault.

"Kane," Vale said, appearing beside him. "Don't listen to her; she's trying to manipulate you."

"But," he started, "I came here to avenge her death, to free her."

Vale frowned. "Is that all?"

Kane took in a long breath. "No, I came to ask her permission."

"Permission?" Vale inquired.

The demon prince nodded. "I came…to ask Seren if I could…remarry."

Vale pulled in a surprised breath. "Fate?"

The demon blushed. "Who else?" Then Kane lowered his gaze. "You're certain it wasn't you who killed Seren?"

The shade took in a shaky breath and nodded.

"How can you be so sure? It was so long ago," Kane said, eyeing him with suspicion.

Vale turned his gaze upward, then replied, "Because…I know who did."

The demon prince felt his knees fall weak as he forced the words out, "Who?"

"Remember when I told you Seren did Sybil a favor many years ago?" Vale asked.

Kane nodded.

"I…lied when I said I didn't know what it was." Vale winced. "Seren found Sybil, dying, wounded from Malus's guards. Seren helped her, she…took her home."

"What!" Kane's head spun, was what he was hearing the truth? Could it be possible?

Vale continued, slowly and in obvious pain. "Sybil was starving, Seren tried to feed her some small animals…but…"

He didn't need to finish, Kane could guess what happened next. Seren's kindness had gotten her killed. Her unselfish, mothering nature had betrayed her.

"Are you sure?" Kane whispered, hardly able to speak. "She would never…I mean…why would she help a shade? She hated them."

Vale shook his head. "It's what Sybil confessed to me before I left. I promised her…I wouldn't tell you." He looked away, ashamed.

That's what Vale had whispered to Sybil on the day they left, Kane surmised. That he wouldn't speak of it.

"Thank you," Kane said honestly. "I know it was hard for you to admit. Thank you."

Now knowing his wife's killer, however, did not help matters further. To free his wife, he'd have to kill Vale's sister.

"We should go," Kane admitted. "There's nothing more I can do here."

Vale looked confused. "Aren't you going to ask her about you and Fate? About asking for her hand in marriage?"

Kane shook his head. "I've decided that I don't need permission, besides, I don't think Seren is well enough to…" His words were suddenly cut short by a painful blast to his back, sending the large demon flying several feet forward.

"Kane!" Vale shouted as the red crowd surged into two different mobs, one attacking Vale, the other, Kane.

The poltergeists ripped at his skin, pulled on his limbs to the point where he thought he'd break into several pieces. Vale's pained cries echoed his own, Seren's malicious laughter sounding over the frenzied horde.

He couldn't see a way out of this. Poltergeists, as far as he knew, could not be killed. He didn't even know if they could be stopped long enough for them to get away, it was a far climb up a steep mountain wall to escape.

"Vale!" Kane called out. "Wisp! Get out of here! Save yourself!"

But he heard no reply.

"Vale!" he yelled as several crimson ghosts sliced his arms and legs with lance-like claws.

Blood dripped over his eyelids, obscuring his vision. Not that he wanted to see the horrible, angry faces of the poltergeists as his last sight.

Seren's vicious giggling resonated in his ears, her hatred and evil tearing at his soul.

She is not the woman I knew, he realized. *And I have to live…for Fate and Ever!*

Despite the pain, the blood, and the betrayal, the warrior chose to fight. He would not back down, not this time. He'd come to this wretched place to help Seren find peace, he'd come for her.

Now he would fight to leave.

Kane forced his arm upward, reaching over his shoulder for his sword. He would try again, he would summon the *power.*

And it had better damn well listen this time.

Staggering to a stand, he raised his black diamond sword to the covered sky, shouting, *"Ego sum Legio!"*

The ebony blade began to quiver, igniting into hot, red flames. The power began to course through him, and somehow, he now understood where it came from.

"Ego sum Legio! I am Legion!" His voice rumbled through the crowd, and they cowered before him, covering their ears and

whimpering. *"I am the sum of all demons; I am the power of the ancients reborn in the flesh!"*

Seren's laughter faded away, the poltergeists retreating. Vale's broken body lay a few feet away, his white eyes wide as he watched tendrils of fire ripple over Kane's body.

The energy of his ancestors exploded through his veins, their magic raging in his blood. He'd never felt so alive, so strong. Like he'd waited all his life to take this first breath.

He *was* power.

He *was* magic.

With his mother gone, he was ready to lead Dark World.

He was ready to take his rightful place…

As the devil.

9

"Ick!" Fate shouted, tears of joy springing to her eyes. "Where are you? How come I can't see you?" Still sitting, she felt the air in front of her, blindly searching for his furry little body.

"Ick," he said, followed by some sort of growling garble.

Suddenly, his emerald orb-like eyes appeared in front of her, just as mischievous and impish as she remembered. Then, the rest of his body appeared, his soft white fur a crazy mess and wings tucked tight to his back.

"Ick!" she cried, grabbing him and nestling him against her chest. "Where have you been? I thought I'd lost you forever!"

He purred like a kitten, nuzzling her neck and pressing his cold, wet triangular nose against her jaw like a kiss. Then Fate felt movement on her legs and glanced down to see five more fluffy gargoyles. They were all about the same size as Ick, but had various colors of eyes and fur.

Two were pure black with sky-blue eyes; another was covered in a calico pattern, all orange, white, and black with an onyx circle surrounding one of her bright ochre eyes like a shiner. The last was the most beautiful, her coat gleamed silver, well-tamed and clean. Her eyes shone pale blue, reminding Fate of the moon on a cloudless night.

All girls. Ick's little harem, Fate thought with a giggle.

Then she realized she'd only counted five including Ick, she was sure she'd seen six carrying the hellish dog away. Where was the last?

She looked around, then from behind one of the girls peeked a tiny set of big green eyes. Far smaller than the rest, Fate assumed he had to be a newborn or at the very least, the runt of the litter. Pure white like Ick, she wondered a moment if he wasn't related to Ick, a little brother perhaps?

"Hello," she offered quietly. "It's okay, I won't hurt you." She presented her hand to him, palm turned upward. "Come here, little one."

Cautiously, nervously, he toddled towards her, sniffing the air around her. Finally, he put his tiny, furry hand in hers and let her pet his head, closing his eyes as though in heaven.

Sighing, Fate smiled. She'd found the best part of being in a supernatural realm. And for once, she was profoundly happy she was there.

"Okay," she said finally, reluctantly, "I guess we should get going. You guys coming?"

Ick tilted his head questioningly, as if to ask where they were headed.

"I have to go to the Guf," she announced. "To get my soul back. Will you help me?"

Ick turned his new littermates, garbling words to them, then turned to Fate and nodded his fuzzy head.

It was probably going to take a lot longer to get there, what with their short little legs, but she didn't care. It was just going to be nice to have company.

She didn't know what was going to happen. If her soul would accept her or reject her. Would she even get there in time? Or would the black, lamia blood eat her alive, tearing her to pieces from the inside out? If she got her soul back, what would she become then? Would she still be a monster? A shade? A lamia?

She didn't care, labels didn't matter anymore. A name for her monstrosity wasn't important. All she knew is she had to try. She had to heal herself for Kane, for Ever, and for Dark World.

This world, this hot, hellish world was now her home—and she was going to do everything she could to help save it.

10

The chanting grew louder, the energy source swimming over Ever's body pulsed and thickened.

This was the moment he'd been waiting for. The moment he could rid Dark World of Malus forever.

Drawing a long silver blade from within the arm of his robe, Vrill closed the distance between himself and the princess.

"Leave us," Vrill commanded of the room and the necromancers filed out, leaving him alone with the helpless demon girl.

He scanned every curve of her body, wondering where Malus was hiding within. Where would the Devil reside? Where inside this vessel did she dwell?

Vrill raised the blade, knowing exactly where evil would take residence.

The heart.

He readied himself to free Dark World of evil. Readied himself for glory, for eternal gratitude. He'd be a hero, a savior, a god.

Myth would surely award him his immortality again. She'd be a proud mother to his silver race once more. Return her love to them.

Vrill pulled in a deep, contented breath, closed his eyes and plunged the blade downward.

Only something stopped him. Something outside himself. Something magical.

Spinning about, he came face to face with Sybil.

"What are you doing?" he asked, confounded. How did the Oracle have such powers?

She smiled darkly, her eyes unnaturally blue for a shade. "I cannot allow you to kill the princess, I need her for myself," she said, her voice not her own.

"What? But I have to, she's the devil! She'll destroy us all!" he cried, pivoting about and attempting again to slay the beast on the table.

Suddenly he was raised into the air, his limbs frozen, his body possessed by magic. Involuntarily, he turned to face Sybil again, drawing closer and closer until he was within inches of her.

"Why?" Vrill asked, silver tears falling over his face at his failure and his fear.

"Because," she growled, producing a short, curved dagger from behind her back and driving it into his heart. "I cannot take over the Surface without my granddaughter."

Vrill's lifeless body fell to the floor, his mouth agape to the horror, the betrayal. Silver blood pooled around his body, the cries of thousands resounding in his head as the other necromancers felt his pain, his death.

His last sight was of Sybil—Malus—placing her hand upon Ever's chest…and completing the transfer of her soul.

11

The monster opened his eyes, scanning the unfamiliar environment with the innocence of a newborn. Red sands rubbed against his naked skin, blistering heat licked his back. He forced himself to sitting, his body not as he remembered it.

What did he remember? Who was he? What was he?

He took inventory of his surroundings, this new, dark world. A reddish haze occupied every horizon, every direction, intolerable heat raged like the roiling innards of a giant—and then there was the sky. Or lack thereof.

The beast gazed at the covered sky, it glared back, its teeth baring as though ready to feast upon him. He averted his eyes, unable to comprehend.

Then he saw his hands, his arms, and his chest. What were these strange markings running the length of his entire body? Ebony tracks spread like a web from the center of his torso, cracked and ran under his skin like a disease. Everywhere. The dark blood was everywhere, all throughout him

Then the hunger hit. A hot, raging pain within, like some ravenous parasite devouring his intestines. Panic threatened him for a moment. What was happening?

He thrashed inside his conscience, beating down the walls of his memory, forcing the thoughts forward. Who was he?

Then it came. Like light escaping from an impenetrable box, it struck him.

He knew his name.

Through trembling black lips, he grinned, uttering but one word—his name, "Rory."

The Pages
Of the
Devil's Bible

Given to the Demons

I

I am legend,
I am lore,
I am the essence of nightmares,
The dawn of fear,
A fallen angel,
A winged beast,
Spawn from the seeds of evil and black magic,
I am Lucifer,
Lord of the Dark

Given to the Necromancers

II

There can be only one,
Upon the throne of blood,
A ruler among fiends,
A leader over beasts,
Old will expire,
New will succeed,
But only one is meant to be,
Meant to reign,
Meant to rule,
The Devil's Heir

Given to the Banshees

III

A secret underworld,
Alive beneath the feet of man,
To rise,
To ascend,
The races must blend,
Must blur the lines of disparity,
Must come together,
With the pages united,
Dark World will be enlightened,
Darkness will meet the Light

Given to the Wraiths

IV

A legend,
A fantasy,
A lore,
Asleep,
She waits to be awakened,
A song of Four,
She waits to hear,
The legend,
The fantasy,
Myth.

Given to the Reapers

V

Yet to be obtained.

VI

Location unknown